Don't miss Irene M. Drago's first novel:

DAUGHTERS OF LONG REACH

2018 Next Generation Indie Book Award Winner

I actually read the novel in one day, unable to stop reading. Irene writes great dialogue, which is something I always admire, because it is not easy to do.

—GEORGE SMITH, columnist

American poet Walt Whitman (1819–1892) once wrote: "As soon as histories are properly told there is no need of romances." But Bath author Irene M. Drago might prove him wrong...This is a shipbuilding, seafaring, family love story, folding in real history and real people, with thoughtful fiction to fill out this clever tale.

—BILL BUSHNELL, literary critic/columnist: Bushnell on Books

I loved it! What a fine line you managed.

—NANETTE GIONFRIDDO, owner of Beyond the Sea

Drago delivers a beautifully written debut novel set in the town of Bath, nestled along the coast of Maine. The story, steeped in local maritime history, deftly weaves past and present honoring core New England values—love of family, love of history, and the importance of fighting for what you believe. Readers will be well pleased!

—JULIE SHEA, owner of The Mustard Seed Bookstore

THE
MAINE POINT

IRENE M. DRAGO

Cover Art
Claudette Gamache, PSA, MCIAPs

Designed and produced by:
Maine Authors Publishing
12 High Street, Thomaston, Maine
www.maineauthorspublishing.com

Printed in the United States of America

For my mother,
Edna Van der Waag Murtagh,
and her three sisters,
Estelle, Marie, and Muriel,
my four musketeers,
who taught me the power of love.

"All for one, one for all."

— *The Three Musketeers*, 1844, Alexandre Dumas (1802–1870)

"All human wisdom is contained in these two words:
Wait and hope!"

— *The Count of Monte Cristo*, 1845, Alexandre Dumas

CHAPTER 1

July 2018

On its final approach, American Airlines Flight 732 glided over Maine's Casco Bay like an osprey in flight. From my seat, I could see the wake of a ferry, and as the plane banked left, I spied two islands dotting the bay. The captain was clearly piloting our plane between those islands as we prepared to land at Portland International Jetport. Peering out the window, I took a deep breath and focused on Portland Head Light. I imagined all the storms it had survived, all the keepers it had protected, and all the sailors its light had saved. Since I'm a screenwriter, I'm always looking for a touchstone, and a lighthouse usually has a secret to tell. Characters were emerging, a storyline was forming, and words were beginning to appear on a blank page in my mind when a commanding voice interrupted my creative flow.

"Sir, please turn off all your electronic devices and stow your briefcase below the seat in front of you."

I didn't hear an apology, but I did hear a click when the man behind me closed his laptop. I folded my hands in my lap, closed my eyes, and wondered why there was always at least one Very Important Person on every flight, then I took a cleansing breath. Maybe four months was too long to be away from Bath, away from Jake. How long could a bicoastal love survive?

My eyes blinked open as the plane touched down with a bump. I looked through the window to confirm that we were taxiing at PWM after that hard landing. When I saw the two-story terminal against the topaz-colored sky, I sighed. Maine looked fresh and clean, so different from L.A. and New York, and it felt good to be home. I stood up to open the overhead compartment and thought of Jake waiting for me, running his hands through his hair, stretching, and checking his phone for updates. That happy thought made me smile, but it didn't give me the strength to free my bag. As I tugged on it for the third time, I heard a magnetic voice say, "Can I help you with that?"

"No, thanks, I've got it," I replied with feigned hubris.

Just as I was about to lose my balance and let that bag come crashing down, the gentleman with the voice reached above my head and caught it.

I glanced at the handsome older man and blushed. "Thank you. I guess I'm not that strong after all. Would you believe once upon a time I played basketball?"

He closed one of his dark-brown eyes and quickly sized me up from head to toe. "Maybe a point guard," he said, "but it's not a matter of height or strength; it's a matter of practice, and I've had a lot of practice."

A little flustered, I nodded, tossed my long chestnut curls in a determined way, and headed toward the exit. As I left the jetway, my phone pinged, telling me Jake had arrived. I was almost home. Walking through the terminal, the gentleman with the voice—and an expensive suit, I noted—caught up to me.

"Are you meeting someone?"

I paused at the top of the escalator and scanned the small crowd below, then answered, "Yes, my boyfriend."

"I'm not surprised," he said.

I didn't react because I had spotted Jake waving a bunch of white daisies over his head like a flag. I jumped and waved back to signal *I see you, too.*

Mr. GQ must have noticed my joy because I heard him chuckle. "Is that sun-bronzed god over there your boyfriend?"

I fixed my eyes on Jake and said, "Yes!"

The moment my feet touched the floor, I ran. In less than a heartbeat, Jake caught me in his arms and the daisies touched my cheek. We kissed hard, then I paused and whispered, "I've missed your lips."

Jake reached down and kissed me again—softly this time. When he looked up, he noticed the gentleman from my flight standing a few feet away.

"Garrett?"

"Hey, Jake, I didn't expect to see you here. Our meeting is scheduled for next week, right?"

"Yes, that's right. I wasn't expecting to see you, either. Can I offer you a ride?"

Garrett held up his hand. "No, thanks. I have a car waiting." He looked at me and teased, "But you could introduce me to the lovely lady you just kissed."

Instantly, Jake let me go and squared his shoulders.

"I'm sorry. This is Anna Malone, my girlfriend."

I turned and smiled.

"Anna, this is Garrett Liston, the maverick who purchased the Pearl Island Light Station and is single-handedly saving it from extinction."

"Whoa! I'm not exactly saving it by myself," he said with a wink and a smile. "Sorry I can't stay and chat, but that driver is waiting. If I don't hurry, he'll think I went home without him."

He started to walk away, then turned back and focused on Jake. "I'm looking forward to our meeting next week. Tuesday at ten. Don't be late."

"I won't."

Taking Jake's hand, I chimed in, "Wait! How do you two know each other?"

Garrett looked at me with those intense eyes. "We met at an auction. It seems Jake and I have similar tastes."

With a raised brow, I softy said, "That sounds cryptic."

Laughing, Garrett replied, "Business is cryptic." As he waved goodbye, he chided, "Jake, you should bring Anna to our meeting. She's pretty *and* smart."

Confused, I watched Mr. Liston stride away and whispered, "That man is either your next best friend or your worst enemy. Tell me, what have I missed?"

Jake planted a kiss on my waiting lips and firmly replied, "Not much." He nibbled my ear—knowing that sends me to the moon—and said, "I booked a room at the Press Hotel in the Old Port, and made a dinner reservation at the Union. Check-in is at three. It's time to catch up. Don't you think?"

I giggled. "Yes, but first we have to grab my other two bags. You do realize I've been gone for four months. I couldn't have survived for thirteen weeks in L.A. and three weeks in Manhattan with only one carry-on."

Jake threw back his head and laughed. "Of course not! I'm surprised you could manage with only three."

"Be nice, Jake, or you'll have to reserve another room at the Press for *yourself*."

"That's harsh," he said pulling me close with his right arm while his left pulled one of my bags off the carousel.

* * *

Twenty minutes later, Jake and I pulled up to the hotel on the corner of Federal and Exchange Streets. At its urban-sleek entrance, Jake jumped out of the Jeep to open my door, then quickly turned to hand his keys over to a young valet. As I stepped out, I let my eyes climb to the top of the seven-story granite building, which was a storied place because for many years it had housed the offices and printing plant of the *Portland Press Herald*.

Entering the lobby, I half expected to see a wisecracking reporter. Instead, I saw the *Swarm*, a collection of vintage typewriters mounted on the wall. This whimsical work of art made me feel the energy of a newsroom; it also made me want to sit down and write. As I admired the *Press*'s dramatic décor, I realized Jake had chosen this hotel to please me.

After checking in at the front desk, he came up beside me and took my hand. "Anna, I know the art is amazing, but I've been missing you for months, so would you like to go up and see our room, or would you rather keep gazing at typewriters?"

"Oh, darlin', I can't believe we're here. I'd love to go up to our room."

He moved his hand to the small of my back. "I've been waiting to hear you say that."

Stepping into the elevator, I caught a glimpse of the *Press*'s signature mosaic—letters of all sizes, fonts, and colors—and I remembered reading an article about it. The letters spelled *resurgam*, which is Latin for *rise again*. As the elevator doors closed, I squeezed Jake's hand and thought about the miles we had traveled to arrive at this place.

* * *

Four years before, I'd signed a deal with Coastline Studios and had been working nonstop ever since that door opened. Before that, I had been a struggling screenwriter, and my creative spirit had almost been extinguished by Hollywood and New York. As fate would have it, when I came to Bath and met Doris Van der Waag—a former New York designer and a champion for historic preservation—everything changed. She put me in touch with the CEO of Coastline, Warren Dunlap. For me, it was a dream-come-true connection that allowed me to write and produce *Daisy Longtree*, the first film to include my name in the final credits. And now, my second feature film, *Captains of the Kennebec*, is ready to be released. After four long years of pounding the keyboard, searching for words, crying, laughing, missing sleep, and missing Jake, the crew had wrapped. To borrow a 1930s expression, it was in the can! With a little luck—okay, a lot of luck—*Captains* will win the hearts of American moviegoers by Christmas.

* * *

Jake looked at me and said, "I feel guilty. Your mom and dad are probably anxious to see you, and I'm delaying your return by half a day."

Stepping closer, I replied, "Only twelve hours? Oh, I think we'll need more time than that. Don't you?"

"Only if we stand here and keep talking." He reached over to press 5. The elevator started to rise and we kissed.

When we stepped out onto the fifth floor, I noticed the twentieth-century headlines scattered across the wallpaper. For a moment, I was transported back to the early 1930s when Prohibition was in full swing and the Great Depression was demanding more alcohol to drown financial woes. My feeling of nostalgia deepened when we entered Room 504 and I sat in a swivel chair with a declarative sentence written across its back—"The quick brown fox jumps over the lazy dog." While Jake tipped the bellboy, who had taken the next elevator, I picked up an unusual blue-glass bottle of water with a W.C. Fields quote hanging around its neck: "Once, during Prohibition, I was forced to live for days on nothing but food and water." I loved the fact that the commas were properly placed. It was grammar perfect. If Jake had wanted to impress me, he had achieved his goal.

As soon as the door closed and we were alone, I jumped up and put my arms around his neck.

In a low voice, he said, "Your hazel eyes touch me like nothing else."

We tumbled onto the bed and into a dream. For the first time in a long time, I stopped thinking about writing and focused on loving.

* * *

Full from a rich dining experience of fresh greens from local farms, shrimp, lobster, and a rhubarb crisp with vanilla ice cream, Jake and I slept in the next morning, showered late, and strolled down to the Inkwell at nine. We sat at a glass-topped table tucked in the corner, breathed in the aroma of our freshly brewed coffee, and peered at the front page of a 1933 edition of the *Press Herald*: "Eighteenth Amendment Repealed! Prohibition Ends!" I shook my head, because less than thirteen hours ago, at this same table, we had enjoyed two glasses of brandy from the bar as a nightcap.

I looked up at Jake and smiled. "What a great use of space: a café in the morning and a bar at night. I guess it's all about the lighting and the beverages, right?"

He rubbed his chin. "This is not the conversation I was expecting. I thought you'd be more focused on us."

"I am, but my mind tends to wander before coffee. I really think if we hadn't been so starry-eyed last night, one of us would have noticed this headline under the glass. Imagine! Last night, eighty years after the appeal of the Eighteenth Amendment, we enjoyed drinking alcohol in a city where it was once forbidden, proving that men and women will always fight for the freedom to be naughty."

"Anna Malone, you see the world in a different light, and I love you for that."

"Oh, really! How much do you love me?"

"Funny you should ask!" Jake replied. "I need to talk with you about something."

"That sounds serious."

"Well, I just want to point out that this may be a good time to move in together. You just finished producing a film, and you've already signed a contract with Manhattan Publishing for your next project. Do you really want to go back to Bath and live with your parents?"

I sat back in my chair. "This subject may require a second cup of coffee. I mean, we've been together for less than twenty-four hours after a four-month separation."

Jake reached across the table and took my hands. His ocean-blue eyes poured into mine. "I know. That's why I can't wait any longer to tell you that I want to share my life with you; I want to live with you, and wake up with you, and go to bed with you over and over again."

My mouth opened, but not a single word passed my lips. Runaway tears ran down my face, but Jake wouldn't let go. Our hands rested on the tabletop with the headline from the 1930s staring back at us.

"Okay," whispered Jake, "maybe I've caught you by surprise, but in your absence, I've had a lot of time to think, and I've come up with a plan that will allow us to live, love, and work together."

"I'm listening."

CHAPTER 2

December 1936

Penélope Solis McGowan, known by everyone in Bath as Penny, tucked her white blouse into her navy-blue skirt for the third time since arriving at the W.T. Grant Department Store on the corner of Water and Centre Streets. She was trying not to bite her freshly polished nails. Her aunt, Mary Rose Goss, had told her that the first day would be the hardest. Waiting at the cosmetics counter, she applied some red lipstick and recalled her aunt's advice: "Be patient with every customer, including the difficult ones, and be brave. Only the brave survive working in a retail shop."

She looked into the mirror and her brown eyes looked back with exuberance. In that moment, she remembered what her aunt had said at the kitchen door: "I believe in you, Penny. My family is my best work, and I know you can achieve whatever your heart wishes."

"Miss McGowan!" the manager shouted.

"Yes, Mr. Harris," Penny responded respectfully.

Augie Harris leaned over the counter until his large, veiny-red nose was a mere six inches from Penny's face. "Don't forget to stock aisle four with long red tapers. It's December, after all, and customers buy candles in December. They'll be looking for red ones."

Penny could smell the alcohol on his breath even though it was early in the day. Biting her lip, she stepped back. She wondered how anyone could sound so annoyed on such a beautiful winter morning. Christmas was only a few weeks away, and she wanted to be merry, but staring into Mr. Harris's bloodshot eyes, she began to doubt the *Daily Times*'s morning headline, "Glimmers of Hope Appear in Bath." Since the Crash of '29, families along the Kennebec had been struggling to keep their heads above water; then the river flooded, and they thought they were literally going to drown. She almost laughed when she realized her mind was creating a metaphor out of two disasters.

For generations, Kennebeckers like her father had sailed down the river to the ocean, but last March during the spring thaw, families feared they would lose their homes and businesses when the rain was torrential and ice jams even threatened the bridges. The ice field moved southward toward the sea carrying with it all sorts of debris—a coal shed, a dead cow, a shanty, and parts of the Richmond-Dresden Bridge. Tasked with breaking up the ice field, the Coast Guard cutter *Ossipee* positioned herself north of the Carlton Bridge. Everyone in the city held their breath while they waited to see if the nine-year-old bridge would survive the force of the moving ice. By the grace of God and the skill of the Coast Guard, the bridge remained standing. When the rain finally stopped, Bath celebrated. On March 25, 1936, Bath Iron Works launched its new destroyer, the USS *Drayton*, and the skies over Bath began to clear. For some indiscernible reason, remembering the history of the Kennebec emboldened Penny. Stepping up to the counter, she chose to be brave and not let Mr. Harris dampen her spirit.

On this clear December day, there were indeed glimmers of hope all over Bath. Festive wreaths trimmed with ribbon, berries, and pinecones hung on almost every door, and the shop windows along Front and Centre Streets were sparkling with glass ornaments, quilted stockings, nutcrackers, and delicate porcelain angels of every size. Bath's deluxe movie theater, the Opera House, was showing *The Great Ziegfeld*, a newly released musical starring William Powell and Myrna Loy. If you looked, there were signs of love and joy all around the city.

From behind the counter, Penny had a great view of the department store's window displays. They were filled with toys: Shirley Temple dolls dressed like sailors in patriotic blue and white, a Lionel train set, board games—Monopoly, Sorry, and Scrabble—finger paints, die-cast model cars, a red wagon, and a deluxe pedal truck. Penny was grateful to have a job close to home, but she wished her grumpy boss would be grateful, too. Why was he so dreadful? Everything was finally looking up for Maine's little city. The Carlton Bridge—linking Portland, Brunswick, and Bath to Wiscasset, Boothbay, and Rockland—was beginning to work its magic: The state of Maine had recently added the word *Vacationland* to its license plates, and the tourists were coming. Optimists like Penny and her aunt believed that wherever tourists went, money would surely follow. If they were right, Bath was headed for a boom in the not-too-distant future. Unfortunately, Mr. Harris was not an optimist. With only fifteen shopping days left until Christmas, he would rather be drinking whiskey at the River Tavern than training a young counter girl.

"I'll do that right away, Mr. Harris," said Penny. But as soon as her boss walked away, she muttered, "If I can figure out where those candles are in that dark and dingy stockroom."

Helene Milhomme, a coworker and her aunt's best friend, suddenly appeared at her side.

"I can help you find those candles, honey. Follow me, and I'll show you how to navigate that maze they call a stockroom in no time."

"Thank you," sighed Penny. "I don't know why, but Mr. Harris reminds me of my ninth-grade algebra teacher. I hated algebra."

Weaving their way between glass counters covered with tartan-red scarves and soft woolen mittens, socks for all sizes, handsome ties for the men, and pretty handkerchiefs for the ladies, Helene and Penny made their way to the northwest corner of the store. As Helene opened the heavy oak door leading to the stockroom, Penny glanced back at the gold-medallion clock hanging over the store's sunny, south-facing entrance, and pouted like a schoolgirl. The store would be open until eight to accommodate all the exhausted shoppers. She had many hours left to go.

* * *

Despite the late hour, Penny's walk home replenished her soul. The night sky glowed with a full moon and a splash of stars, and all the windows along Washington Street were shining with holiday candles. The eighteenth-century homes—large Italianates, Greek Revivals, and federal-style colonials—were dressed up for the holidays. Ten-foot-high doors were decorated with wreaths, and wrought-iron railings and fences were wrapped in evergreen roping. Even though the workdays could be heavy and dull, the December nights glowed with good will. Penny looked up the street to see that her Aunt Mary, as usual, had left the porch light on. She smiled. Her aunt would be sitting in the front parlor waiting to hear about her travails at Grant's.

Penny opened the side door and stepped quietly into the Goss's warm kitchen. She could still smell the meatloaf and mashed potatoes that her aunt had prepared for dinner hours ago. There was a plate, covered with a clean dishcloth, waiting for her on the counter, and her stomach growled as soon as she spied it. After a long day of standing under bright lights in a noisy, wide-open space, it felt good to be entering a cozy, softly lit room. She sat down on a bench near the doorway and removed the rubbers protecting her good leather pumps. She stood to take off her matching red hat and scarf and her calf-length, charcoal-gray swing coat, hanging it on a peg near the back staircase. It was the nicest coat she had ever owned. Her sharp new work clothes and this stylish wool coat signaled that the worst days of the Depression were behind them and better days were on their way.

"Is that you, Penny?" called Aunt Mary from the front room.

"Yes, Aunt Mary. Who else would it be at this hour?"

By the time Penny had completed her rhetorical question, her aunt was already heating up her supper. "So, tell me, darling, how did your first day go? Was the store busy?"

Penny laughed. "Oh, yes, the customers, men and women, were lined up at my counter."

"And what counter would that be?"

"Mr. Harris, in his great wisdom, thought I would be well-placed at the perfume and cosmetics counter," answered Penny with a touch of sarcasm.

"So, you had men at your counter?" asked Mary Rose.

Penny pulled a tortoise comb from her hair and an avalanche of long dark tresses fell over her right eye. She peered at her aunt with one clear eye and giggled. "Yes, most of them were buying gifts for their wives or daughters, but a few of them were just waiting there to tell me I was pretty or to ask me out for coffee."

It was her aunt's turn to giggle.

"Men will act like boys whenever they're around a pretty girl."

Penny sat down at the kitchen table. She fixed her eyes on the candle that was glowing by the six-over-six window and sighed deeply.

"It seems funny now, but at five o'clock it was highly annoying. I was tired and hungry, and my feet were aching. Besides, most of them weren't the least bit attractive."

"Most?" teased Aunt Mary.

"Now that I think about it, not a single one of them was attractive. They were awful except for the few who were buying gifts for their daughters. Those darling ones made me miss my own father."

"I'm sorry, Penny. The holidays are always difficult when it comes to missing a loved one. Your father has been gone for sixteen years, but it seems like yesterday that he was standing in the doorway."

Penny picked up her fork and played with the mountain of milky-white potatoes on her plate.

"You and my dear cousin Stella have been all the family I've needed. My parents left me in good hands. I'm not complaining; I'm just not sure I can stay in Bath much longer. Maybe I should call Stella tonight. She's doing well in Manhattan. She's working, saving a little money, and making plans. I have to find my way, too. Don't we come from a long line of daring shipbuilders and sea captains?"

Mary Rose shook her head and gently said, "Penélope, you may not look like your father, but you certainly share his wanderlust. My half-brother, Daniel, was never truly happy unless he was navigating around Cape Horn, sailing to an exotic port, or saving a beautiful woman like your mother from a cruel life. He was strong, smart, and incredibly brave, but he could also be starry-eyed, especially when it came to your mother and you."

Mary Rose fell silent. She shifted her weight on the rush seat of her old shaker-style chair, folded her arthritic hands on the pine table between them, and focused her gaze on the kitchen sampler hanging over Penny's head. She was remembering Daniel's charming smile and emerald-green eyes. Those unforgettable eyes had come from their father, Captain Robert McGowan.

Their father had spent most of his life at sea and had been seasoned by his experience. By definition, he was an old salt. He would rather smoke his pipe than discuss another person's business. Shortly before his death, he had told Mary Rose that life was as rough and unforgiving as the sea. She remembered sitting at her father's bedside waiting for a loving goodbye, but he only whispered about heavy gales, crashing waves, broken masts, and lost sailors. Once, he cried out for Clare, his first wife, but that was his only reference to family. In her heart, Mary Rose knew that her father had loved the sea and his ships, but that he also mourned the time he had lost with those he had loved.

Despite her fatigue, Penny noticed her aunt's thoughtfulness. "Are you okay, Aunt Mary?" she asked softly.

Mary Rose nodded. "I was just thinking about your dad, and my dad, too. Even though Christmas is supposed to be merry, it also evokes memories—some sweet and some bitter. Let's be cheerful. Call your cousin. I have no idea what crazy scheme the two of you will cook up, but I know you both will travel far and will find your way home."

Penny stood. "Thank you for dinner, Aunt Mary, and for always keeping the light on. I'm going to call Stella Rose right now. She's a night owl, so I'm sure she's still awake."

CHAPTER 3

July 2018

When Jake and I pulled up in front of my parents' antique colonial on Washington Street, I noticed the front door right away and feigned outrage.

"What happened to Essex Green? I thought my mom and dad were traditionalists. Didn't my mother spend a year researching this house's history with her Nequasset Preservation, Inc. friends? Unless I'm mistaken, sky blue is not a historic color."

Jake grinned as he stepped out of the Jeep. When he reached the passenger side, he opened the door and teased, "You're impossible—you miss nothing and comment on everything."

The blue door opened and my five-foot-two mom called my name. "Welcome home, Anna! I've missed you. How do you like the front door? It's Whipple Blue."

We all laughed, but Jake laughed the hardest. "Ellie, you're using your super powers again. Not fair."

"Okay, Jake. I'll abstain. I've missed you, too."

While Jake unpacked the Jeep, I rushed up the granite steps and hugged my blond and bubbly mom. From the corner of my eye, I could see that Jake was studying us from afar. He was probably thinking we couldn't look more different, yet act so alike.

Respecting Mom's wishes to always keep the entryway with its curving staircase free of clutter, Jake and I carried my luggage upstairs to the bedroom at the back of the house—my quiet place. As I set my bags down on the wide-planked floor, my gaze fell on the quilt covering my wrought-iron bed, and I felt instantly at home and at ease. Jake sensed the sweetness of the moment and pushed me onto the mattress, covering me with kisses.

When he rolled away, he murmured, "To be continued."

I sighed and brushed his lips with one more kiss before we both stood up and descended the back staircase to join my parents outside on the deck. It was early afternoon, and the day's forecast was hot and sunny, but even Freckles, our dachshund-sheltie, was relishing the breeze rising off the Kennebec less than a hundred yards away. As I witnessed my mom and dad enjoying the splendor of Maine's short summer, I realized how tough the last few months had been for me. After risking my life and sanity in the chaos of L.A. and New York City—scurrying under heavy metal scaffolding; waiting at traffic lights with horns blaring and people raging; stepping in dog poop on city sidewalks; standing in long lines for expensive coffee—this covered deck with its two wicker couches and matching chair was paradise. I knew I was really home when my mom poured the perfect Arnold Palmer: a little ice tea with a lot of lemonade.

"Ellie, your deck is blooming!" Jake said as he fell into a soft cushion and reached for a handful of potato chips that were waiting in an orange bowl on the glass table. "You make everything look and feel so beautiful."

Sitting down next to Jake, I saw my mom tilt her head and smile.

"Oh, Jake, I almost forgot how charming you are. Where have you been while Anna has been toiling away in California and Manhattan?"

"I'm still an engineer for Maine DOT, but on my days off, I've been helping a firm that restores historic lighthouses."

Mom laughed. "Does this mean that Nequasset Preservation, Inc., Doris Van der Waag, and I have convinced you that historic landmarks are worth saving?"

"Yes, but others...have had some input, too," stumbled Jake.

"Well, I'm just glad you've come over to the bright side."

With a glint in his eye, Jake said, "Full disclosure, Ellie, I've been hunting for an old lighthouse to rescue, so I've teamed up with a true preservationist."

My dad sat up in his chair. "This is a new development. I'd like to hear more."

"Don't worry," Jake chuckled. "I haven't found one yet, but I've attended a few auctions, and I think I've found a good mentor."

That was my dad's cue to ask the next question. "Who would that be?"

"Garrett Liston. He's the go-to-guy when you're looking for a lighthouse to save. He's a smart businessman who happens to be passionate about Maine's maritime history. He's also an excellent poker player, giving him an advantage at a high-stakes auction."

Nodding, my dad said, "I read about him in the paper. He was given credit for saving the lighthouse on Pearl Island. In the interview, he talked about the extreme weather that hits that island and the obstacles his team had to overcome to restore the lighthouse and the keeper's quarters to their 1950s condition. If I recall, his project is going to be featured in a documentary film on vanishing maritime treasures. Am I right?"

"Yes, the restoration of the Pearl Island Lighthouse is quickly becoming the gold standard. Garrett's an amazing guy."

Fearing Dad was leading Jake into a technical discussion that would put us all to sleep, I changed the subject.

"Jake and I are going to drive up to Port Clyde tomorrow to see an apartment. Maine DOT has been keeping him busy on Route 1 between Thomaston and Rockland, and that's probably why you haven't seen him these last few months. He's going to sign a lease on the place we're looking at if I approve."

Before my parents could react, Jake chimed in, "Would you like to join us? It's just a day trip. I have a meeting in Portland on Thursday, but otherwise it's an easy week. You know how I love spending time with the Malone family."

My intuitive parents looked at each other, then looked at us, and said, "Yes."

* * *

The next day, we loaded up the Jeep with water bottles, sunscreen, trail mix, and Panama hats. Jake had spent the night in my parents' guest room because we wanted to get an early start. The weather station was predicting blue skies, which meant all the cars heading north on Route 1 would be stopping in Wiscasset. If only Red's—the iconic lobster shack—wasn't located at the west end of the Davey Bridge, happy motorists would be able to cruise over the Sheepscot River to Edgecomb and all points Down East without a headache. But by noon every day during the high season, traffic slowed to a crawl in "Maine's Prettiest Village," so we had to leave Bath early if we didn't want to face that traffic.

When I slid into the backseat, I noticed Mom was wearing her white hand-embroidered blouse from Oaxaca and I had to smile. Even though she'd fallen in love with Bath the moment she saw the white steeple of the Winter Street Church, Mexico was still her favorite destination when snowdrifts in Maine reached toward the sky.

"*Te ves muy Buena, Mamá,*" I said in my best Spanish accent. "Are you missing your Spanish class?"

Mom shot me one of her classic don't-make-fun-of-me looks so I clarified my observation.

"You look just like you did when you left the house every weekday to teach at Laurel High School."

"Oh, honey, you're full of sugar in the morning," she said rather curtly without cracking a smile. Then her voice softened. "Thanks for reminding me. Those days were far from easy, but they were definitely rewarding, and I remember them well."

Twenty minutes later, Jake shouted over the 1980s music playing on the radio, "We're passing Red's and there's no line."

"That's because it's not open yet," I shouted back and everyone laughed, including my no-fooling-around-in-the-car dad.

Jake stepped on the gas and continued on to Port Clyde. Less than an hour later, he pulled into a parking space in front of the Village Creamery and Bakery Shop on Port Clyde Road.

"I have a rule," my dad said quietly as soon as Jake turned off the motor.

"What's that rule, sir?" asked Jake.

"No ice cream before lunch."

Still seated in the back of the car, Mom and I both shook our heads in unison.

Jake flashed his winning smile. "I agree with that rule, but this creamery is also a bakery, and a cup of their

French roast is worth the trip. Besides, the apartment is five minutes away and we're running early."

As soon as we stepped inside the shop, we felt its charm. The wooden counter was painted blue. Behind it, there was a wall covered with a large blackboard divided into two columns. The first, written in pink chalk, was a list of bakery items; the second, written in white chalk, was a list of the ice cream flavors for the day, and we all studied that list in silence.

After scanning the list, Dad boldly stated, "I know what Anna will be having."

I jabbed him with my elbow. "Just wait, Dad, I might surprise you."

"Oh, really?" he teased. "You're not going to order the blueberry-lemon scone?"

"Okay, you're right as usual, and a mug of dark roast."

"I thought so," he said with a grin. "Place your orders, everyone! I'm buying."

Jake stepped up to the counter and ordered a chocolate chip muffin, and Mom couldn't resist the chance to tease him.

"Would you like that with a scoop of coffee ice cream?"

"No, Ellie, but I'll take my coffee with a little cream and sugar."

Mom shrugged her shoulders and said, "Of course."

Pulling his wallet out of his pocket, Dad intervened. "What do you say, Ellie? Would you like to share one of those wicked sticky buns?"

"No, I'll have my own, thank you."

He answered her with a smile while a big man with a scruffy white beard handed each of us a red coffee mug.

"Good morning. I'm Tate," he said in a gravelly voice. "Find a table with chairs that suit you. My wife, Becky, will bring over your coffee and sweet rolls. She's the baker and deserves all the credit. "

I noticed all the chairs were different, striking me as quirky and endearing. For some people, this little cream-ery might be located in East Overshoe—way out of the way—and sorely deficient in Wi-Fi service, but I liked everything about it and gave Tate a big smile.

We found a table with two blue and two green chairs and sat down to enjoy the local ambience. I looked over at Jake and he winked. That's when I realized he was feeling confident and was ready to share our plan with my par-ents. I wanted to raise my hand and say *stop*, but instead I gently shook my head.

Jake must have caught my *no* because he took a big gulp of coffee, tipped his chair back, and said, "I like this place."

He paused, and I focused on the old oak table—etched with *I love Violet*—until he continued.

"From this sweet spot, I can see why artists come to Maine. What do you think, Ellie?"

My mother's eyes turned soft.

"You don't say much, Jake, but what you do say tends to surprise me."

Jake grinned. "Everyone likes surprises, right?"

"That depends on whether they're good or bad," said Mom with a hint of a smile.

"Well, today, I'm going to show you an unusual apart-ment."

Dad closed one eye and queried, "Is that 'unusual' in a good way or a bad way?"

We all laughed, but I laughed the hardest. My dad, Dr. Tyler Malone, a PhD in political science, had a magical power: He could make my worries disappear. All morn-ing long, I had worried that my parents would think an apartment at Marshall Point was too remote. I also worried that I would come to the same conclusion. My family and I were accustomed to living near a college campus, a major airport, and a big medical center. That's why it was easy for us to be happy in the City of Bath, but we were also accustomed to moving. On the brink of change, I made a wish, then took a bite of my blueberry-lemon scone and enjoyed the flavor of the day.

CHAPTER 4

September 1937

On an apple-crisp morning, Mary Rose was at the wheel of her new Packard Six automobile when her twenty-seven-year old niece, who looked every bit of seventeen, screamed, "Watch out! That truck is slowing down."

Mary Rose slammed her foot on the brake and gasped, "I can see that truck, Penélope. Don't ever scream at me like that again!"

After a fleeting moment, she put her foot back on the gas and continued driving and talking.

"There's no need to shout. I'm a good driver. Your Uncle Thomas taught me. He could sail any square-rig, pilot any tugboat, and drive any motorcar; he was the captain of my heart."

Glancing sideways, Penny admired her aunt's enduring devotion. Uncle Thomas had died over ten years ago, but he was still her true love. She was right; he had taught her well. In fact, Aunt Mary was the only woman she knew who owned a car and was willing to drive from Bath to Portland. For a woman of her age, she was fearless and skillful. She could repair a broken chair, fix a faucet, read a map, change a flat tire, and drive an auto-mobile. Almost everyone in Bath referred to Mary Rose Goss as a woman ahead of her time, and Penny agreed.

An hour later, when they arrived at Union Station, Mary Rose parked her $800, state-of-the-art Packard behind a beat-up old Ford and turned off the engine, but neither she nor Penny moved. Instead, they both stared straight ahead, as if they were still driving, because they didn't want to say goodbye.

Finally, Penny turned her smooth, dark-skinned face toward her aunt and whispered, *"No puedo decir adiós, mi tía."*

Mary Rose shook her head and chuckled. "My dear, you always speak Spanish when you're nervous. I'm glad your mother taught you to speak her native language, but I don't want you to be nervous; I want you to be excited. You may look like your mother, but you have a lot of your father in you, too, and you're ready to set sail for Manhattan and beyond."

Reaching into her bottomless purse, Penny grabbed a handkerchief and blotted the tears that were ruining her mascara.

"I'll miss you, Aunt Mary. I'll miss our walks along Popham Beach, our countless trips to the library, our long talks at dinnertime, and your home cooking. I doubt there's a single person in New York who can cook like you."

Mary Rose swallowed and blinked, but there was no stopping the wave of emotion. Trying to escape her feel-ings, she opened the car door. Once her feet hit the ground, she breathed deeply and watched Penny step out of the car and walk around its shiny hood. When Penny opened her arms, she fell into them.

Between sobs, Mary Rose struggled to speak. "I should be consoling you. This whole day is upside down.

Sometimes life is so filled with misfortune. Your mother died before she had a chance to teach you how to fly. When you were born, she asked me to be your godmother. Since her passing, I've tried to keep you close and safe, but I know she wanted you to see the world like she did with your father. If you don't leave now, you may never have the chance to go to New York, and that's the bold life your mother wanted for you."

Penny patted her aunt's back as if she were a child, consoling her in a dulcet voice, "I know, Aunt Mary. You've been a kind, loving guardian. I would have been lost without you. Now please don't cry. I'll have a big adventure in New York City, then I'll come back."

Mary Rose squared her shoulders, smoothed her skirt, and stroked her niece's raven-colored hair. "It will be all right. We'll be all right, and you must believe you can go wherever you want."

"I do, Aunt Mary. I do."

"Well, now that we've cleared that up, I'm supposed to tell you that Stella will be waiting at Grand Central. I bet she'll be wearing a bright-yellow raincoat, rain or shine, and a black hat with a wide brim. In other words, she'll be impossible to miss."

Penny laughed. "Even in a crowd, I'm sure she'll stand out."

Mary Rose chuckled. "She always does. Now let's get your luggage out of the trunk and buy your ticket to Manhattan."

* * *

Screeching, the *New Haven* came to a halt at Grand Central and Penny peered through the small dusty window. She smiled at the mere thought of seeing her glamorous, strawberry-blond cousin. They were opposites, and that's why they got along so well. If anyone could help her find an avenue to success in New York City, it was Stella Rose Goss. Some women had a talent for knitting, baking, singing, or dancing, but Stella had a gift for patching up scraped knees and making dreams come true. Since graduating from high school and losing her last parent, Captain Daniel McGowan, Penny had been searching for something or someone to give purpose to her life. When she boarded the train in Portland that morning, she knew she would find a piece of home at her cousin's apartment, but she wasn't sure she'd like her new job in a skyscraper in midtown Manhattan.

It had been a long travel day. The *Flying Yankee* had carried her from Portland to Boston's North Station; then a trolley had taken her to South Station, where she had caught the *New Haven* to New York City. She was tired when she spied Stella. Her curly blond hair was easy to spot, and she was wearing a red dress to die for. As soon as Penny spotted her, she stood up, grabbed her valise, and headed toward the exit as fast as her fellow passengers would allow.

Stepping onto the platform, she was met by a throng of people, and she was glad she had seen Stella before exiting the train. If she hadn't, she wouldn't have known to push straight forward into the center of the crowd. She stretched her arm over her head and waved to signal her arrival. Within a minute, Stella spotted her and started to push through the crowd as well. At last, they met in the middle and hugged and squealed with unabashed affection. After years of living in separate cities, it was a happy reunion.

Penny stepped back to admire her cousin's belted dress with its cap sleeves, full collar, and slightly flared bottom. "Oh, Stella, you look divine! That dress is the cat's meow! I love your haircut, too! It suits your personality."

Shaking her head, Stella said, "Enough about fashion! I fear you worked too long at that department store. It's definitely time for a change. Let's get out of here so we can talk."

Penny grabbed her bags, and the two made their way to the stairs. Once outside, Stella took Penny's hand and led her to the curb.

Looking up, Penny observed the immensity of Manhattan for the first time. "Where are we going?" she asked in an awestruck voice.

"We're going to my place on West 61st Street, but first we have to hail a cab. It's too late for the trolley. Besides, it's a special occasion. Your coming to Manhattan is worth the fare."

"Okay, if you say so, but how do we hail a cab?"

Stella winked. "Watch and learn."

With New York–style chutzpah, Stella walked to the curb, raised her arm, and positioned her right leg so that more than her ankle showed. Penny quickly realized that her cousin's provocative position was carefully orchestrated to stop a taxicab driver from passing her by. In a minute, the signal was received, and Stella and Penny climbed into the backseat of a yellow cab.

The driver turned his head to the side, just enough so Penny could see his profile, and spoke to them over the back of the front seat. He had a Roman nose, unruly gray hair, and a shaggy beard. Penny thought she detected a foreign accent and suspected he was Italian, but he didn't seem at all like Machine-Gun Vito or Lucky Luca, characters she had seen on screen at the Bath Opera House, and she was relieved. Perhaps men like that only existed in the movies; if that was not the case, she prayed she would never meet them.

"Where to, ladies?" asked the cab driver in a smoker's voice that made him sound tough and old.

Stella replied boldly, "530 West 61st Street. We're not in a hurry, so please drive slowly around the circle. It's a great night to enjoy the scenery."

"Will do, miss," said the cabbie as he started the meter.

In a blink, they were headed up Madison Avenue. Penny was about to get her first look at Central Park and Columbus Circle—two landmarks that looked fabulous on starry nights. Even though the cousins had a lot of business to discuss—like what Penny's job at National Screen Service would entail—tonight's ride was all about the view. Besides, Stella believed that becoming acquainted with the city was an important part of Penny's training as the newest receptionist at National Screen. Stella had never intended to stay at an office job for more than a few years, but much to her surprise, her coworkers on the tenth floor of the Film Center had become her second family. It was a great place to work, and it would be even better with Penny at the front desk, but she still planned to leave at the end of next summer. Her plan was to submit her application to Lenox Hill Hospital's School of Nursing by the December deadline. After working as an executive secretary for almost four years, she was more certain than ever that she wanted to care for the sick, not take dictation. Penny would understand. Even though she was two years younger than Stella, she had always been the pragmatic one. Penny didn't dream about sailing around the world and helping strangers in faraway places; rather, she would be happy riding a bike down a dusty road with someone she loved.

The cab pulled up in front of a four-story brick building.

"Here's your stop, ladies. That will be three bucks."

Stella pulled out a five from her black leather wallet and handed it over the front seat to the driver.

"Keep the change," she said as she slid toward the curb side of the vehicle.

"Thank you," he said as he stepped out of the cab to get Penny's bag out of the trunk.

Seconds later, the yellow cab sped away, and Penny looked up the granite steps in amazement. The address was written in cursive on the blown-glass window at the top of the tall oak door. Penny stared at that door as if she was commanding it to open, and suddenly it did. A young woman, followed by a cute guy, came out, looked up and down the street, took each other's hands, and walked toward the corner. Between Stella's building and the end of the block, there were two more apartment buildings, a tailor shop, a Chinese restaurant, and a drugstore. Despite the late hour, the street was humming. Penny could only imagine where that couple was headed. The possibilities in a city this big were endless.

Stella's sweet-sounding voice drifted over the city's noise. "Hey, Penny, don't just stand there. Come on up and see your new home."

Penny rushed up the steps and entered the building, but she still had three flights of stairs to climb before she could step over the threshold of Apartment 3C and begin to unpack. Tomorrow would be her first day at National Screen Service.

CHAPTER 5

July 2018

As my parents, Jake, and I drove away from the Village Creamery, I couldn't help but wonder if I was heading in the right direction.

"We're off like a herd of turtles," shouted Jake as the tires screeched on the asphalt and headed toward Marshall Point.

Driving along the coast of Maine was usually relaxing, but Jake was racing down Port Clyde Road as if he was on patrol in Iraq. Fortunately, I had warned my parents about his aggressive driving. I blamed it on his military experience, and they seemed to understand. My mom comes from a Navy family. During World War II, her mother and father served in the South Pacific. They were both in harm's way. I never met my grandmother—she died too soon—but according to my mother, I have her eyes, and that's proof that love survives. Maybe Jake feels at home with my family because he knows we're survivors. I think he sees surviving as our great common denominator.

Like Jake, my dad is well acquainted with the anguish of war and the challenges veterans face upon returning home. When he graduated from the College of the Holy Cross's NROTC program, he was commissioned an ensign and sent to Southeast Asia to pilot a patrol boat, a PBR, through the weed-choked rivers of Vietnam. My dad had told my brothers and me that his boat engaged in frequent firefights with the enemy and was charged with inserting and extracting Navy SEAL teams. If anyone could understand Jake's desire to live life "full up" like Hemingway's bullfighters, it was my dad.

When Jake pulled his fire-engine-red Jeep into the parking lot at Marshall Point ten minutes ahead of our ETA, my parents didn't bother to read the sign. They slowly stepped out of the car and stretched. I opened my door and heard my mother's voice.

"Is this Marshall Point? Where's the apartment?"

As Jake nodded and cleared his throat, I looked toward the brick-and-granite tower and let my eyes climb the twenty-four feet from its base to its crowning light and prayed Jake could convince my parents that his zany idea to live on the second floor of an old keeper's house was intended to be inspiring, romantic, and a gesture of love.

"Yes, this is the Marshall Point Lighthouse Station," answered Jake. "From here, you can see the entrance to Port Clyde Harbor."

Dad raised his hand to block the sun, then he volleyed back, "I've got a clear view of the harbor, but where exactly is the apartment?"

I started to hum—something I do when I'm nervous.

Jake pointed up the hill. "It's on the second floor of the keeper's house. Remember when I called it 'unusual'?"

"Yes," answered Mom, "I remember."

Dad echoed, "Yes," and went silent.

"Well, I meant amazing and historic. The St. George Historical Society restored the keeper's house in the 1980s, and the second-floor apartment has been rented since 1989. In fact, the same couple, a photographer and his wife, lived in it from 1989 until 2002 and published a book of photographs and memories. St. George assumed ownership of the entire station in 1998. The lighthouse is still a Coast Guard aid to navigation, but the keeper's house is a museum with an apartment upstairs."

"And you want to live out here through the winter?" asked Mom in a rising voice. "The museum will close in October. Won't you feel isolated?"

"No, the former tenants told me that visitors keep coming to take pictures, commune with nature, talk to the waves—"

A gust of wind tossed his unruly hair over his eyes. He brushed it back with his hand and kept defending the Point. "There are some year-round residents along the coast, and the Black Anchor Restaurant and Port Clyde General Store stay open. It will be quiet in winter but not dead."

I raised an eyebrow, sealed my lips, and watched the whitecaps rise and fall on the water. My dad suggested we take a look at the apartment. I nodded, relieved that my parents were going to reserve judgment. If Mom unraveled, Dad had a way of rolling her back. If Dad came unglued, Mom had a way of sticking him back together. The longevity of Eleanor and Tyler Malone's marriage was a clear case of yin and yang.

Inside the museum, I began to feel the station's charm. The keeper's summer kitchen had been converted into the museum's entrance hall, and there was a lot of history to see in the long narrow room. As I wandered around the first floor, I noticed a print of the Marshall Point Light signed by the artist himself, Andrew Wyeth, and I took a deep breath. The volunteer standing nearby told me

Wyeth had painted the original watercolor in the 1930s when he was in his twenties. He and his family had spent many glorious summers in Port Clyde. Standing before his work, I could see how the quiet fishing village had provided him with a bounty of inspiration. I turned my head and looked through a sea-facing window to see powerful waves crashing against the stone tower.

On the drive up, I had checked my phone and learned that the lighthouse was rebuilt in 1857 because the original tower, built in 1832, was made of rubblestone and laid up with poor lime mortar that was soft and penetrable. In winter, it was plagued by ice, and it fell into disrepair, but it continued to keep watch over the harbor. At the height of the Great Depression, the leaky lighthouse at the edge of the Point inspired a young Andrew Wyeth. When so many Americans were plunged into darkness, Wyeth saw the enduring strength of the rocky coast of Maine. I was beginning to see why Jake felt such a strong affinity for this light at the southern edge of St. George. My grandmother, Stella Rose, would have liked Jake. She had stitched a lot of wisdom into kitchen samplers, like "Sorrow can burn you to bitterness or spin you to gold," so I believe she would have sensed the gold in Jake.

My dad must have been thinking a similar thought because he suddenly called out to Jake. "Look at this photo of Forest Gump!"

Jake went to his side, and they laughed like two sailors on liberty. Once again, the volunteer on duty shared some rich local lore. One of the most memorable scenes in the 1994 movie *Forrest Gump* was filmed at the Marshall Point Lighthouse Station. Forest's cross-country run had ended at Marshall Point. I glanced at my dad and witnessed his reaction. Tyler Malone, a retired college professor, was dazzled by a photo of Tom Hanks in costume as Forrest Gump standing at the Marshall Point Lighthouse.

"You may be right about this place," said Dad as he slapped Jake on the back in a supportive way. "Let's go upstairs and take a look at the second floor. I'd like to see this apartment you're so eager to live in."

I found my mom admiring a display of miniature lobster buoys that were painted in the local lobstermen's colors by a founding member of the museum. When I tapped her shoulder, she turned and gave me a look reminiscent of a teacher who had just discovered a new lesson.

"What a clever way to show visitors how the lobstermen identify their traps!"

"Mom, I think you're still in the arena. Have you really retired?"

She tilted her head, then glanced at Jake. "I'll always be a teacher, just like he'll always be a Marine."

Jake waved, and that was my cue to bring Mom over to the main counter where they kept the keys to the apartment. Jake had phoned ahead so the property manager was expecting us.

"Okay, Mom, follow me. Let's go see what has captured that Marine's imagination."

* * *

On the second floor, we all gathered around Noah, the son of the first Coast Guard keeper at Marshall Point, and listened to him praise the durability of the keeper's house. Standing in the middle of the sun-drenched apartment, Noah explained how the original house had been destroyed by lightning in the spring of 1895 and replaced by November with the colonial revival–style house we were visiting today. The one-bedroom apartment was spacious and freshly painted. The white appliances in the kitchen were dated but functioning; and the bathroom had been updated with new tile and an oak cabinet. The spectacular view of the bay and harbor was enticing, but my mom and dad acknowledged the elephant in the room.

"What does the heating bill look like for a place like this?" asked my dad.

Noah was ready for that question. "It's oil heat, of course, but when the house was updated in 1986 they installed forced air so there are no radiators to deal with. The house has been well insulated, too. The historical society invested in the heating system to preserve the local artifacts on the first floor. That's good and bad. Heat rises. Some people say it gets too hot up here."

Taking my hand, Jake asked Noah if we could have a few minutes to poke around and discuss our options. He agreed, but he also cautioned us about taking too long to decide.

"This place will go fast and folks tend to stay. It has only turned over a few times since its opening in 1989. I'll be downstairs if you have any more questions."

Jake squeezed my hand. "Thanks. We won't be long."

As soon as Noah closed the door, I seized the moment. "Jake has asked me to move in with him, and I think this apartment is perfect for us. I can write here, and Jake will be close to his Maine DOT jobs in Waldoboro, Thomaston, and Rockland."

Silence filled the room. Jake squeezed my hand again—a little harder—and I could feel his tension.

"What about your connection with Garrett Liston?" asked my dad. "Isn't he based in Portland? This place could be hard to get in and out of, especially in winter."

Jake paused, running his fingers through his hair, then he replied in a clear, strong voice, "Garrett has offered me the use of his private jet, and the Knox County airport is just three miles south of Rockland. Distance won't be a problem."

My dad put his arm around my mother's waist and pulled her close to his side, smiled at Jake, and said, "God knows you're both smart, and I think you know what you want…If you think Marshall Point will work for you, it probably will, but don't forget Bath isn't far away. You can get there from here, and we hope you'll visit often."

Then Dad reached out his hand and Jake shook it.

"Thanks for the vote of confidence, sir. Don't worry. We'll visit Bath often."

"But not because we're cold or lonely," I teased.

Jake finished my thought. "We'll be nice and cozy here, but I'll miss your vegetarian lasagna even though I'm not a vegetarian."

Mom laughed. "Ty's lasagna is the best in the state, and it's worth a trip to Bath."

I winked. "No argument."

With sunshine streaming through every window, I continued chatting like a bird.

"I'm going to write my novel here, and it won't be stygian. It's going to be filled with the light and history of this place. I started it today."

My dad looked puzzled. "*Stygian*? And when did you have a chance to write?"

Jake chimed in. "I don't know what *stygian* means, but I do know that first Anna sees the story in her mind's eye, and then she puts the words on paper."

"He knows me too well," I said with a giggle. "*Stygian* means dark and gloomy, the opposite of a keeper's house."

CHAPTER 6

December 1937

At the Film Center Building in midtown Manhattan, Stella sat in a hunter-green chair across from Simon Miller's mahogany desk. She crossed her legs, opened her steno pad, and let her hand fly over the page to create an elegant set of symbols that could be easily read by anyone who understood the Gregg Shorthand System. Later she would have no trouble transcribing her notes because she was National Screen Service's best stenographer. In fact, she had mastered Gregg in less than six weeks of training—a company record.

Stella's boss was speaking quickly. He was a native New Yorker to whom time was money and a minute was less than sixty seconds. While Simon spoke, he stared out the window of his corner office on the twelfth floor of the thirteen-story building. He was weighing his words. This letter was supposed to close the deal with Hollywood's leading motion picture company. He didn't want to look directly at Stella, his Girl Friday. Over the past few years, she had become his right hand. She took dictation at 280 words per minute, was a champion speller and a whiz at grammar, made the best coffee, and had a mellifluous phone voice. The only drawback was her desire to leave the job. Two weeks ago, she had asked him to write a letter of recommendation; a few days ago, with a heavy heart, he had penned a glowing one.

The stoic president of NSS willed his emotions away and continued to dictate a trailblazing letter of agreement to Global Pictures, but because Stella had uncrossed and crossed her shapely legs, it was difficult for him to focus. Her sheer nylons with their single straight seam enhanced the allure of her exquisite calves. She was wearing dark-blue heels and a gray dress with a crisp white collar and thin red belt. Her curly hair was pinned up with two tortoise-shell combs, and her lips were painted cherry-red. In a word, she was stunning.

When Simon fell silent, Stella picked up the thread. "National Screen Service looks forward to…"

Her silver-haired boss continued, "…looks forward to providing the best trailers for Global Pictures for many years to come. Sincerely…"

Closing her steno pad, Stella asked cheerfully, "Will that be all, Mr. Miller?"

Simon slowly removed his wire-rimmed glasses, set them down on the desk, and stood. When he cleared his throat, Stella stood up, too, because she sensed her usually confident boss was suddenly nervous.

Reaching into the pocket of his well-tailored pants, Simon said, "No, there's something more." He pulled out a small blue velvet box and offered it to Stella.

She didn't move and fixed her gaze on Simon's weathered face and noticed the fine lines beneath his warm brown eyes.

After an awkward pause, she managed to stammer, "What's this?"

Simon swallowed hard before answering in a hushed voice. "It's a gift for the holidays...nothing more. Please take it."

Stella raised her hand and touched the box, then shook her head and whispered, "No, I can't."

"You deserve it. I wish you weren't leaving."

Placing her steno pad down on the desk, she reached for the gift. When she opened it, she found a silver brooch, a delicate bow with a deep-blue sapphire set on top of the knot.

She gasped. "Mr. Miller, this is too much!"

"No, I'm afraid it's not enough. I chose it because the sapphire accents your eyes. I want you to know how valuable you are; how you've changed this place. You've made everything better, especially me."

Stella looked up and her sparkling eyes lit up the room.

"Mr. Miller, your wife died over five years ago. By the time I arrived, you were already through the worst of it. I've just listened."

Simon stepped around his desk to stand beside her. He didn't dare touch her, but he asked, "Would you let me take you to Barbetta's tonight? It's not far from your place, and maybe I can convince you over dinner that you're too good at stenography to go to nursing school."

Setting the gift on the desk, Stella laughed lightly, grabbed her pad, and turned to leave.

Standing in the middle of his private office, Simon asked, "Where are you going?"

"You wanted this letter to go out today and it's almost five. I need to start typing."

"What about dinner?"

"I'll have to take a rain check. The girls are taking me out after work. They want to celebrate my applying to Lenox Hill Hospital's School of Nursing. I mailed the application this morning. Thank you again for the recommendation. And I'm sorry I can't accept your gift, Mr. Miller. It's just too much."

Stella walked out the door, and Simon's empty gaze landed on the blue velvet box sitting on the corner of his desk where the steno pad had rested.

* * *

At five o'clock, Penny buzzed Stella's phone from the reception desk, which was located by the dramatic Art Deco elevator doors. The Film Center Building was one of the finest examples of Art Deco in the city, and the bold and varied colors extended from the walls of the lobby to every radiator grille. Penny felt lucky to be working in such a modern building in the Hell's Kitchen neighborhood of Manhattan. Coming from Bath, Maine, she had a great appreciation for American architecture and had already researched Ely Jacques Kahn, the building's brilliant architect. Ever since her arrival in mid-September, Penny had been dazzled by the glitter of New York. It was a marvelous place, and she was grateful that her cousin had paved her way to a front-desk job in an exciting industry. What could be more exciting than working for the motion picture business in Manhattan?

Stella noticed the blinking red light on her desk phone and picked up the receiver.

"Hello, National Screen Service, Mr. Miller's office, Miss Goss speaking."

Penny giggled. "It's Penny. Are you ready to leave? It's not too cold, so the girls want to walk over to the Landmark on Eleventh Avenue. The exercise will be good for us, and afterwards we can all catch a cab home."

"Give me ten minutes to wrap up. I'll meet you in the lobby."

"Okay, but don't be late. Sometimes you're too loyal and hardworking for your own good."

"I promise! I'll be there in ten." Stella hung up and kept typing.

* * *

One receptionist, two typists, and two executive secretaries, all from National Screen Service, and all young and fashionable, walked into the Landmark Tavern just after five thirty. They were seated promptly — Alice O'Connor, the vice president's secretary, had called in a reservation and she knew the owner. Their gum-chewing waitress asked for their drink order and Alice didn't hesitate.

"That will be four whiskey sours and one gin and tonic." She looked around the table and loudly asked, "Am I right, girls?"

"Who's the gin and tonic for?" Stella asked.

"Me, silly. I've graduated to a more sophisticated drink. I'm through with sweet cocktails. They leave me with a terrible hangover."

Taking out a cigarette, Carole chimed in, "Well, you should know, Alice, because this place has become your favorite hangout."

Penny looked aghast. "That sounds a bit mean...don't you think?"

Carole fixed her eyes on Penny. "You're still kind of new. Just wait. You'll soon find out how social Alice can be. Look! There's the owner. He's coming straight to our table because Miss Alice O'Connor is with us."

"Hi, Alice, hi, girls," said Denny Murtha. "It's good to see you all looking so well, and I have to tell you someone at the bar noticed. That man over there, the one with the broad shoulders in the herringbone suit, is sending over a bottle of champagne for your enjoyment."

"Whoa!" whispered Evelyn, one of the sweeter girls from the typing pool. "Who is that handsome stranger?"

Penny cleared her throat delicately and replied, "I know him."

Stella practically squealed. "Well, tell him we accept and we think he should join us!"

Penny blushed a deep shade of crimson and everyone noticed.

Evelyn was seated next to Penny at the middle of the long rectangular table. She reached over and quietly asked, "Who is he and where did you meet him?"

As Penny watched the young man stand and approach them, she answered in a hushed voice, "His name is Sal Leone. He's the top salesman of the month. I chatted with him this morning at the office. He covers all of New England, from Hartford, Connecticut, to Providence, Rhode Island; from Boston, Massachusetts to Portsmouth, New Hampshire; from Portland, Maine, to Burlington, Vermont. If there's a movie house in New England, he's been there and sold them a trailer with a poster to go with it."

Carole and Evelyn tried to conceal their amusement by covering their mouths with their napkins, but Stella just laughed.

"Oh, my goodness, Penny, you're certainly familiar with that man's territory."

Starstruck, Penny added one more city to her litany of praise: "He even covers Bath, Maine."

The "Italian stallion" with dark curly hair and a knockout smile arrived. He stood at the head of the table next to Alice, and even though his chocolate-brown eyes avoided Penny, the girls of National Screen felt the connection between the dashing salesman and the ingénue of the office.

Stella was about to say hello when she spotted Simon Miller and Alan Wyman, the company's newest VP, push through the tavern's frosted door. She bit her lip like a nervous teenager wondering how cozy things would get before it was time to go.

A few minutes later, Simon and Alan found their way over to National Screen's unofficial table at the Landmark. Of course, they were greeted so warmly they decided to join the group. And of course, Simon sat next to Stella.

* * *

At eight o'clock, Alice, Carole, and Evelyn said good night, and Alan stood as well.

"Let me hail a cab for you ladies," he said.

Alice answered for the group, "Thank you, Mr. Wyman; that would be lovely."

Before leaving, Alan's eyes swept the table. Only four remained.

"This was fun. I'll see you at the office."

As soon as Alan and the girls departed, Sal touched Penny's hand and whispered, "I don't want to go home yet. Would you like to take a walk and maybe grab a nightcap around the corner?"

Penny nodded, and they both stood to leave.

Smiling, Stella cautioned her cousin, "Don't be too late. Tomorrow is a workday, and the alarm is set for six."

"Yes, *Mom*," Penny called back.

Stella laughed, and Simon loved the sound.

When she turned to look at him, he said, "So, it's just the two of us."

CHAPTER 7

July 2018

The drive from Port Clyde to Bath seemed long. The traffic along Route 1 came to a complete stop on the Davey Bridge thanks to the line at Red's. While tourists on foot waited for a lobster roll, tourists in their cars were treated to a delicious view of Wiscasset, the seat of Lincoln County and a tourist attraction widely known as the "Prettiest Village in Maine": It even said so on the signs. Unfortunately, we weren't tourists; we were Maine residents on our way home, and we were stuck in an old Jeep with an air-conditioning system that was clearly failing. No one was comfortable, and I sensed that my parents were beginning to think that during the summer, Port Clyde would only be accessible by boat, and they didn't have one. I didn't want to make them unhappy, but Jake and I were definitely moving to Marshall Point in October. At least the high season would be over by then and the traffic would disappear. I knew my parents wanted me to settle in Bath—our home of five years—but this change in plans wouldn't surprise them too much. After all, our family had rolled from city to city for decades, and I had grown accustomed to moving.

Whenever I was in trouble, my parents called me Anna Rose; whenever I was in *big* trouble, they called me Gypsy. But they had to accept my wanderlust because it was inherited. My affinity for bold new experiences was in my blood. I knew I'd be happy living at the water's edge — at least for a while. The keeper's house would infuse my fiction with history and romance, and I wouldn't be alone. Truth be told, Jake Summers was the surprise. Just when I thought I would never find the right person, I'd found this man who wanted to live life to the fullest. We were a good match, and we were ready to live at a lighthouse for a year, maybe more.

When Jake finally parked his Jeep in front of my parents' house on Washington Street, it was 3:15 and we were all a bit weary from the long drive.

"Would you like to come in for a cold beer and a snack, Jake?" my mom asked.

"No thanks, Ellie. I've got a meeting in Portland tomorrow with Garrett Liston and I need to get ready, but I'll see you soon."

My dad opened the car door and said, "Thanks for inviting us today. Regardless of age, your kids are still your kids and it helps to see where they're going."

Jake nodded as we got out of the car. While my parents walked quickly to the front steps, I put my head through the driver's open window and planted a kiss on his cheek.

"Don't worry. They love you."

"I hope so," he said with a serious look. "Will you come to the meeting tomorrow?"

"Why?"

"Garrett invited you, and he never says anything he doesn't mean. For some reason, he wants you there."

"Well, in that case, I'll be there. Just tell me when and where."

"I'll text you the address, but it starts at ten. Don't be late. He admires punctuality."

"I'll be there five minutes early. Now drive safe. I can tell you're preoccupied."

"I'm a Marine, remember? I can drive and think at the same time."

He flashed his wicked smile, and I kissed him again before saying goodbye. "See you tomorrow, sweetheart."

He laughed. "I love it when you call me that. Don't forget, ten sharp—and I love you."

* * *

The next morning, my alarm went off at 6:15. I showered, dried my hair, put on some eye shadow and a little mascara, and stood in front of my closet. What was I supposed to wear? I thought about texting Jake, but he was probably out on his morning run. Besides, he was rarely any help in the wardrobe department. Wearing a uniform for eight years had warped his sense of appropriate attire. The decision was all mine. I tested three outfits and chose the first: a short light-blue skirt paired with a tangerine scoop-necked top and strappy brown sandals. I checked my watch, and since it was only 6:55, I headed down the back staircase for my usual cornflakes-with-banana breakfast. I caught Mom coming in the side door with our dog Freckles. It was hard to know who had woken up first, Freckles or Mom, but they were always out on their morning walk by 6:30. It was a comforting routine and I was happy to be home to witness it, especially since I had been living in hotels with no-pet policies for too long.

I bent down and rubbed Freckles's ears. In return, she wagged her tail and licked my wrist, which made me happy because I knew she felt safe, and that's what a rescue dog yearns for the most. In 2012, she was found wandering a country road and taken to a shelter. She was sick, but an organization called Hope 4 Paws stepped in, nursed her back to health, and put her up for adoption. My parents were lucky because they were the first to call. I think rescue dogs can smell true love; I wish people had the same sense.

When I stood up, I realized my mom had paused to enjoy the moment.

"Freckles missed you."

"I missed her, too. It feels good to be home."

Pouring a cup of coffee, Mom asked, "Where are you off to this morning? You look more put-together than usual."

"I've been invited to a meeting at One Portland Square."

I pulled a box of cornflakes from the pantry; Mom took a bottle of milk from the refrigerator and two bowls from the cupboard, and we sat down at the kitchen table to discuss the plan for the day.

"I'm impressed," my mother said quietly. "May I ask who invited you and why?"

As I sliced a banana, I replied, "Garrett Liston invited Jake and me. We're meeting with the board of directors of Keepers of Maine, Inc. As for *why*, I'm not sure."

We sipped our coffee, looked out at a hummingbird feeding by the window, and weighed our next words.

My mother broke the silence. "I'd like to talk with you about your plans to move in with Jake, the timing and whatnot, but you could hit traffic on 295, so I don't want to keep you...but could you just tell me how this morning's invitation came about?"

"It's kind of weird," I said with a shrug. "Garrett sat behind me on my flight from La Guardia, and after we got off the plane, he was behind me on the escalator. He was still behind me when I met Jake. I was surprised when they recognized each other and started talking like they were business partners."

"Are they?"

"I don't think so, at least not yet. Jake works full-time for Maine DOT and Garrett is focused on restoring an abandoned lighthouse station in Casco Bay, but Garrett mentioned this meeting, then asked me to come, too."

Mom took a nibble of her ginger scone and continued to question me. "Didn't you and Jake talk about this over the weekend?"

"Yes and no. At the airport, Garrett told me they had met at an auction, so I asked Jake about that. He said it was a Coast Guard auction. Garrett was looking for a military-grade responder boat to plow through the ten miles of sometimes rough weather between Yarmouth and Pearl Island. Jake helped him decide on a twenty-five-foot Defender-class vessel. Garrett's company is so pleased with that purchase, they may want to engage Jake as a consultant."

"I can see why Keepers of Maine, Inc. is interested in Jake. He's a veteran, a graduate of Worcester Polytech, and a Maine DOT engineer, but that still doesn't explain why they're interested in you."

"Maybe they just want to meet his significant other before they make him an offer. You know, some people actually think you're more reliable if you're in a committed relationship."

For a moment, I thought I was going to be sprayed with coffee, but Mom managed to swallow before laughing.

"If that were true, a lot of people would be out of work! Seriously, do you think Jake is looking for a new job?"

"Honestly, I don't know. Like the ocean, Jake is sometimes unfathomable."

I looked at the clock and cleared my place.

"Don't worry about the dishes," Mom said in her upbeat way. "I'll clean up. You don't want to be late for your *very* important date."

Now it was my turn to laugh. "So true! Jake told me to be on time because Garrett admires *punctuality*."

"It's always best to keep the boss happy."

With that advice ringing in my ears, I grabbed my purse and hurried out the door.

* * *

When I pulled into a parking spot a block away from One Portland Square, I thanked God for my good karma. In southern California, I never had to worry about parking because the studio provided me with a driver. In New York, I relied solely on public transportation and occasionally hailed a taxi or called an Uber. Now, even though it felt good to be back in the driver's seat, I had to deal with the challenge of parking again. Today I was grateful my Subaru Outback, loaded with auto-stopping, intelligent cruise control, lane detection, and a rearview camera, navigated country roads and city streets like a modern-day sailing ship.

I pressed the door lock and walked down the street humming, but my happy thoughts disappeared when I looked up to see a towering building that shouted *work*, not play. KOMI's offices were located on the top floor of the ten-story building. As I admired the shimmering glass and dark red bricks, I suddenly realized why Garrett Liston, the president of KOMI, had invited me. He was hoping to impress me because he wanted Jake to work for him full-time. He needed Jake's unique set of skills, but he knew KOMI was risky and Maine DOT was safe.

Jake's career with Maine DOT was rock-solid. When he'd negotiated a compromise with Nequasset Preservation, Inc. to allow for a major road improvement project in Bath, he'd proved his worth. Like Garrett, he managed to save a piece of Maine's history. When Maine DOT was about to bulldoze the oldest section of the Beacon Hill Cemetery—Bath's final resting place for nineteenth-century sea captains and shipbuilders—Jake proposed the creation of a Memorial Garden to honor the city's founding families, making him a local hero. He wouldn't leave Maine DOT for KOMI, would he?

"Anna!"

When I heard my name, Jake was standing less than six feet away from me, but I hadn't noticed.

"Jake!"

"You're early," he said as he gave me a peck on the cheek.

"I wanted to surprise you."

"Mission accomplished. I'm surprised—and nervous, too."

I took his hand. "Don't be! You've got me on your side, and according to the boss, I'm pretty *and* smart."

"Well, Garrett's not my boss, but I agree with his taste in boats and women."

"But tell me, why do you always put boats first?"

"I don't answer *why* questions this close to Friday. Ask me on Monday. Right now, we're going into this fortress of steel and riding the elevator all the way to the top."

As Jake pressed the up button, I took a moment to evaluate our situation. This was not Disney World and we weren't in the Tower of Terror. Garrett was a respected entrepreneur, and he probably saw a bright future for Jake. I took a breath and felt a bump as the elevator began to rise.

When the doors opened, a middle-aged man in a dark-blue suit was standing in front of us. His hair was dark with gray sideburns, and he looked like he had just stepped away from a *Gentleman's Quarterly* photo shoot.

"Good morning. I'm Oliver Hayden, one of the vice presidents here at KOMI. You must be Jake and Anna."

"You're right on both counts," Jake said as he shook Oliver's hand. "I'm Jake, and this is my girlfriend, Anna."

"Hello," I said with the sweetest smile I could muster. I shook his hand as firmly as I could. It was warm, and I wondered what kind of man stood next to Garrett Liston. What were his responsibilities? Was he KOMI's official greeter? Was he Garrett's personal scout, in charge of sniffing out good or bad intentions?

Oliver let go of my hand as if he could detect my skepticism and focused on Jake.

"Garrett asked me to show you around before the meeting gets started," he chuckled. "That's office code for 'Take them to the coffee room, then go up to the rooftop patio and show them the best view of Portland.'"

Jake glanced at me and I smiled. He looked at Oliver with a poker face and exclaimed, "That sounds like a brilliant idea!"

We all laughed, and that broke the ice. The morning sun was shining on us, and I was beginning to feel optimistic.

"I could use a cup of coffee," Jake said.

"I could, too, and I've never been on a rooftop in Portland. We'll follow you."

"Anywhere?" Oliver asked with a grin.

I shook my head. "No, just up to the roof," I said in an extra-high voice.

Jake shot me a look. "And back down again," he added rather firmly.

Jake filled his mug with coffee and a hush fell over the room. I felt a sudden chill. Maybe this was the Tower of Terror after all, and we were going to be stuck here for a long time, or until we came crashing down.

The coffee room's glass door swung open, and Garrett's booming voice shattered the silence. "So, you've arrived and you've met Oliver. Have you seen the rooftop?"

Jake smiled. "Not yet. I'm ready to hear what KOMI is planning, and how I can help. If your office space is any indication, your business must be doing well. I'm excited to be here."

In a heartbeat, Jake was the man in the arena. I saw his eyes change from sky-blue to steel-gray. He had put on his armor and was ready to enter the fray, but I was worried. Jake and I had known each other for five years; I knew him well enough to know he only had two speeds: fast and faster.

With Jake on fire, I decided to downshift. "Garrett, why don't you show us the view from the roof? We'd like to see Portland and Casco Bay the way you see it."

"Well, Anna, that would be my pleasure. Thank you for asking. Besides, Oliver has a presentation to fine-tune before our meeting. Don't you, Oliver?"

"True. I'll see you in twenty minutes. In the meantime, enjoy the patio."

I looked at Jake and he winked back. The games had been postponed. A part of me was waiting for the director to take his seat and shout, "Action!"

Moments later, we stepped out of the stairwell and into the light. Garrett spun around and shouted, "Look at that azure blue! Doesn't the sky above Casco Bay inspire you to save the planet?"

I looped arms with Jake and said, "Yes, it does," then whispered, "That man is *in charge*. If he says 'leap,' think first!"

Jake whispered back, "I will."

—

CHAPTER 8

December 1937

In the middle of a recurring nightmare where she was chased by a stranger on a dimly lit street strewn with bottles, tin cans, and mewing cats, Stella woke with a fright. The one-bedroom apartment was dark except for the light from the street lamp that slipped through the venetian blinds. She looked across the room to see if Penny was asleep and immediately sat up when she realized the chenille bedspread hadn't been pulled back, and the twin bed was empty. With a feeling of imminent doom, she looked at the alarm clock on her nightstand and noted the time. Where could Penny be at this hour? It was Friday, a workday, not a holiday. She swung her feet to the floor and into her slippers, pushing her curls away from her eyes. She reached for her robe, but as she opened the bedroom door, she heard a key turn in the apartment door's lock. She froze in her tracks when she heard a man's deep voice.

"I don't want to go. Could I stay for a while?"

"No, you can't. I have a roommate, my cousin, and she's probably sleeping right now."

The man responded with a chuckle. Then there was a long, silent pause. Stella imagined a goodbye kiss.

"Okay, but I'm leaving on Sunday for Boston and points north. How about a movie tomorrow night?"

"On one condition."

"What's that?" he asked in a hushed voice.

"You let me pick the film."

"I'll agree to that if you promise to sit close and share my popcorn."

Stella stepped back into the bedroom. She heard a giggle, then another silent pause, longer than the one before, until Penny's voice passed through the door and filled the apartment like music on the radio.

"Thank you for tonight. It really was unforgettable. Now I'm going to dream about you. Good night, Sal."

"Good night, pretty Penny," he replied.

Stella waited for the door to open and shut. She stepped into the hall, flipped on the light, and scolded her cousin. "Where have you been? It's late!"

Startled, Penny blinked and tried to explain. "We...we went on a carriage ride through the park...Central Park," she stammered.

"For *five* hours? Who goes on a—"

"Shhh! Calm down," Penny said quietly. "You're going to wake the neighbors."

"Don't you hush me! You're the one coming home in the wee hours of the morning."

Rolling her eyes, Penny took off her hat and coat and hung them on the hall tree.

"It's not that late," she said over her shoulder as she walked into the kitchen. "We had a nightcap at the Empire Room. Why are you so upset? Didn't you have a nice time with our *boss*, Mr. Miller?"

Stella felt as if she'd been slapped. "What is that supposed to mean? Never mind. I'm tired and I'm going back to bed. We both have to be in the office at nine."

Penny was filling a glass of water at the kitchen sink, but she stopped and turned to face her cousin. "I'll be there on time, but you don't have to worry. *You* can be late."

Stella dropped her eyes to the floor. "That's not fair. You think you know, but you don't. We can talk about it over lunch maybe."

Now it was Penny's downturned eyes that focused on the linoleum. "Okay, I'm sorry," she said.

* * *

Sal Leone and Simon Miller stepped out of the elevator onto the twelfth floor. They were side by side, and both were smiling. Before they parted, Mr. Miller turned toward Sal and shook his hand.

"Congratulations, Sal! You've had a great quarter. Keep up the good work, and you'll be a VP before you turn forty."

"Thank you, sir, but I couldn't possibly wait that long."

When both men laughed out loud, they seemed more like father and son than boss and employee, but that wasn't surprising. Simon was loved by many because of his kindness. He was the founder of National Screen Service, but sometimes he acted more like the friendly janitor than the owner of the company. He always wanted to fix whatever seemed broken—a typewriter, a stapler, a telephone, a contract, or a heart. Blessed with a crown of snowy hair, he would have been called Santa Claus at NSS if he wasn't so fit, clean-shaven, and devotedly Jewish. In the entertainment industry, he was truly unique, and on this twenty-first day of December, he was even jollier than usual.

Simon walked into his sprawling corner office, and Sal sauntered over to the reception desk. Penny saw him coming and smiled.

"Good morning, Mr. Leone," she said cheerfully.

"Best morning ever, Miss McGowan. Let's celebrate with a cup of coffee. What do you say? Can I pour you a cup of Maxwell House in the break room? You know, it's 'good to the last drop.'"

Penny laughed. "Of course, I'd love to, but give me a minute. I have to wait for Alice to relieve me."

Sal winked his approval and headed for the break room.

Penny's fawn-like eyes followed him, and a few minutes later she hurried down the hall in pursuit of hot coffee with a little cream and lots of sugar. When she found Sal standing alone at the counter, however, she didn't need the extra sugar. She only needed him.

"Hi, lucky Penny," said Sal as soon as he saw her.

Taking her hand and pulling her close, he said, "I wish I could kiss you right now, but since that's against office policy, let me hand you this cup of coffee, and we'll pretend we're here for caffeine."

Penny giggled and grabbed the mug. They both stood at the stainless-steel counter stirring their coffee. Sal had even added the cream and sugar. Penny looked into her mug and grinned.

"I was thinking we should see the new Gary Cooper film, *Souls at Sea*."

"Oh, really," Sal chuckled. "Are you a fan of Gary Cooper?"

Avoiding his midnight eyes, Penny looked across the room and softly answered, "No, not exactly, but my aunt wrote to me that a Bath-built ship is featured in the film. It's a bark, the *Kaiulani*, and it was launched in December of 1899 from the Arthur Gannett and Company shipyard, which used to be behind our family's home on Washington Street. The *Kaiulani* was the fifth steel vessel that the Gannetts produced, and one of its last. The yard closed in

1903 after launching the *Kineo*, its only steel schooner. The *Atlas*, the last square-rigger built at the shipyard, slipped over the ways in 1902, and that's the year square-riggers began to sail out of sight."

"How do you know so much about ships, and what's a bark?"

Penny shrugged, but her reddened cheeks revealed her embarrassment. Talking about home was her Achilles heel, and her fascination with maritime history was a borderline obsession. No one in Manhattan could possibly match her passion for tall ships.

"A bark is a type of square-rigger," she said matter-of-factly. "It's a sailing ship; I know about these things because I come from Bath, the City of Ships."

Sal put his hand under Penny's chin and gently tilted her face upward. "Bath—that's in Maine, right?" He broke into a grin. "I'm just teasing. My mom was born in Lubec, and she comes from a long line of shipbuilders and sea captains. Don't let the name Leone fool you. My mother was a Winslow."

Penny shook her head and gasped, "No! I don't believe you. How on earth did your parents meet?"

Feigning injury, Sal answered with a question. "Do you think I would ever lie to you?"

Penny set her coffee mug down on the counter. "No, but I don't think many Italians immigrated to Lubec. It's practically in Canada."

"You don't say," quipped Sal. "My dad was a stonemason, and…"

His eyes darted to the clock on the wall. "I've got a meeting with Alan Wyman right now, so this love story will have to wait."

He glanced at the door, and seeing no one, planted a quick kiss on Penny's cheek before leaving the break room.

* * *

The first light on Stella's phone blinked, which meant her boss was calling. She picked up the receiver.

"Good morning. Miss Goss speaking."

"Good morning, Stella. Please bring me my mail—only what I *need* to read—and a cup of coffee."

"Of course. Heavy on the cream and light on the sugar?"

"Yes, you know me better than anyone."

Stella replied briskly, "Right away, sir."

Entering Simon's office with coffee in one hand and the mail in the other, Stella had to use her left hip to close the door. Simon looked up from the contract he was reading just in time to see her graceful motion, and he sat back to enjoy the view.

"What took you so long?" he asked with a twinkle in his eye.

Stella smiled as she set the mail and coffee down on the cluttered desk. "I'm sorry. The phone has been ringing off the hook this morning. All our salesmen and most of our clients want everything yesterday, and Christmas is only four days away."

"I'm kidding," said Simon. "You're right on schedule, just like Christmas."

Blushing, Stella quickly looked down at her scuffed leather pumps and said, "Thank you, Mr. Miller. Will that be all?"

Simon took off his glasses, leaned back in his chair, and breathed in Stella's scent—*Shalimar*, a holiday favorite—before responding.

"One more thing…I had a nice time last night."

Stella dropped her guard and looked directly into her boss's engaging eyes.

"I did, too," she murmured.

"Sometimes it's good for the boss to see his staff enjoying themselves outside of the office. The food was good, the drinks were better, and the conversation was the best of all. No harm was done."

"I agree," said Stella, looking out the window and fixing her gaze on the skyscraper across the street.

"What's troubling you, Stella? You don't seem like your buoyant self today. Sit down for a minute and talk to me."

"I don't know," answered Stella as she sat down and faced Simon. "Maybe I'm homesick, or maybe it's just the holidays. New York is a big crowded city, but at times I feel alone here even though I have Penny."

"Everyone feels that way, even me. Since Naomi's passing, my brownstone in Brooklyn feels more like a cell than a home."

The office fell silent until Stella gently said, "You have your boys."

"My boys are in college, one at Princeton and the other at Penn, and quite independent."

Now it was Simon's turn to gaze out the window. "Naomi used to say, 'Your children are only loaned to you. They're not yours to keep,' and she was right."

"I can't even imagine how much you must miss her."

Getting out of his chair, Simon practically shouted, "Listen to us! We sound like two lost souls. I'd like to fix that."

Stella shook her head. "Mr. Miller, you are a man of many talents, but just how do you plan to accomplish that?"

As he walked around his desk, Simon smiled. "With Sunday dinner! I'll send my driver to pick you up at five. Is it a date?"

Speechless, Stella stood up, nodded, and left the office. Simon had managed to have the last word.

* * *

On the corner of 42nd Street and Seventh Avenue, in the heart of New York City's theater district, Penny and Sal stepped out of the subway to find a growing line in front of the Rialto Theater, a new Art Moderne building with a glass-block façade. At the second-floor level, the blue and white glass had strips of aluminum protruding like metal fins on a big engine. Still new to Manhattan, this was Penny's first trip to the Rialto, and she was thrilled to be holding Sal's hand as they joined the line.

Looking up at the eighty-foot tower, also made of glass, she gasped, "Is this really a movie theater? It looks more like a modern-day palace."

Sal chuckled. "Oh, it's a movie theater all right, but the building also houses offices, shops, and a restaurant with a dance floor. It was built to replace the old Rialto, which used to be at Times Square on the corner of Broadway and 42nd Street, and was designed by two master architects, Thomas Lamb and Rosario Candela. I think it's a little over the top, though, even for New York."

"Really? You don't love it? I think it's amazing," said Penny with her eyes fixed on the illuminated signs all over the building.

Glancing over her shoulder, she exclaimed, "Look at this line! Since we arrived, it's wrapped around the corner. I hope the show doesn't sell out."

Sal noticed she was shivering. It was beginning to snow, and the temperature was dropping. He took off his tartan scarf, wrapped it around her neck, and whispered in her ear, "Relax. This theater has seven hundred and fifty seats, and we're getting close to the box office."

Penny laughed and stomped her feet. "Okay, but could you please put your arm around me and share some body heat?"

Sal put his arm around her waist and didn't let go until they stepped up to the ticket window.

"Two for *Souls at Sea*," he said.

The man in the booth responded, "That will be fifty cents."

Sal reached into his pocket and pulled out two quarters. "Thanks," he said as he handed the ticket seller his money. Penny looped her arm in his, and they passed through the double glass doors into the Rialto's lobby for a night at the movies with Gary Cooper and Frances Dee.

Penny sighed. It was almost Christmas and she was on a date with a tall, dark, and handsome man in New York City. How did she get to be so lucky? How she wished she could tell her mom and dad, but that wasn't possible. Like the tall sailing ships of Long Reach, they had passed out of her sight. Suddenly, she felt a chill; then she heard Sal's steamy voice.

"The show doesn't start for twenty minutes. Let's get a bucket of buttered popcorn. What do you say?"

Penny giggled. "I say yes."

By the time they entered the theater, they were lucky to find two seats together in the middle section, and only had to climb over a half dozen people. As soon as they were settled, Penny reached into the bucket and pulled out a handful of popcorn. Munching, she took a moment to absorb the theater's romantic glow, then playfully poked Sal with her elbow.

"So, when are you going to finish your story?"

"What story?" he mumbled, his mouth full.

Penny shook her head and leaned toward him until their shoulders touched. "You know," she whispered, "the story of how your Italian father met your mother, a Mainer."

"You don't let go of much, do you?" he chuckled.

"No, no I don't." Penny answered with a grin.

"Okay, but the movie is going to start in five minutes, so I'm going to give you the short version. No frills."

"That's all I need."

Sal shifted in his creaky seat and looked into her warm, chocolate eyes. When he swallowed hard, she knew he was keeping his emotions in check.

"My dad was a young, talented stonemason in New York City. He worked on several jobs for the Roosevelts. In 1907, Mrs. Roosevelt requested him for a job at Campobello in New Brunswick, Canada. My dad, Salvatore Leone, went up there for several summers in a row, and during one of those summers he met my mom, Melanie Winslow, an American girl who lived in Lubec, Maine, but took a boat over to the island every morning to work at the Roosevelts' cottage. The rest is a long, circuitous road that leads to me, my four brothers, and my sister, Madeline."

Penny's eyes, brimming with emotion, locked onto Sal's face. "Your parents certainly defied the odds. When they married, they merged two different worlds, and I think their story would make a fabulous movie."

"I agree, but it's not over yet. They're both still living on Staten Island. But maybe I'll write their story someday." He looked down into the bucket of popcorn and swallowed hard for a second time. "I hope somebody does," he said gently.

The theater lights dimmed and Penny took Sal's hand before the curtain opened and the lights went out. She reached over and kissed his cheek. He turned, found her mouth, and kissed her with passion as the theater filled with sound and the first trailer started to play.

CHAPTER 9

July 2018

Jake and I sat next to each other at the middle of a long mahogany table that looked as if it had just been shined with a soft cloth and a dab of Old English polish. From our leather-cushioned seats, we enjoyed a bird's-eye view of one of Portland's busiest squares. This old port city reminded me of Philadelphia, a vacation destination for my family when my dad was teaching at Loyola of Maryland. Like Benjamin Franklin's City of Brotherly Love, Portland had a colonial feel, and I half expected to see men wearing tricorns and women wearing fancy bonnets as they strolled over streets paved with red bricks. Despite its charm, I didn't see any haberdashery shops in the Old Port district that morning. Rather, I saw a lot of casual, twenty-first–century young people scurrying about in comfortable shoes and jeans or chinos with cotton shirts. It was clearly an old city with a fresh attitude, and I liked it. I liked it a lot.

Garrett was seated at the head of the table with his eyes glued to his smart phone; Oliver sat to his left with his hand on the mouse of a Dell laptop, and a slightly older man sat to his right with a green folder in front of him. He looked important in his pinstriped suit and Hermes tie, but I had no idea who he was or what he did for KOMI. There was a total of seven men sitting at the table, including Jake. I was the only woman and I felt alone, but Garrett had invited me and Jake was beside me, so I took a deep breath and waited for the director to call "Action."

"Okay, it's ten o'clock, so I'm calling this meeting to order," said Garrett in a strong, calm voice.

His eyes swept around the table until they landed on Jake. He nodded, shuffled a few papers, cleared his throat, and continued.

"Before we get under way with a progress report on our Pearl Island Project and delve into the financials, I've invited two guests, Jake Summers, who some of you have already met, and his friend, Anna Malone. I'll let Jake explain why they're here today."

Glancing to my left, I saw Jake's serene face and wondered how he could look so calm when my knees were shaking. Then I heard his voice, smooth as Irish whiskey, and I felt better.

"Good morning, gentlemen, and good morning, Anna," he said.

I blushed, but Jake didn't notice. He put his hands on the table and paused dramatically before addressing the board.

"I'm here because I love Maine lighthouses as much as you do, and, apparently, I have some skills that KOMI can use to fully restore Garrett's lighthouse at Pearl Island. Hopefully I'll be able to assist you in helping other lighthouse owners as well."

Jake paused to read the room, then grinned and added, "Truth be told, I'm not really sure why Garrett invited Anna, but you should know that she's a screenwriter, a movie producer, a documentary filmmaker, and a soon-to-be novelist. In her spare time, she hangs out with me and keeps me from misbehaving too much."

Smiles rippled around the table, and Oliver seized the moment to jump into the deep end of the agenda.

"Except for Garrett, our CEO, I'm the only other KOMI exec to have had the privilege of meeting *both* of you before today's meeting. I'm delighted you're able to join us for our discussion on Pearl Island, especially as it pertains to the keeper's quarters."

Next, the mysterious gentleman seated to the right of Garrett took off his glasses and welcomed us as well.

"Good morning, Jake and Anna. I'm Lincoln Morrell, a board member and Garrett's favorite brother-in-law. He was married to my sister, Sophie, for twenty-four years…" He paused and put his glasses back on before continuing. "I hope I'm not being presumptuous when I say, 'Welcome aboard.'"

Jake dropped his right hand beneath the table, and I took it without attracting anyone's attention except Garrett's.

"Let's not get ahead of ourselves, Link," said Garrett with a smile. "We don't want to spook this Marine. He has some mad skills with power tools, and Oliver, our naval architect, *likes* him."

Jake chuckled. "Marines don't spook easily, but I'm anxious to see Oliver's presentation and hear what Keepers of Maine, Inc. is planning to do this coming year. I know Pearl Island was scheduled to be a three-year project, and you started in 2016. Will it be done by the end of December? What does your next project look like?"

"Those are good questions," said Garrett. "Oliver will show us the answers."

"I believe that's my cue," said Oliver as the lights dimmed and a white screen appeared at the far end of the conference room.

* * *

Almost two hours later, Jake and I stepped into the elevator and he pressed the button to send us to the lobby. When the doors opened, we stepped out and exited the building. Neither of us had spoken a single word since saying our goodbyes to the board. Just before leaving, Garrett had pulled Jake aside and given him one more pitch for the road, and Jake had promised he would consider KOMI's offer.

I was dumbstruck. I had just learned that KOMI had signed a contract months ago with the Marshall Point Lighthouse Committee and the Town of St. George to reproduce the station's original barn, update the keeper's house, and repair the light's tower. Jake's silence confirmed my suspicion that he knew all about the contract. I was hoping some fresh air would clear our heads, and maybe our hearts would resume their steady beating when we had a chance to talk privately, away from the Tower of Babble.

"The Corner Room is only a few blocks from here," said Jake quietly. "What do you say to hashing this out over lunch?"

It was high noon, and I had to shield my eyes when I looked up at his handsome face. His good looks were always disarming; I had to catch my breath before I agreed.

"Okay, but I have to feed the meter first. I wouldn't want to get a ticket. It would add insult to injury."

Jake put his hands in his pockets and kicked a stone down the sidewalk.

"You're here because of me, so I'd feel bad if you had to pay a fine." He looked up with an impish grin and said, "I'm parked in the garage...Garrett gave me a KOMI spot."

"Oh, I bet he did," I volleyed back.

Still smiling, Jake shook his head. "I can tell you've recently spent time in New York City because your sarcasm is sharper than usual."

I rolled my eyes, took his hand, and pulled him toward my car. "I'm getting hungry. Let's feed this meter and get a booth at The Corner. Maybe my tongue will sweeten to your liking after I have some food."

Jake threw back his head and laughed "Now that sounds wicked! Let's do it!"

* * *

Spread out in a booth that could have squeezed six, I took a gulp of water, perused the menu, and prepared to do battle with my six-foot-two Marine. Of course, I knew from the start that I would lose. In a second, the attractive young waitress headed over and asked if we would like to order drinks.

I smiled and said, "Yes, please. I'd like an Arnold Palmer."

"Is he in Portland today?" Jake kidded.

The pretty waitress chuckled, but I frowned and stepped on Jake's foot.

Jake sat up straight and ordered. "I'll have a glass of lemonade, please," then added "without the Palmer."

I shook my head and said under my breath, "Sometimes you're impossible."

He reached across the table and took both my hands in his.

"Sometimes I'm worth it. Come on, Anna. Don't be angry."

He waited for me to smile, but when I didn't, he continued. "Okay, I've known about KOMI's plan to start work at Marshall Point for weeks, but I wanted you to see the station before we attended the board meeting, and before they asked me to oversee the project."

"That's all good, Jake, but you've been working with Garrett for months and haven't said a word to me about it."

Leaning over the table as far as I could, I fired away. "How could you? I thought your idea to live at the keeper's house was inspired by love, but now I see it was driven by ambition. You're about to change careers. You want to restore lighthouses for a living, but you've kept me in the dark."

When Jake lowered his eyes, I knew he was raising the white flag. For me, the restaurant fell silent, and I wanted to cry, but I didn't.

Jake tried to explain. "It's been tough navigating without you these past few months. I wanted to tell you about the opportunity at KOMI, but Maine DOT has been so good to me, and I was ambivalent about leaving one for the other. I guess I wanted to wait until I was sure."

He lifted his eyes and seemed to look past me. "The truth is, Garrett's work has stirred my soul. You, of all people, should understand how invisible forces can move us. You feel that way about maritime history and Bath's Long Reach."

I sat back and said, "Oh dear, I'm sorry. I haven't been here for you. Text messages, Face Time, and rushed phone calls with bad cell service aren't the best way to communicate with someone you love. I'm the one who's guilty of blind ambition, not you."

Jake reached for my hand again. "Ambition is not a sin. In fact, I think it's a virtue we both share, and I don't want us to change, but we need to talk more and text less."

I looked at Jake and said, "How crazy is this? I'm the writer, and you're the one launching words like arrows. You're a puzzle, Jake Summers, an irresistible puzzle."

At that moment, my head cleared, my heart spoke, and I knew what I wanted.

"Jake, remember that question you asked me at the Farmer's Market in Bath four years ago?"

He leaned back and blew out some air. "How could I forget? It's not every day you ask a woman to marry you and she turns you down."

"Would you ask me again? Would you ask me right now?" I whispered.

Stunned, he sat up and managed to produce a single word: "What?"

"Okay, let me be perfectly clear. Jake Summers, will you marry me?"

He threw up his hands. "Of course you'd ask me on a day I don't have the ring in my pocket!"

I slid out of my seat to sit beside him, then I said, "I don't need a ring; I just need a *yes*."

"Yes! I'll marry you, and I'll put that ring on your finger as soon as I can!"

As he kissed me, the waitress returned with our drinks.

"Are you ready to order?" she asked.

We both said no, and Jake kissed me again as if no one was looking.

* * *

On Friday morning, my phone rang, and I answered it with my eyes closed. "Hello, Anna speaking."

"Did I wake you?" asked a husky voice.

I blinked and looked at the clock. "Jake?"

He chuckled, "Who else would be calling you at this hour?"

I stretched in my bed and answered in a lilting voice, "Only you."

Suddenly, the phone went quiet. When I heard Jake's voice again, his tone was a tad more serious.

"Garrett would like you to join us on our boat ride to the island this morning. Can you meet us at the Yarmouth Marina by eight fifteen?"

I threw off the covers. "I'm up for that."

"Are you really?" he quipped. "Don't be late."

"Don't worry; I'll be early. I'm anxious to see how one saves a lighthouse!"

"I bet you are," said Jake with a belly laugh.

I couldn't see his face, but I heard the sunshine in his voice, and that pushed me out of bed.

Through my window, I could see the raspberry sky over the Kennebec, and I was inspired to tease. "Red sky at morning, sailors take warning. See you soon."

"As soon as you can," he replied.

I put the phone down, rushed into the shower, and twenty minutes later scurried down the back staircase to grab a Thermos of coffee and breakfast to go. Of course, Mom and Dad were already in the sunroom enjoying bacon and eggs and watching their favorite morning show. They acted as if they were surprised to see me.

"To what do we owe this early-morning appearance?" asked my mom.

I tried to answer nonchalantly. "Jake called and invited me out to Pearl Island this morning. I'm finally going to see Garrett Liston's famous lighthouse and find out what part Jake has played in its restoration."

"Oh *that*," said Dad with a smile.

"There's a ginger scone in the cupboard," said Mom in her insanely cheerful voice.

She was the quintessential morning person. Sometimes that annoyed me, but today I was grateful.

"Thanks, you're a lifesaver."

"Not really," she said with a grin. "I just buy them by the dozen at the Farmer's Market and freeze them. I had a feeling you might *need* one this morning, so I defrosted it last night. Take it; scones travel well."

I grabbed it and said, "True. See you guys later. I don't know when, but I'll be back."

As I flew out the door, I heard my dad's reply: "We're counting on it."

* * *

About thirty-five minutes later, I pulled into the Yarmouth Marina and spied Jake talking with Garrett next to the boat that had started their alliance, a 25-foot, Safe Boats International Defender-class vessel. From a thousand feet away, I could tell it was formidable, capable of crashing through rough seas to carry workers and supplies to a small island mostly made of ledge, 9.5 nautical miles east of Portland, just as Jake had described. I waved as I approached the dock, but neither Jake nor Garrett noticed as they disappeared into the pilothouse. Clearly, Jake wasn't expecting me to arrive on time, so he had told me 8:15 instead of 8:30. My early arrival shocked him. Suddenly, "The Things We Do for Love," the song I'd been listening to on Sirius Radio, started playing in my head. I was humming when I stepped onto the dock.

When Jake emerged from the pilothouse, I saw the sun touch his face and stopped to admire him.

"Ahoy!" I shouted with a dramatic jump and a wave; then I noticed Garrett standing at Jake's side and felt foolish.

"Well, good morning, Miss Malone. Welcome aboard!" said Garrett in a sunny tone.

I started to wonder if my first impression was wrong. On that flight from La Guardia, I had thought Garrett Liston was full of himself, but Jake had great instincts—they had saved his life more than once in Iraq—and he believed Garrett was a leader worth following. My inner voice told me to trust Jake. Besides, even the press was calling Garrett's project a Casco Bay miracle. Who was I to disagree?

With my chin up, I smiled and said, "Happy to be here, sir."

* * *

Our state-of-the-art watercraft sped through the water, and in less than twenty minutes, we landed at the 150-foot dock that Garrett's crew had built two years earlier despite challenging weather. I could tell Garrett was proud of the achievement because he mentioned it right away.

"We couldn't begin restoring the seventy-six-foot granite tower and its boathouse without resurrecting a dock. It's peaceful today, but that's not typical. The wind and the sea have managed to sweep away almost everything that has been built here. In the 1960s, there was a helicopter pad on this island; it didn't last long."

As I looked up at the lighthouse, I noticed at least a dozen seals sprawled on the rocks. I heard the waves splashing against the ledge and the humming motors of lobster boats. All my senses led me toward the mighty tower that had brought so many sailors safely to shore.

Garrett noticed how charmed I was by the beauty of his private island and was obviously pleased. I saw him tap Jake on the shoulder and tip his head in my direction. Within seconds, Jake was at my side. He was eager to give me a tour of the station, including inside the tower and boathouse—I remembered him telling me that KOMI was doing a painstaking renovation and the keeper's quarters, boathouse, and galley were all being restored to their 1950s condition—and I was anxious to see it all through his eyes.

Standing outside the tower, Garrett explained how the lighthouse had been commissioned in 1871 and abandoned by the Coast Guard in 1975. While I was still processing that information, I realized that Pearl Island's beacon of light had been abandoned for forty years before Garrett rode in and saved it. I could see why so many viewed him as a miracle worker.

As soon as Garrett left us, Jake showed me the keeper's quarters. He was especially proud of the fact that they had pulled the walls back to reveal Douglas fir paneling and had found a bottle of whiskey that was signed and dated "Christmas 1938." He told me the date was significant because it was the last year that the Lighthouse Service was charged with the station's care and operation. In 1939, the organization was disbanded and the torch was passed to the U.S. Coast Guard.

"Why do you think the keeper hid a good bottle of whiskey in the wall?" I asked.

"Keepers were not allowed to drink on the job," Jake said with a slight smile, "but this one probably knew his service was coming to an end, so he hid it with the hope of drinking it on Christmas. Perhaps some colossal event prevented that celebration from happening, and the bottle stayed in its hiding place, waiting to be found."

"Now that's a story I could tell!"

Jake put his arms around me and pulled me close. He kissed me gently and quietly said, "I hope you *do* tell that story. I hope you capture the character of our sailors, fishermen, and lighthouse keepers because our maritime history needs to be told. There are probably more stories than pieces of sea glass along the coast of Maine, and they're waiting for you to find them."

"Ah, Jake, I love it when you show your sentimental side."

"I'm glad you think so because I *am* sentimental when it comes to Maine *and* you."

He reached into his pocket and pulled out the ring he'd been keeping since I had said no that hot July day four years ago. Slipping the solitaire on my finger, he said, "I want you to be my muse forever." Then he kissed me again and I melted in his arms.

We stepped outside and I took his hand. "You're already mine."

I couldn't help but notice how my solitaire sparkled in the summer sun.

CHAPTER 10

April 1938

The sun was streaming through the tall blown-glass windows of the Film Center when Stella answered the phone.

"National Screen Service, Mr. Simon Miller's office. Stella speaking. How can I help you?"

A woman's silvery voice answered, "Good morning. I'd like to speak with Mr. Miller, please."

"Who should I say is calling?"

"A...friend," said the woman with just enough hesitation to spark one's curiosity.

"Of course; please hold for a moment," replied Stella.

After using her index finger to firmly press the hold button, she used her ring finger to buzz her boss.

"Miller."

"Mr. Miller, there's a woman on line one who would like to speak with you. She didn't give her name, but says she's a friend."

Stella couldn't see him, but Simon leaned back in his

chair. There was something in Stella's voice that had made him blush, and that was unsettling.

He cleared his throat and said, "Okay, I'll speak with her."

When the light for line one stopped blinking, Stella reluctantly put down the receiver. She wanted to listen in on the conversation, but her conscience wouldn't let her, so instead she glanced at the clock on the wall and began to time the call.

Meanwhile, the mystery woman said, "Hello, Mr. Miller," a whole octave lower than she had just said good morning to Stella. "I hope I'm not disturbing you. I feel a bit foolish because I just disguised my voice while speaking with your secretary—"

"Why would you do that?" asked Simon brusquely.

"Well, I'm Stella's mother. I was afraid she would recognize my voice, and I don't want her to know I'm calling you. Can we keep this between the two of us?"

Simon rested his elbows heavily on the desk. Holding the receiver in his left hand, he rubbed his forehead and said, "Of course we can. You must be Mary Rose. Stella has spoken of you so often that I feel as if I know you." He chuckled nervously and quickly added, "She always describes you in glowing terms—"

"I'm calling to invite you to lunch the Sunday after next at the Tavern on the Green. It's at Central Park West and West 66th Street. My friends who visit New York frequently tell me it's a lovely place. They've even seen a few movie stars there."

Stunned, Simon swallowed hard before answering. "Well, that's a wonderful invitation, Mrs. Goss. Frankly, it's surprising."

"I hope it's not too surprising. Perhaps Stella hasn't announced it yet, but last week she received her acceptance from Lenox Hill's School of Nursing. I'm coming down to celebrate with her and my niece, Penny McGowan. I'd like you to join us because you've been so supportive. You gave Stella and Penny their first jobs in Manhattan, encouraged Stella to go to business school and promoted her, and wrote a letter of recommendation so she could go to one of the best nursing schools in New York. We owe you so much, Mr. Miller. Please come celebrate. Let's toast to Stella's bright future."

Simon spun around in his swivel chair and looked up at the ceiling. Overcome with emotion, he wasn't sure he could respond.

"Mr. Miller? Are you still there?"

"Yes, I'm here. Of course I'll come to your celebration." Sitting still in his chair, he took a deep breath and filled his next words with genuine feeling. "Nurse Stella will bring comfort to so many people in need. I know she'll be able to ease their suffering because, on occasion, she has eased mine."

Simon's candor surprised Mary Rose. For a moment the line went silent again. She gently said, "Thank you, Mr. Miller. I look forward to meeting you in person. Come to the Tavern at noon. I've reserved a table by the window. According to the hostess, we'll have a great view."

Trying to camouflage his emotion, Simon pushed back from his sturdy desk and resorted to small talk. "Yes, we'll have an amazing view. Did you know that the building that houses the Tavern was built in 1870 from a design created by Calvert Vaux? It was the sheepfold that used to house the flock that grazed at Sheep Meadow."

Mary Rose stifled a giggle. "Now I know why Stella loves you so! In Bath, we value history, architecture, and the Kennebec River."

Without missing a beat, Simon chuckled and said, "Well, give me a minute and I'll tell you about the East River, and the Hudson River, and a place called New York Harbor!"

"Oh, Mr. Miller, I'm looking forward to meeting you and listening to your unabridged history of New York Harbor. Believe it or not, I may have a few Goss details to add. See you at the Tavern on the seventeenth at noon. It's a surprise party, so Stella won't arrive until twelve thirty. Mum's the word!"

"Yes, ma'am," he said. "I'll bring a yellow rose, and I'll be smiling."

"Stella was right. You *are* charming. Goodbye, Mr. Miller."

"Goodbye, Mrs. Goss."

Simon hung up the phone and Stella saw the blinking light turn off. The unidentified woman had spoken with her boss for a total of seven minutes, not too long, but long enough to further pique her curiosity. Now she had to wait and hope Simon would reveal the identity of his friend, intentionally or not.

Through a fog of muddled thoughts, she heard a clear, light voice.

"Stella, wherever you are, come back."

When she looked up, she saw Penny standing at her desk. Trying to chase her cares away, she tossed her head and smiled.

"I'm sorry. What were you saying?"

"Nothing," answered Penny, "except we've missed three minutes of our coffee break and you're usually the one standing at my desk reminding me it's time for sugar, cream, and Maxwell House."

Stella looked at the clock and pushed away from her desk.

"You're so right. This morning I could use more than sugar; I could use an *Irish* coffee."

Penny feigned shock by placing both her hands over her heart. "Stella! I can't believe you just said that. What's going on? I want to know everything."

Pushing a few curls away from her eyes, Stella stood and said, "Follow me and I'll fill you in on all the scathing details."

Fortunately, no one was in the break room, so Stella closed the door and sighed deeply.

"You're not going to believe this, but a woman called Mr. Miller this morning, and she refused to give her name."

Penny responded with a frown and a silent pause.

"She said she was 'a friend.'"

"Okay," said Penny calmly, "and why does that trouble you?"

Stella sighed again, then dropped into a chair, buried her face in her hands, and started to cry. "I don't know," she said between sobs.

Penny put her hand on her cousin's shoulder and sat down beside her.

"Are you sad about leaving? Have you told Mr. Miller you were accepted into the nursing program? What's going on, Stella? Tell me."

"No, I haven't told him, but I will. It's just that…"

As she struggled to explain, she was hit by a second wave of tears.

"But what? You hardly ever cry. Now you're starting to scare me."

Stella pulled a handkerchief out of her pocket, dried her eyes, and blew her nose. "Don't worry, Penny. I'll be fine."

"*Fine* isn't a good word when it's used to describe the way a woman feels. Saying 'I'm fine' usually means 'I'm in big trouble.'"

Nodding, Stella whispered, "You're right. I *am* in big trouble."

"Oh, no. I was hoping I was wrong. So tell me."

"I think I'm going to miss Simon. We've been having Sunday dinners together, and I've started to look forward to them more and more."

Penny raised an eyebrow and asked her cousin the obvious question. "How long has this been going on?"

"Since December, shortly after that night he walked into the bar with Alan Wyman; when we were there with the girls from the office, and Sal took you on that carriage ride through Central Park. It was Christmastime, and I was feeling a little homesick."

"So you started going over to your boss's place for Sunday dinners?" asked Penny.

"He was feeling lonely, too. His wife has been gone a long time. It seemed like a nice thing to do."

"I'm not sure *nice* is the right word," said Penny with a growing sense of alarm.

* * *

Later that afternoon, it was Penny who found herself watching the clock on the far wall of the reception area as she directed countless calls to the appropriate offices and greeted clients and salesmen alike. There was only one salesman she was waiting to see. Sal should have returned from his road trip through New England last night, and she had expected to see him in the office before lunch, but he still hadn't arrived and she was starting to worry. She knew he liked to make a grand entrance, but it was almost four thirty and the workday was almost over. Typically, when Sal returned from two weeks on the road, they celebrated with dinner out at a fancy restaurant. Penny tapped her pencil on the desk and fretted. This was turning out to be the worst day ever at National Screen. Whoever said, "April showers bring May flowers" was wrong. April was a stormy month that threatened to wash away every hope for crocuses and daffodils. At this rate, nothing would bloom in May.

The elevator doors opened just before five, and a handsome gentleman in a blue pinstriped suit and freshly polished shoes entered the office, his dark-brown eyes fixed on Penny. She looked up to catch his gaze and her whole face glowed.

"Welcome home, Mr. Leone," she said with a lilt.

"Thank you, Miss McGowan. It's good to be back in town."

"What's so special about it?"

"You're here and it's almost dinnertime," said Sal in his most seductive voice.

Giggling and feigning surprise, Penny asked, "What exactly does *that* mean?"

"It means I would like to take you out for a meat-and-potatoes dinner, if you'll let me."

"Yes! Let's go to P.J. Clarke's. I've been longing to go there, and I need to end this workday on a high note."

Sal raised an eyebrow and tried not to laugh.

"I'm all for ending the workday, but P.J.'s is on the Upper East Side, and getting there at this hour will be horrendous. How about that mom-and-pop diner near your place?"

When Penny merely nodded, Sal sweetened the invitation. "The booths are cozy there."

Penny shrugged her shoulders, but her eyes said *yes*. "Okay, big guy, you win."

Sal chuckled. "Ah, pretty Penny, I hope I can keep you happy."

After looking to the right and left, he placed his hand over hers and said, "I've got to talk to the boss, but I'll meet you down in the lobby in twenty minutes."

* * *

An hour later, Sal and Penny were sitting in a booth on benches covered in red vinyl at the West Side Diner. Penny was a regular so she didn't have to look at the menu, but Sal pretended to study it as if there were scores of dishes to choose from instead of two specials and six everyday favorites. His attention to the bold print was just a show because he always ordered a flank steak, medium rare, with a baked potato and sour cream, and a side of green beans. Tonight's dinner wouldn't be any different, but Penny was content to sit and admire Sal's curly brown hair as he bowed his head and read the menu from cover to cover.

When the waitress finally arrived at the end of the table, Penny smiled politely, but the haggard waitress, who was new, didn't smile back; rather, she bluntly asked, "What will it be?"

Penny couldn't guess her age, but she had obviously passed her prime. As Sal placed his order, Penny read the waitress's name tag and wondered how Myrna, a woman about her Aunt Mary's age, could survive in New York City on tips and a paltry wage. She made a mental note to ask Sal to be extra generous when it came to the tip, then ordered as nicely as she could.

"I'll have the same, please, but I'd like my steak medium, not medium rare, and I'd like butter, not sour cream, with my potato. Thank you."

"What would you like for drinks?" asked the waitress curtly.

Sal looked at Penny, and Penny nodded.

"Two beers, please. Rheingold, if you have it."

That last remark won half a smile from Myrna. "Yes, we do. I'll be right back with those."

Sal sat back and instantly relaxed. "What was so terrible about today?"

"Oh, nothing and everything." Penny shook her head, and her long, raven-colored hair flew from side to side. "I'd rather not talk about it. Why don't you tell me all about your trip to Portsmouth, Biddeford, Old Orchard Beach, and Cape Elizabeth? Did you get up to Bath?"

He shrugged. "I'd say it was lucrative. I didn't get further than Portland, though. I'm targeting New Hampshire, Maine, and Vermont this spring, and I'll pull back to Connecticut, Rhode Island, and Massachusetts at the end of June. It's a lot of driving, and the roads can be dangerous, especially when it's foggy or late at night. They're not well lit, and they twist and turn and dare you to drive over forty miles an hour."

"It sounds like hard work, but you must have had some fun along the way."

"Well, I did meet some movie stars at Old Orchard Beach," said Sal with a grin.

Penny's eyes opened like two full moons. "Who? How? I want to know all the details."

For a fleeting moment she thought she detected a blush on Sal's flawless olive complexion.

"Well, I met Bette Davis and a few of her costars from *Jezebel*. Apparently, there's a contingent of movie stars who summer in Maine, but this group came early to celebrate *Jezebel*'s premiere away from Hollywood."

"Oh, I see. And how was Miss Davis?" asked Penny coyly.

Sal answered with a single word: "Aggressive."

Penny's brow furrowed with concern, and she spoke haltingly. "I suppose that makes sense...She's a talented actress, a huge draw at the box office...and beautiful."

"I don't think I'd go that far," said Sal. "Let's just say she's not the ingénue she once was. I think she smokes and drinks too much."

Penny looked into Sal's eyes and asked, "Exactly how much time did you spend with her?"

Sal's eyes twinkled. "Do I detect a hint of jealousy?" He chuckled, then reached for her hand. "I didn't spend *any* time with Miss Davis because I wanted to hurry back to you."

Myrna returned with their cold beers, and Penny waited until she left to respond.

"Good! That's the right answer."

He winked. "We should toast to my good sense."

They raised their glasses, and Penny said, "To us."

Sal echoed her words and added, "To love."

Penny smiled like a movie star.

* * *

The sun came sliding through the blinds, and Penny opened her eyes to a lazy Sunday morning. She looked at the clock and yawned. It was eight o'clock, luxuriously late. Monday through Friday, the alarm was set for six. She peered over the nightstand to see if Stella was still asleep. When she saw a few strands of wild blond hair sticking out from under the covers, she smiled sleepily. Even on the hottest summer day, Stella would burrow into bed by pulling her soft bedspread over her head. Penny understood. The matching bedspreads were a gift from Stella's mom, and they were the sweetest reminder of home because they had once covered their matching twin beds on Washington Street. She closed her eyes and allowed herself to dream a little longer. She envisioned her aunt's federal-style colonial with its gently turning staircase, pumpkin-pine floors, and six-over-six blown-glass windows that played with the light in the most beautiful way. She could almost smell the blueberry pancakes and cinnamon scones.

Somehow the dream of her aunt's kitchen sounded a silent alarm. She suddenly remembered the importance of the day. It was Sunday, the seventeenth of April, and her aunt had planned a surprise party for Stella. She had to get up. She was responsible for bringing Stella to the Tavern on the Green at half past twelve. Mary Rose, Sal, the girls from the office, and even Mr. Miller would all be there to greet *Nurse* Stella Goss! In a blink, Penny was up and in the shower.

After drying her long hair with a towel, Penny wrapped it up and put on her robe. She wiped off the mirror with the edge of her sleeve. Her plan was to put on her makeup, get dressed, then wake up Stella and suggest they attend the eleven o'clock mass at the Church of the Blessed Sacrament on West 71st Street. She knew Stella would agree because she often commented on how much she liked the *feel* of Blessed Sacrament. New York City could be such a big, impersonal place, but in church one could feel connected. In many ways, Blessed Sacrament reminded Stella and Penny of Saint Mary's in Bath, and they felt at home there.

Penny's plan worked like a charm. They were both dressed in their Sunday best, sitting in their favorite pew, and singing the closing hymn at noon. By twelve thirty they were walking into Central Park at West 66th Street, and Stella wasn't the least bit suspicious. Miraculously, the party was going to be a surprise, but Penny was nervous because she knew Mr. Miller would be at the restaurant, and she wasn't sure her cousin would be okay with *that* surprise.

* * *

All the invited guests were seated at a large, round table in the middle of a room surrounded by windows looking out on the Tavern's patio and soon-to-bloom garden. They popped up and shouted, "Congratulations, Stella!" as soon as she arrived. Stella stood frozen with her mouth wide open—and her eyes found Simon almost immediately.

Penny put her hand on the small of Stella's back and gently pushed. "Stella, your mom planned this. We're all so proud of you."

Stella looked back at Penny and for a moment considered fleeing the room, but she knew that would be an ungrateful act, so she faced her guests and smiled with all the grace she could muster.

"Thank you! You've surprised me." She laughed and looked at Penny. "How did you pull this off?"

In turn, every one of her guests, including Simon, laughed with her, and they all sat down to enjoy an enchanting lunch at Central Park's crystal palace. Stella sat between her boss and her mother. She placed her napkin on her lap and wondered how she would manage the next ninety minutes without crying. Why was it so hard to turn the page?

CHAPTER 11

October 2018

Long ago, I had decided that moving was worse than having my wisdom teeth pulled. When I was seventeen, I had the opportunity to compare both of those events. If life had a replay button, I'd rather have the oral surgery. Of course, at seventeen, it was my parents' decision to move. Now, two weeks shy of my thirty-sixth birthday, the choice was mine. In 2008, I had promised myself I would only move once a decade, but I'd moved twice since then. Each time, regardless of how much I planned, something went seriously wrong: The moving truck showed up after dark; there was a downpour as they unloaded my antique dresser; and I lost a few precious items, like a jar of sea glass and a photo album from my eighth-grade musical, *Bye-Bye Birdie*. Today, even though it was the thirtieth of October, the day before Halloween, I was oddly optimistic. This move was going to be different. I was moving to Marshall Point with Jake for love and art—they often go hand in hand—and nothing bad was going to happen. We were going to lift the curse of moving once and for all.

Anxious, I woke before the alarm, but I lingered in bed because it was hard to leave the comfort of my grandmother's quilt. I would miss the Panama Room (my mother names rooms the way other people name pets and boats). My sanctuary in Bath was painted Windham Cream, and it was filled with mementos from trips to Latin America. There was a reason I became a writer. My mother, Ellie Malone, is a fan of Albert Einstein and puts his words into action. Before my brothers and I could even pronounce the name *Einstein*, our mother taught us, "Imagination is more important than knowledge." She expanded on Einstein's message by adding, "Traveling sparks imagination." As kids, we had made that connection naturally.

"Anna, it's time to get up," my mother called from the foot of the stairs. "You're moving today, remember?"

There was no escaping the march of time. I threw off the quilt and stepped into my soft L.L. Bean slippers, which helped ease the transition from cozy bed to hardwood floors.

"I'm up!" I shouted. "I'll be down in a minute."

I hurried into the back bathroom, which I've shared with every guest who has slept in the Flag Room—so named because of its red, white, and blue décor. Truth be told, my favorite visitor was my four-year-old niece, Stella. She loved to wake up with the sun and jump on the bed until someone promised her a stack of pancakes. Oh, to be in the presence of a morning star. Waking up today, I could have used a little of Stella's sparkle, but I was alone and beginning to doubt my grown-up self. At the Marshall Point Light Station, the second-floor apartment was 800 square feet; it had one bedroom, one bathroom, a kitchen, and a sitting room. I wondered how well Jake and I would share the space. Since moving to my parents' house on Washington Street, I had become accustomed to living large. Looking into the mirror, I noticed the dark rings under my eyes and sighed. My stomach rumbled. Food would help. I quickly brushed my teeth, splashed some cold water on my face, ran a brush through my hair, and gave my reflection a pep talk: "Reach! Don't be afraid!" I slipped on my grungiest pair of jeans and my beloved NYU hoodie and went downstairs to face a day of change.

As I stepped into the kitchen, my mom greeted me with, "*Buenos Días, Sol!*" without even looking up from the *Portland Press Herald*.

"Oh, please," I whined. "Could you bring down that cheer just a little?"

"Why? Today's a momentous day. You're moving into the keeper's house with your fiancé. It's a new beginning."

Reaching for my favorite coffee mug, I quietly moaned. "I know, and that's why I'm feeling conflicted."

Mom folded her newspaper and set it on the kitchen table. She looked at me with her eyes wide open and told me to sit down, then launched her to-the-point question.

"What are you conflicted about? Jake?"

"No, I love Jake. I'm just not sure moving to Port Clyde is the right move to make. I mean, the premiere for *Captains of the Kennebec* is two weeks away in L.A.; my publisher is in New York City; and I won't be close to a major airport. Have I lost my mind?"

Mom shook her head and poured herself another cup of coffee. She took a long, slow sip before responding.

"No, but sometimes you think too much and feel too little."

I felt like a wounded bird: I wanted to fly, but I couldn't.

"That's harsh. I wrote a screenplay for a romantic film and now I'm writing a novel—also a romance."

"Anna, my dear, writing about love and being in love are not the same."

My shoulders caved and I listened.

"What are you afraid of?" she asked.

"I'm afraid of failing. I'm afraid of failing at love."

Facing me across the table, my mother sat up straight and squared her slender frame.

"When I was young, my father told me the only thing I had to be in life was brave. It was good advice, and now I'm sharing it with you. Be brave, Anna. Love deeply and trust that a good life will follow."

"Oh, Mom, you talk like I write, but it's not that simple. I've signed a contract with one of the biggest publishers in Manhattan, and they want thirty thousand words by the end of February."

"The words will come. They always do. Besides, the keeper's house at Marshall Point is historic *and* romantic. Wait and see; it will inspire you. My God, they shot a scene from an iconic movie there. Don't forget, in the 1930s, the Wyeth family summered and painted in Port Clyde. There's a reason the Marshall Point Lighthouse has graced the cover of *Maine Magazine* more than once."

"That may be true, but it's a bit remote, and Jake and I haven't even set a date yet. Maybe moving in together is premature."

Mom laughed. "You're kidding! You're about to turn thirty-six, and he's forty-one."

"Who's counting?" I asked defensively.

"No one, but this isn't premature. Stop overthinking every decision you make."

Now it was my turn to laugh. "Okay, you win. I don't want to be a stress ball forever. I just want to be with Jake, wherever that is, and write a best-selling novel."

"Don't change too much. You may be a stress ball, but you're also the greatest dreamer I know."

"Thanks, Mom. You keep me sane."

I checked the time on my phone. It was almost half past ten.

"I haven't heard from Jake. He was supposed to call me when the movers finished at his place; he's planning to follow the truck here. I have some boxes and my writing desk to add to the load, and that's all. I hope you're okay with watching Moose. I think dogs hate moving more than humans...if that's possible."

On cue, my phone rang. I picked up and said, "Hello!"

"We're passing Freeport now. If I'm lucky, I'll see you in thirty minutes. Still love me?"

"Still."

* * *

When the doorbell rang, I was in the Flag Room folding the clothes I needed to pack. Dad was working in his office at the top of the front staircase, so he was the first one to reach the door, but I wasn't far behind.

"Good morning, Jake. It's still morning, right?"

Expecting to see me, Jake shifted his weight and stammered, "Yes, sir...Good morning...I hope I'm not disturbing you."

"Disturbing me? Not at all," chuckled my dad. "I saw the bling you put on my daughter's finger, so I know you're serious. Come in. I think congratulations are in order."

By the time Jake stepped inside, I was there and Mom was beside me.

"Well, Anna and I need to get moving...literally." He cleared his throat and kept talking. "The movers are waiting in the truck. As soon as they load Anna's stuff, we'll be on our way, and hopefully we'll be settled in by nightfall."

My mom chimed in, "I knew you'd be in a hurry, so I packed some sandwiches, apples, and a half dozen chocolate chip cookies."

"Homemade chocolate chip cookies?" asked Jake with a boyish grin.

"Yes, they're my famous Mrs. Malone cookies."

Jake laughed out loud. "The best! Thank you."

My jacket and plum scarf were hanging on the hall tree, and I seized that lighthearted moment to grab them. Dad noticed. He looked down and pinched the bridge of his nose. I knew we had to move the boxes and the desk out fast. Our family was accustomed to moving and making tough choices, but we weren't immune to the feelings that come with change. We were fully aware of how painful transitions could be.

My dad swallowed. "Time is money. Tell the guys in the truck to come on in, and I'll carry out a box or two myself."

"Thank you, sir, but that's not necessary."

"I know," said Dad in a commanding tone, "but my only daughter is moving today, and I am determined to help."

Jake stood up straight. At six-foot-two, he was an inch taller than my dad. He nodded and quietly said, "Of course, sir."

"Call me Ty. We're going to be friends…as long as you're good to Anna."

"Roger that, sir…I mean Ty."

Smiling, Dad put his hand on Jake's shoulder, looked him in the eye, and said, "You're quick. We're going to get along just fine. Now let's load up that truck and get you on the road."

* * *

Jake and I pulled out of my parent's driveway shortly before noon and followed Ron and Dicky in their Two-Men-and-a-Truck van over the Sagadahoc Bridge, heading northeast on Route 1 to Waldoboro, and continuing on to Thomaston. At the Knox Mansion, we turned right onto Route 131 heading south. From my copilot's seat, I chuckled as we passed the welcome sign by the side of the road.

"What's so funny? We've been driving for over an hour, and I've been up and moving since five *o' dark early*, as your dad would say."

"I know. That's why you're so grumpy. But that sign we just drove past was hysterical."

Jake hit the gas pedal, then he shot me an annoyed look and said, "Care to share?"

"Sure, honey. The sign said, 'Discover a bit of unspoiled Maine.'"

"And?"

"And nothing. It just strikes me funny that this peninsula should be described as *unspoiled* because everyone knows it's the home of Forrest Gump's lighthouse and the Port Clyde General Store. In other words, it has been well advertised and it's on the tourists' radar."

Jake shrugged. "Well, I agree with the sign."

"And that's why we're moving here."

He glanced at me and his face brightened. "Wait and see. You're going to love it."

I fixed my eyes on the road. "I will…as long as you're with me."

* * *

Snow was falling, giving us the first glimpse of winter, as we pulled into the upper parking lot of Marshall Point. We jumped out of the car and scurried like children to the water's edge. Standing on wave-swept rocks, I savored the view: A 24-foot tower, crowned by a seven-foot wrought-iron lantern, stood against a blue-gray sky and a dark-gray sea with waves crashing like cymbals all around it; and a wooden walkway, supported by two granite walls, stretched over the rocks from the door of the lighthouse to the small front yard of the keeper's house. Except for its light, the cylindrical tower resembled the turret of a medieval castle. It reminded me of

Camelot and Disney castles. I lifted my gaze and shouted into the wind.

"Look! It's Monhegan Island!"

Jake took my hand and kissed it. Without letting go, he shouted, "Come on!"

We ran along the creaking walkway to reach the light-house—glorified by postcards for over a century—and stopped to look back at the keeper's house. Nestled between the St. George River and the Atlantic Ocean, we admired its *unspoiled* beauty from a distance. The deep but narrow front porch was covered by a white balcony that could only be accessed by climbing through a second-floor window. I asked Jake if we could do that as soon as possible, but he didn't say yes. Instead, he put one arm around my waist and said, "It's beautiful. Isn't it?"

"No, it's divine!"

"I'm not going to argue. The only point that matters is the second floor is ours for a whole year."

"What are we waiting for?" I smiled. Gazing into his eyes, I asked a follow-up question. "Do you have the keys?"

Jake paused and reached into his pocket. He shook his head. "No, I don't."

My stomach flipped. "You don't?"

He grinned. "The museum's side door has a push-button lock. That's where we'll enter and exit. This antique has been updated, but it's also *unspoiled*."

I shook my head and took his hand. "Let's unpack before I change my mind."

We greeted our movers at the side door of the keeper's summer kitchen, an 1879 addition. I had discovered that fact and a lot more after Noah gave us our tour in July, explaining that the original house had been destroyed by lightning in 1895 and replaced by November of that year. When I learned that Garrett wanted Jake to oversee the reconstruction of the light station's barn, my interest in the history of Marshall Point was piqued. I did some research at the Maine Maritime Museum and discovered some fascinating stories about the lighthouse and its long line of courageous keepers, including Charles Clement Skinner, a Civil War veteran, who served for forty-five consecutive years as the keeper at Marshall Point. His tenure from 1874 to 1919 was remarkable for a single station. The lighthouse was automated in 1971 and the keeper's house was boarded up in 1980, but the St. George Historical Society was entrusted with its restoration in 1986. Skinner's two daughters—Eula, born in the first dwelling in 1891, and Marion, born in the new keeper's house in 1895, attended the grand opening in 1990.

Now, the summer kitchen's side door served as the main entry to the lighthouse station's museum and our apartment. I held my breath as Jake punched in the code and opened the door to our first home. Even if I had known those numbers, I wouldn't have remembered them at that moment, but Jake was always calm under fire. Noticing the lumber stacked behind the house, I knew Jake would soon be busy and at his best. This old station was about to be renovated again, and this time Jake would be at the helm. I was used to recording history on paper, but Jake and I were about to *enter* history and hopefully make some more. As we stepped over the threshold, I felt giddy with excitement.

We had arrived at our destination and had two competent movers behind us. As we passed through the hallway between the summer kitchen and the main part of the house, Ron and Dicky stopped. They were staring at the *Forrest Gump* poster hanging on the wall and were obviously surprised by the fact that two photographs of Tom Hanks—dressed as a disheveled long-distance runner—had been casually taped to the poster.

Finally, Dicky, the quiet one, said, "Don't you think someone should have found a frame...for Tom Hanks."

We all shook with laughter. It was getting late, and we were tired, but the big belly laughs revived us. I suspect our clamor stirred up the old keeper's house, as well. Magically, the tall narrow staircase at the front of the house seemed less daunting. Ron and Dicky had transformed our moving day from bearable to unforgettable.

* * *

Three hours later, under a full moon, Two Men and a Truck pulled away. Jake and I went upstairs and climbed through our bedroom window to stand on the Romeo-and-Juliet balcony. We looked out over a river, an ocean, and a lighthouse. The cherry on top of this delicious moment was a night sky filled with constellations.

Looking up, I whispered, "Can you imagine anything more memorable than tonight?"

Jake took my hand and studied the sparkling diamond he had placed on my finger just a few months ago. "Maybe. Twenty-eight days from now we're going to be at the Dolby Theater in Hollywood, California, at the premiere of your second feature-length film, *Captains of the Kennebec*. That will be unforgettable, too."

I giggled in his arms. "I guess you're right."

Jake kissed me and let his lips linger.

"Imagine that—I'm right twice in one day. The Town of St. George *is* unspoiled Maine."

We paused to fill our lungs with Port Clyde's salty air, then we kissed again for twice as long.

CHAPTER 12

August–September 1938

On the Upper West Side, at Columbus Circle, traffic didn't roar quite as loudly on Saturday or Sunday as it did Monday through Friday, especially during the dog days of summer. From the Fourth of July through Labor Day, every New Yorker who had the weekend off tried to escape to the beach, whether it be Coney Island, Fire Island, Jones Beach, or, if you were really fortunate, the Hamptons. This was Penny's first summer in the city, and she was in love so she didn't mind waiting for Sal to return from another sales trip on a scorching Saturday in August. Of course, by the time he pulled into a parking spot in front of her apartment building, he wasn't inclined to fight beach traffic, so they decided to pack a lunch and take a stroll to Central Park.

Dressed for the city's high humidity, Penny was wearing her beach-pajama pants. She loved them because their wide bottoms and high waist reminded her of sailor pants. They were aqua, the color of summer, and she paired that fashion statement with a long plum-colored vest over a tucked-in sleeveless white blouse. To complete her outfit, she wore a straw hat trimmed with a white ribbon and a silk flower from B. Altman and Company's flagship store on Fifth Avenue. For Penny, the eighteenth of August was a picture-perfect day. For Sal, the heat was challenging. He didn't seem quite as confident or relaxed as usual.

As they approached Columbus Circle, Penny took Sal's hand. "You're quiet. How was your trip to Bean Town and all points north? Is everything okay?"

"Yeah, it was okay...hot, but okay. Sometimes I wonder..."

Penny stopped. "What? What do you wonder?"

Standing on the sidewalk surrounded by happy-go-lucky tourists and cynical New Yorkers, Sal opened his mouth, then closed it. Out of the corner of his eye, he spotted a young artist near the park's entrance. He was wearing a French beret and sitting on a stool next to the wrought-iron fence, clearly waiting for a subject—anyone who would pay a few bucks for a portrait. There were always dozens of vendors lining the fence, and all were selling something they thought was valuable, such as flowers, hats, souvenirs, and sometimes their own talent. Sal was a salesman, not so different from any one of the vendors outside the park. Today he saw them all in a striking light, especially the young man with the sunburned face and the brooding dark eyes.

To get his attention, Penny nudged him with her elbow and whispered, "Sal?"

He looked at her and in a mellow voice said, "Let's have our portrait painted by that artist over there. I think he's waiting for us."

Penny looked at the man wearing the beret and a tattered red-and-white shirt, and chuckled. "Oh, really! How long has he been waiting?"

"All summer long, Mariposa. It's our turn."

She raised her hand and touched Sal's face.

"What are you talking about, and who is Mariposa?"

He looked up at the azure sky as if he was ready to fly. "*Mariposa* is the Spanish word for butterfly. When I first met you, I wanted to get to know you, so I asked Stella if Penny was a nickname, and she told me your full name was Penélope Solis McGowan. Penélope Solis seems like an unusual name for someone from Maine. It has a Spanish ring to it, and I've learned a few words from my Spanish-speaking neighbors. In my mind, I started calling you Mariposa. A butterfly is free and happy, and that's how you make me feel. But until today, I've never called you Mariposa out loud. Do you like it?"

Shaking her head, Penny said, "I don't *like* it;" then she giggled, "I *love* it."

"Really?"

Gripping her basket, which was chock-full of bologna sandwiches, watermelon, oatmeal cookies, and a Thermos of sweet tea, Penny cried, "Yes! I'd love to have our portrait painted by that skinny artist over there, so he'll be able to afford some lunch, too."

Sal grinned like a schoolboy and reached for the basket. "Okay, *Mariposa*, I'll carry your basket wherever you want to go."

In less than a minute, the two lovebirds were sitting on chairs placed so close their knees touched in front of the shaggy-haired artist.

"Let me see a summer kiss!" shouted the painter with a strong French accent.

Sal put his lips on Penny's ear and whispered, "He's wearing a beret; you know he's going to be famous. I think we should give him what he wants. Maybe he'll remember us."

In reply, Penny turned her face to meet his lips and surrendered.

"Beautiful," said the lanky artist under his breath but loud enough for his subjects to hear.

When they came up for air, they looked at the painter and smiled as if they had a secret. Minutes later, the Frenchman handed them his work, a portrait in charcoal that captured the passion of a sizzling-hot day in New York City.

"My name is Paul Lemieux. If you look closely, you'll see I've signed your portrait, and I've named it *French Kiss*."

Awestruck, Penny and Sal showed their approval with silent nods.

"How much do we owe you?" asked Sal.

Paul quickly replied, "Two dollars."

"No!" cried Penny. "Your art deserves more. I think you've captured our kiss divinely."

Sal reached into his pocket and pulled out a five-dollar bill. "I wish I had more to give you. Thank you."

He tried to hand Paul the bill, but the proud artist just shook his head.

"I charge two dollars for a portrait, and that's all."

"Today," chimed in Penny, "you will accept five dollars because you managed to shine a light on love. Considering our world's dismal condition, I'd call that a miracle. It's certainly worth more than two dollars."

At the end of her rant, Penny grabbed the bill out of Sal's hand and placed it firmly in Paul's then stood on her toes and gently kissed his cheek.

Paul bowed his head and quietly said, "*Merci!* I will remember you—the both of you."

"Thank you, or *mil gracias*, as my mother used to say."

With a hint of a smile, Paul said, "Ah, your mother must have been an exotic beauty. I suspect you resemble her."

Feeling a bit uneasy, Sal stepped forward.

"Now we should say goodbye. I'm afraid, monsieur, your talent coupled with your charm could prove irresistible, and I want to keep my girl."

They all laughed, and Paul nodded. "You are both smart and kind-hearted, and I predict you will hold on to each other for a long, long time."

Sal and Penny walked away but turned back for a final look. Paul saw them and placed his hand over his heart.

* * *

Stella was at her desk reviewing the day's schedule when the phone rang. She quickly picked up the receiver, but before she could say good morning, Simon requested her presence. He sounded upset and she knew why. It was Friday, the twenty-sixth of August, her last day at National Screen Service.

"Yes, Mr. Miller, right away."

As she hung up the receiver, she grabbed her steno pad and stood up, smoothing her skirt before marching into her boss's office.

He was waiting.

"Close the door, Stella, and take a seat. You didn't have to bring your pad; I'm not going to dictate a letter. Today's your last day and I'm going to beg you to stay."

"Mr. Miller, my classes at Lenox Hill begin the day after Labor Day. I have to move out of my apartment, and I want to go up to Bath and visit with my mom—"

"No, that's not the point. And for God's sake, call me Simon!" Softening his tone, he added, "I think we know each other well enough, don't we?"

Stella lowered her gaze. She looked at her hands, folded in her lap, and said, "Yes, Simon, we know each other well enough."

"Why are you leaving?"

"I want to be a nurse. There's a war coming, and whether we like it or not, we'll have to get into it."

"You may be right, but you have to realize what you're leaving. I know you want to save the world, but why not start by saving one man. Save me, Stella."

He looked out through his office window and seemed far away until Stella's words pulled him back.

"I want to save you, Simon, but not at the expense of all the others who will need me. I can't think of only one man right now."

"That's why I love you, Stella. I want you to understand what you're giving up for the unknown soldiers you hope to help. Since the 1920s, this company has been growing by leaps and bounds. It survived the crash and kept on going. Now we're producing and distributing trailers for all of the major movie studios. Last year, we did our first test printing of posters. This year, we're taking over that accessory and other forms of paper advertising as well. In a few years, we'll monopolize the industry. Stella, the sky's the limit. Just wait…wait with me! *We* can have a future."

Stella stood up and walked to the window. Now it was her turn to look out over midtown Manhattan and dream. Tears came to her usually smiling eyes and Simon noticed. He came up behind her. Ready for his loving embrace, she leaned back then turned and cried in his arms.

* * *

On Labor Day, the fifth of September, Stella and Penny should have been playing at Rockaway, but instead they were working hard at home. Kneeling on the floor of their apartment, dripping with sweat, they were packing boxes for Stella's big move across town to the nurses' residence at East 76th Street between Park and Lexington. It was well past noon, and they had been working steadily since nine. The heat was beginning to affect them.

"I'm afraid our fans aren't keeping up with this heat wave," said Stella with a whistle that sounded like a tea-kettle at high boil.

Penny sighed, "I know; I think it's time for a glass of lemonade."

"I think it's time for a boat ride to Havana," said Stella as she stood up and headed for the icebox.

Penny popped up and followed her cousin into the galley kitchen, refusing to let her have the last word.

"I'm afraid the only boat captains we know are in Bath, and today that city seems as far away as the China Sea."

Both cousins, two sides of the same coin, started to laugh.

"You're right, of course. We're not going to escape in a windjammer, we're going to roast in this apartment," whined Stella.

She set two glasses on the tile countertop and filled them slowly as if she was pouring the last drink they would ever enjoy together.

Penny raised her glass. "Let's toast to our future. May it be exciting and rewarding."

Listening to the clink of their glasses, Stella added, "May love find us…wherever we go."

Penny laughed to lighten the mood. "Don't be gloomy, Stella. You're about to begin a great adventure."

"Yes, and I *am* ready," she said quietly. "But I'm worried, too. I mean I'm not twenty-one anymore. I'm thirty."

"Well, you're the youngest-looking thirty-year-old I know."

Stella chuckled. "How many thirty-year-old people do you know? Let's count them. Is that handsome sales director thirty?"

Penny blushed. "Oh, I don't know for sure, but I think Sal is a little over thirty."

"Sal? I was referring to Bill, the director for National Screen's mid-Atlantic region," said Stella in a serious tone, then she burst out laughing.

Penny scowled. "You're impossible. You know that, right?"

Still laughing, Stella walked over to one of the tall living room windows and pulled back the curtain.

"Speaking of handsome salesmen, Sal just pulled up in front of the building. It looks like he's driving a company car."

"I don't believe you," said Penny as she rushed to the window and pushed her cousin aside. "Let me see!"

Sal stepped out of a dark-blue four-door Chevrolet sedan and stepped onto the sidewalk. He was wearing a green button-down shirt with tan pants, and his dark hair was slicked back. From the window, Stella saw two girls walk past him, and they glanced back for a second look.

"He looks like a movie star in those sunglasses," she said.

"Well, he's here to help, not to show off his good looks. He volunteered to take us over to Lenox Hill with as many boxes as we can fit in the car."

Stella looped her arm through her cousin's and said, "I hope you keep this guy. He's more than handsome; he's good."

Penny said, "I'll try."

* * *

An hour later, Sal pulled up in front of the 76th Street entrance to the nurses' residence. Penny jumped out as soon as he turned off the engine, but Stella sat frozen in the backseat despite the ninety-degree heat. Shimmering in the afternoon sun, the sprawling hospital loomed like an imposing palace. Its façade of light-colored bricks was trimmed with limestone, and its oldest section stood eleven stories high. The probationers had been instructed to enter through the double doors of the hospital's two-story addition. The entrance was flanked by tall windows covered with elaborate wrought-iron grates, and the second-floor windows had large wrought-iron baskets covering their bottom halves. Established in 1857, Lenox Hill Hospital occupied a solid square block between Park and Lexington Avenues in a predominantly German neighborhood along the East River. Stella was clearly impressed by its prime location and stately architecture—so impressed that she couldn't move. Finally, Sal opened the car door and offered his hand.

"You can't become a nurse unless you get out of the car," he said with a kind smile.

She took his hand and chuckled, "Thanks for reminding me." As she got out, she tilted her head toward two girls who were exiting a cab behind them. "They must be probationers, too. They look so young."

Sal studied them for a moment, and then he turned back to Stella. "It's not your age that counts; it's your spirit. And you have plenty of that."

Stella nodded. "Okay, let's unload these boxes."

She called out to Penny, who was already carrying a box filled with toothpaste, shampoo, curlers, and other sundry personal items toward the building.

"Have I told you how much I like this man of yours?"

Penny called back, "Yes. Twice already. Now let's get moving. You're about to meet your future."

CHAPTER 13

November 2018

As I rolled my suitcase across the parking lot toward the Portland bus terminal, I was reminded of a book my mother used to read to my brothers and me, *Cars and Trucks and Things That Go* by Richard Scarry; I wondered if my childhood quest for the gold bug—hidden somewhere on every page—had sealed my fate. Was I born to travel, or did my family encourage me to roam? Even if I could retrace all my steps, I was certain I couldn't answer those questions.

When my parents, Jake, and I boarded the bus to Logan Airport to catch an evening flight to L.A., I was tempted to pinch myself. How did I manage to write a screenplay good enough to land an A-list director? I thought I had made all the wrong moves. For over ten years, I had walked through the wrong doors, I'd fallen down and screwed up, but now I was on my way to Hollywood as a respected screenwriter and executive producer.

There was a time when I thought I had quit the entertainment business for good—when I stopped working for

Ben, a conniving producer who stole my work and broke my heart. Truth be told, I wound up in Maine because I'd lost my way. I remembered driving north on I-95, crossing over the Piscataqua River, and reading the welcome sign: "Maine—the way life should be." At that moment, I had connected the slogan to the lyrics of an old *Chicago* classic: "Does Anybody Really Know What Time It Is?" I thought about writing a letter to the governor because I wanted to know exactly how life should be, but I wasn't in a writing frame of mind five years ago. Since then, I'd come to realize that there was an upside to living far away from gridlock traffic. My imagination functioned better when I wasn't stuck in a car or a subway every day. In Maine, there was room to think and create. Of course, the downside to living near the storied coast was that it inspired my work so much that Hollywood filmmakers began to notice, and that had brought me back to traffic.

By this time tomorrow, I would be having breakfast with Jake, my parents, my brothers, their wives, and my darling niece, Stella, on the patio of a luxury hotel in Los Angeles. A few hours later, we would be dressing for the world premiere of *Captains of the Kennebec*. I asked myself another rhetorical question: How did this happen? Yet I had always believed in movie magic.

Before boarding, we all grabbed a bottle of water from a bin next to the bus. As I walked past the driver, I held up the bottle and smiled.

"Thank you for the made-in-Maine gift. Poland Spring is my favorite."

He laughed and said, "Maine has crystal-clear water."

"Yes, it does, and that's why I'm happy I've got a round-trip ticket."

I chose a window seat in the middle of the bus and Jake sat next to me. Mom and Dad sat across the aisle. As soon as I fastened my seat belt and opened my paperback, Jake nudged me.

"Garrett and Oliver are meeting us all for breakfast tomorrow morning. I invited them; I hope that's all right."

I turned my face toward his and tried to read between the lines.

"Are we all staying at the same hotel?"

"Yes. Why?"

"I don't know. Maybe I'm still surprised they're coming."

"You're kidding. A world premiere is a *big deal*, and Garrett is more than a boss. He's a mentor and a friend."

I bit my lip and weighed my words.

"You're right. Garrett has been good to both of us, and I'm glad we were able to invite him to a red-carpet event. It's probably the best invitation he's had all year."

"Maybe in his whole life," chuckled Jake.

"And Oliver? I thought you didn't like him."

"He's growing on me," said Jake with a shrug. "Besides, he's Garrett's right-hand man, and this is a business trip for them. They flew out three days ago to meet with naval architects in San Diego. They're driving up to L.A. today."

Suddenly, the sound system crackled and we heard the driver's gravelly voice. "Welcome aboard! If you enjoy today's ride from Portland to Boston, I'm Stan, and this is the Concord. If you don't, I'm Chuck, and this is the Eagle. Now buckle up and enjoy the ride. The movie today is *Overboard*."

I opened up my book and glanced over at Jake. His eyes were already closed, and I felt happy all over. Long bus rides were great for reading and sleeping, but California was less than a day away, and all I could do was dream with my eyes open.

* * *

When I woke up the next day, sunshine was streaming through the sliding glass doors of our hotel room. Feeling as though I had slept until noon, I sat up in a panic and checked my phone. It was only 7:00 a.m., Pacific Standard Time. I fell back on the pillow and rolled toward Jake.

Pressing my nose against his bare back, I whispered, "We're here."

He stirred, and I put my arms around him.

"Good morning, Mr. Night Owl. Wake up. You don't want to miss a minute of today."

He rolled onto his back and without opening his eyes reached for me.

"Have we missed breakfast?" he asked.

I watched him blink his long lashes until he was fully awake, then I rolled on top.

"No, we have time to play for at least an hour."

"That's good," he mumbled as I kissed him.

We didn't talk any more until the alarm on his phone went off.

"When we checked in last night, I made a breakfast reservation for nine. Do you want to jump in the shower first?"

"Yes, please," I said as I swung my feet out of bed. "You know I need more prep time than you."

He came up beside me, and I couldn't resist the urge to run my fingers through his tousled blond hair.

"You know, it's not fair. All you have to do is smile, and you're ready to go; I have to wash and dry my hair, put on makeup, a cute outfit, and earrings."

"You're exaggerating," he said. He kissed my cheek and chuckled, "I have to put on clothes, too."

I hit him with a pillow and jumped into the shower.

* * *

Walking into the Sunset Hotel's sleek, upbeat café, I spotted Garrett right away. At six foot three, he stood above the crowd, and his thick salt-and-pepper hair was impossible to miss. As predicted, Oliver was standing beside him. They were in a huddle with my father and brothers at the far side of the restaurant next to floor-to-ceiling windows that looked out on a manicured garden. The ladies were sitting at a table sipping their coffee and perusing the menu, except for four-year-old Stella, who was coloring her placemat. I quickened my step and Jake followed.

"Good morning," I said a little too loudly.

Jake echoed, "Good morning," with equal intensity.

The men turned and the ladies looked up, all responding with cheerful greetings.

I gave my dad a hug and filled the silence, "So I see you've met Garrett and Oliver, the leaders of Keepers of Maine, Inc."

Oliver shook his head in protest. "I'm just Robin," he said, pointing at Garrett and clarifying, "he's Batman."

We all laughed, especially my brother Joe, who was a huge fan of Batman. The men and I took our seats at the table. As the lively banter continued up and down the table, I made a mental note that Oliver Hayden was quick-witted and charming. Now, if I found him to be genuine, I would understand Garrett's inclination to keep him close. Peering over the top of my menu, I caught my dad assessing the dynamic duo, as well, and I wondered if the KOMI executives would pass the professor's examination. Remembering my father's reputation at Loyola of Maryland, I knew they would not get an easy *A*.

A waitress brought over two large baskets of sweet rolls and returned with two large pitchers of fresh-squeezed orange juice. My brothers looked at me and smiled. They must have placed an early order for starters because a waiter arrived with two bowls of cornflakes and a plate of sliced bananas for Mom and Stella.

It was no secret that grandmother and granddaughter resembled each other, including their need for cornflakes every morning.

As little Stella picked up her spoon, Joe asked a parental question. "What do you say, Stella?"

"Thank you," she answered.

Before Stella could take a bite, my mom asked another question. "Stella Grace, could you help us say grace before we eat?"

Like magic, my little niece lowered her spoon back into her bowl, bent her head, and recited grace with her grandmother. Everyone at the table was quiet, and Garrett and Oliver looked like deer in the headlights.

After placing our orders for pancakes, sausage, french toast, bacon, and eggs Benedict, my sister-in-law, Tess, posed the question of the day: "When do we have to leave for the theater?"

My heart skipped a beat. The longest day was about to begin. I swallowed a bite of my pumpkin muffin and scanned the table. Everyone's eyes seemed to be on me, so I lifted my chin and spoke boldly. "The celebrity limos will start arriving at the theater at five, but since writers, producers, and studio bigwigs like Warren are supposed to arrive closer to six, I've asked our driver to pick us up at five thirty. It's a short ride, but this is L.A.; the traffic is always brutal."

"Are you girls going to spend the day getting beautiful?" asked Joe.

Frank laughed and shook his head. "I don't know, Joe. For a smart guy, you ask some obvious questions. Of course, the women are going to spend the day at the spa, and we're going to play in the pool with Stella."

"He's right," I said. "You can play with Stella and enjoy the California sun with the men while we ladies spend the day getting our nails painted and our hair blown out."

Always the joker, Frank volleyed back, "Hey, Joe, what's that song in *Bye-Bye Birdie* about being a woman? You remember that song from Saint Benedict's, don't you?"

Joe opened his arms wide, and for a moment I was afraid he was going to start singing. In high school, he used to play baseball and star in the musicals. Who does that? As a pediatrician, he still enjoyed shocking people with his hidden talents, but today, thank God, he decided to spare us.

"'How Lovely to Be a Woman,'" he said, giving me a wink.

Dad sat up and put his hands flat on the table, a sign he was going to share a story.

"I remember the first time I saw *Bye-Bye Birdie* and heard Ann-Margret sing that song. She was a knockout!"

Mom flipped her hair and huffed. "Oh, really? Well, I guess that's my cue to get beautiful. What do you say, girls? As soon as we finish consuming lots of calories here, let's go to the spa and ask these Hollywood stylists to make us glamorous, like Ann-Margret."

"Who is Ann-Margret?" asked Tess.

My mom's eyes widened. "A movie star from the sixties," she answered. "Think Jennifer Lawrence with red hair and well-placed curves."

Blushing, Tess said, "Oh, got it. She must have been *something* back in her day."

Garrett was laughing so hard he slapped his knee. Oliver joined in. Clearly, the masks were officially off.

Our breakfast order arrived and the impromptu comedy act ended. As soon as the servers unloaded their trays, we all dove into our morning favorites. I felt instantly better. A day that begins with laughter is bound to end with applause.

* * *

Eight hours later, we gathered in the lobby to wait for our stretch limo. When I thought no one was looking, I seized the fairy-tale moment and twirled in front of a full-length mirror. Jake saw me and grinned like a Cheshire cat.

"You don't fool anyone; you love wearing high heels, and you love the Hollywood glitter."

"Oh, yeah," said my brothers in unison, "she does."

"Who wouldn't?" chimed in Oliver. "I mean the Hollywood part, but I'd hate wearing heels."

Garrett slapped his back. "We know, Oliver. No need to explain."

Dad cleared his throat. "I think our limo has arrived. To borrow from the score of *My Fair Lady*, let's get her to the theater on time."

One by one, we walked through the revolving door—eleven starry-eyed movie buffs, including Stella—to ride in a stretch limo, walk a red carpet, and see my dream come true on the big screen.

When we arrived at the Dolby Theater, the cameras were already flashing. Mark Hartmann, who had brought Captain Henry Goss to life, had just stepped out of the limo in front of us, and the beautiful Jessica Lane, who plays Celia Gannett, was already talking with the press. As I viewed the media frenzy through the tinted windows, I swallowed hard and reached for Jake's hand. Suddenly, I wanted to ask the driver to turn around.

Jake sensed my panic and tried to defuse the situation by being funny. "Is there a drive-thru close by? I feel a need for a loaded cheeseburger right now. How about you, Frank? Joe?"

Distracted by what he saw out the window, Frank replied slowly. "Yeah, anything but this. There must be an In-N-Out Burger around here."

Joe disagreed, though. "No, it's not burger time; it's Anna's time to hear the applause, and we'll be behind her."

The limo stopped. It was, in fact, our turn. We took a collective breath before our driver opened the door. I stepped out first and heard a roar. *This* was happening!

Strangers reached out their hands to shake mine, and I stopped to sign a few autographs along the way, but I was fairly certain that no one knew who I was. Most moviegoers can't name the screenwriter of their favorite movie, so the best writers in the business are free to walk down Hollywood Boulevard without a disguise. However, my handsome escort and glowing entourage attracted a lot of attention. The crowd greeted me like a celebrity, so I acted like a star. I waved, smiled, and hugged strangers as if they were close friends. By the time I reached the Dolby's door, my head was spinning and my hands were trembling. I didn't remember this level of excitement at the premiere of *Daisy Longtree*, and I was genuinely shocked by the turnout.

As soon as I reached the entrance, Warren Dunlap, the head of Coastline Studios, stepped out to greet me.

"Thank God you made it through the mob," he said as he gave me a quick hug. "I was afraid those adoring fans were going to swallow you up."

I patted my hair to see if my French twist was still intact, squared my shoulders, and pursed my lips. "I'm alive and unharmed, and I'm reporting for duty, sir."

Dad chuckled, "You sound like a commander's daughter." He stepped toward Warren and shook his hand. "Good to see you again, Mr. Dunlap. From the size of the crowd, it looks like Coastline Studios has another hit on its hands."

"If we do, your daughter is largely responsible. And I'm Warren, remember?"

"How could I forget? You're the moviemaker who made Anna's dream come true. That makes you *family*."

Mom smiled. "Speaking of family, we'd like you to meet our two sons, Joe and Frank, their wives, Natalie and Tess, and our granddaughter, Stella."

"Pleased to meet you all," said Warren with an approving nod. "I remember Anna's entourage was considerably smaller at *Daisy*'s premiere."

Jake feigned a cough and my dad chuckled. "Warren, have you met Jake, Anna's fiancé?"

Pumping Jake's hand, Warren said, "No, I don't think I've had the pleasure. In fact, I didn't know Anna was engaged. Congratulations!"

"Thank you," said Jake with his signature half smile. "It's a recent development."

Anna chimed in, "We haven't set the date yet. I've just started writing my first novel, and Jake is working on a big project, as well."

"Speaking of projects," said Jake, "I'd like to introduce you to my boss, Garrett Liston, the president of Keepers of Maine, Inc., and his VP, Oliver Hayden."

As the men shook hands and exchanged greetings, Mom asked a serious question. "Warren, do you know where we'll be sitting?"

"Yes, they're center seats—Row J."

"Wow, that's amazing. I wonder who will be sitting in rows I and K?"

My brothers and I shook our heads. Dad responded, "Well, Ellie, let's go see."

Warren chuckled. "Anna, I believe you have the best entourage of any screenwriter I know. Enjoy tonight. You've earned it. I have to wait here for the director—you know he's always the last one to arrive—but one of the ushers will help you find your seats. I'll meet up with you later at the after-party."

I gave him a peck on the cheek and said, "Okay, boss."

I turned and told my family to follow me. As soon as I gave that command, I thought of Fred MacMurray in the classic 1966 film, *Follow Me, Boys!* I wanted to hug my mother for taking me to the movies as soon as I was old enough to sit still for the length of a feature film. I also wanted to thank her for watching all of those old Disney classics on VHS tapes with my brothers and me on snow days or sick days.

When we arrived at Row J, I let my family file in ahead of me. Mom was the last one. I put my hand on her arm for a moment.

"Thank you, Mom. I wouldn't be here without you. Hollywood didn't make this possible, you did. You introduced me to Bath and Grandma's story. You taught me to fly."

My mom shed a tear, and I kissed it away—just like she used to kiss away mine. The lights dimmed. Surrounded by the stars of *Captains of the Kennebec*, my mom didn't notice the actor Mark Hartmann sitting in front of her. However, my brother Frank quickly realized he was sitting behind Catherine Belen, the starlet playing Mary Rose McGowan. He looked at me and mouthed, "Oh my God." As I winked back, I spotted Jessica Lane, our leading lady, sitting next to Garrett at the other end of the row. Just before the lights went out, I saw her lean over and whisper something in his ear. Then she placed her hand on his knee.

CHAPTER 14

September 1938

Stella pushed the heavy door open and rushed out of the nurses' residence as if it were on fire. She was wearing a gray uniform with a white collar and a white apron. She looked like every other probationer except that her curly blond hair was blowing in the wind. If she hadn't slept through the rising bell, she would have tied it back and pinned it up as her instructor had told her to do on the first day of orientation. She was twenty-six days into her three-year nursing program, and she was exhausted. Her Nursing Arts classes were challenging, but she was eager to work on the wards although frustrated by all the rules and regulations.

During their first month of training, probies were required to memorize the contents of laboratory and supply closets; pass exams in anatomy and physiology; learn how to feed and bathe patients; perform a physical examination; make a hospital bed; and give shots. Until they acquired some basic skills, they weren't allowed to touch patients. Stella had overslept because she had spent half the night tossing and turning as she began to doubt her decision. At three o'clock, the school would post the names of the women who would be invited to attend the capping ceremony on Friday night, signifying the official start of their hospital training. If Stella's name was not on that list, she would not be able to set foot on a ward as a student nurse.

Racing across the courtyard, Stella clutched a composition notebook and a hair tie. She wanted to arrive at the lecture hall with a minute to spare so she could slip into the back row and fix her hair before the instructor noticed. As she reached the door, she checked her watch, and collided with a young man in a long white coat.

"Hey, look where you're going," the doctor said tiredly as he raked his fingers through his unkempt hair. "It's early, and some of us haven't been to bed yet."

Stella blushed and stammered, "I'm sorry. I'm about to be late—"

"Let me guess. You're a probie, and your morning lecture starts at seven, but you have a five-minute grace period before the class officially begins." He looked at his watch. "And it's a little after seven, right?"

Still out of breath, she gasped, "Yes, that's correct, doctor. That's why I have to go right now."

Stella grabbed the door handle and pulled, but before stepping inside, she looked back at the irritating, albeit handsome, doctor and gave him a mea culpa. "Next time, I'll watch where I'm going."

Once inside, she flew down the stairs—two at a time— and slipped into the lecture hall just as the doors were closing. She wasn't quick enough, though. As the doors closed behind her, a piercing voice called out her name from the front of the hall.

"Miss Goss, I'm so glad you could join us today."

She turned around to face her instructor.

"Why is your hair falling in your face? How do you expect to care for patients when you can't see them?"

"I'm sorry, Nurse Conley. I was running a little late this morning. I'll try harder."

"Yes, I expect you will. Do you realize Friday is your class's capping ceremony?"

Stella nodded. "Yes, Nurse Conley."

The hall was silent. Every one of her classmates sat with their hands folded in their laps and their eyes fixed on the instructor, a petite RN who could inspire fear.

"Let's talk more about your disheveled appearance in my office at one this afternoon."

"Yes, Nurse Conley," replied Stella in a steady voice as she willed herself not to cry.

"Good. Now take your seat. Let's begin today's lecture. In four days, *most* of you will become full-fledged student nurses."

* * *

At one o'clock, Stella knocked on Nurse Conley's office door.

"Come in, Stella. Close the door and have a seat."

Stella sat down in the wooden chair next to the director's desk. Her hair was wrapped in a neat bun at the nape of her neck, and her face was scrubbed without a hint of makeup. Clearly, this afternoon's meeting was a moment of reckoning, and Stella was ready to hear the conclusion.

In silence, Nurse Conley opened a manila file and reviewed it carefully then looked at Stella with inquisitive eyes.

"Stella, I'm perplexed by your file. You're thirty years old, the oldest in the class, but I never would have guessed that."

Stella opened her mouth as if to speak, but Nurse Conley held up her hand.

"I haven't finished. You've passed all the written exams with the highest scores in the class, but you have trouble following simple rules. Are you willing to take orders? You've proven yourself adept at all the skills required to work on a hospital ward, but you lack discipline and confidence. What makes you doubt yourself?"

Nurse Conley waited for an answer, but Stella remained stoic and silent. The head of Lenox Hill Hospital's School of Nursing, however, wasn't about to give up on a student with so much potential. She leveled her gaze and weighed her words.

"In a hospital, there's a pecking order, a well-established hierarchy, and a nurse is not at the top. A nurse stands when a doctor enters the room; she obeys his orders; she has a soft voice and a light touch; and she is never the center of attention. Some of the best nurses on a ward are almost invisible. So why do you want to be a nurse, Stella?"

Stella wrung her hands and took a deep breath, then she raised her chin and met the clear-blue eyes of Lenox Hill's top nurse.

"I want to be an Army or Navy nurse. America will eventually help Britain and France defeat Nazi Germany. The Third Reich has already taken over Austria; Adolf Hitler is sending innocent Jews—men, women, and children—to work camps. We have to stop him. If I can't join the armed forces to fight, I want to take care of those who do."

Nurse Conley listened with wide eyes and when Stella paused to take a breath, she quietly said, "Now I see a student whose thoughts run deeper than most of the graduate nurses I know. Heck, you may even grasp world affairs better than some of our politicians in Washington. How do you know about the treatment of Jews in Nazi Germany? Your file tells me you're from Bath, Maine."

Looking out the window, Stella replied, "Until a month ago, I worked for National Screen Service at the Film Center Building on Ninth Avenue. The president of the company is Jewish and so is the vice president." Turning her head, she focused once again on Nurse Conley's calm, empathetic face, and continued talking.

"National Screen makes movie trailers for the biggest film companies in Hollywood. I've met some amazing producers and even a few directors. Some of them are Jewish, as well. On occasion, those accomplished men talked with me about trying to get their family members out of Europe. They desperately wanted to bring their aunts, uncles, and cousins to America, but it's a difficult process and they fear it's taking too long."

"I suspect they're right," said Nurse Conley with a heavy sigh. "I live in Brooklyn and many of my friends and neighbors speak English with an accent. Some of them are Jewish. Hitler is a monster, and I wish one of my tough brothers would meet him in a dark alley—that would be the end of him."

For the first time in a month of Sundays, Stella laughed out loud.

With a hint of a smile, Nurse Conley studied her student's face.

"Stella, I believe you know where you want to go, but I'm not sure you know how to get there. You've excelled in your classwork, and there's no reason to deny you a cap. You've earned a chance to prove yourself on the wards. If you want to be a nurse, however, you'll have to learn how to follow orders. Do you think you can do that?"

"Yes, I know I can."

"Well then, it's decided. Your name will be posted on the bulletin board with all your classmates. It's a promising group."

Nurse Conley stood, and the two women shook hands.

In the hallway, Marie Capelotti, Stella's new best friend, was waiting for her. When Stella spotted her, she thought of Penny. The two could have passed for sisters, but Penny's hair was darker.

Marie shot her a how-did-it-go look, and Stella responded with a nod and a smile. Marie approached her and mentioned their appointment in the lab.

"We're supposed to get our TB vaccination at two o'clock, and it's already a quarter to."

"Then we better hurry because I just promised Nurse Conley that I'd never be late again."

Rolling her eyes, Marie quipped back, "That's going to be a hard promise to keep."

"But I will," said Stella.

Marie quickened her step then glanced at her friend and chuckled. "Maybe we should run. The clinic is at the other side of the hospital."

"Oh no, I'm not going to run. I tried that this morning and almost flattened a doctor."

"That doesn't sound so bad," said Marie with a giggle. "I'd like to run into a handsome, doctor, especially if that doctor happens to be Peter Novack."

Stella stopped. "You're kidding, right?"

"No, I'm dead serious," answered Marie with a wicked smile. "He's new on staff, and our whole class is talking about him. He's not the one you bumped into, is he?"

"I didn't catch his name," said Stella. The two probies linked arms, and together they walked briskly down the hall.

As they passed through the hospital atrium, Stella poked Marie with her elbow and whispered, "Sometimes I have to pinch myself."

"For heaven's sake, why?"

"To prove I'm really here."

Marie tilted her head and grinned at her friend.

"Who knew there would be so many benefits to being a student nurse? We get free shots every Monday, and sometimes we run into a young doctor who looks like Cary Grant."

* * *

On Friday evening, Stella and Marie gathered with their twenty-eight classmates at the back of the hospital's main auditorium to practice for their capping. All the women were dressed in their newly issued blue-and-white-striped uniforms with crisp white collars, aprons, and bibs; no one was chewing gum or wearing lipstick. Their hairdos were neat and off the collar, the shoes were sensible, and every student nurse was blushing with pride, but they were not quiet. Over the past few weeks, these women had become a close-knit group, and they were buzzing, but as soon as Nurse Conley entered the hall, the noise stopped.

"Nurses," she said in a loud, clear voice, "I need your undivided attention for about fifteen minutes. When we're finished, I ask that you go directly to the dining hall to eat something light and hydrate. If someone faints during the ceremony, too many doctors and nurses will rush to your side, and they're apt to collide and hurt themselves. Please remember, we cannot afford, nor do we wish, to lose any medical personnel this evening."

Laughter rippled through the room as Nurse Conley bowed her head, and the combined stress of thirty young women evaporated.

"Class, please form two lines in alphabetical order. The first line will begin with Abernathy and end with Murtagh. The second line will begin with Neiman and end with Zapf."

When Nurse Conley stepped to the head of the first line, her assistant moved to the head of the second line, then both nurses held up their clipboards.

"If you don't know where your name falls on the class roster, Nurse Coleman and I can help you. Okay, ladies, start moving."

Within a minute, the class was standing in two straight lines ready for their next set of instructions.

Nurse Conley walked up and down the rows to inspect the uniforms and overall appearance of her student nurses. When she was satisfied that everything was correct, she stood in front of Lenox Hill's newest class of student nurses and praised them.

"Well done. Please note who is in front of you and who is behind you. Nurse Coleman and I will lead you in at seven o'clock sharp. We'll assemble here at the back of the hall at a quarter to. As you can see, your seats are arranged in three rows of ten with five chairs on each side of the aisle. You'll be receiving your caps row by row. When it's your row's turn, either Nurse Coleman or I will stand at the end of the row and signal you to rise. Understood?"

"Yes, Nurse Conley," the nurses replied in unison.

"Good. I have one more item to mention. You won't receive your capes this evening. On Sunday after your class meeting, I'll visit the residence hall and distribute them personally. You should wear them over your uniforms when you're walking to and from the hospital. The weather is turning chilly. You need to care for yourselves so you can care for others."

Nurse Conley's eyes swept over the room and everyone held their breath. After a long, silent pause, the top nurse nodded with approval. "All right, then. Go to the cafeteria and nourish your bodies. Remember, we want you all to be strong and healthy. We'll meet back here in twenty-five minutes."

There was an audible squeal of excitement before thirty young women rushed toward the two large doors at the back of the hall. Marie found Stella and grabbed her hand before they reached the exit.

"Can you believe it? We're going to be capped in an hour!" shouted Marie.

Stella squeezed her hand. "Let's go have some chicken and salad...no potatoes. They want us to be strong, not chubby."

Nurses-to-be Capelotti and Goss were at the back of the crowd. In fact, they were the last two nurses to exit the auditorium. When they did, they were giddy with excitement.

"Hey, don't you ever look where you're going?" yelled an irritated voice.

Touching her forehead, Stella said, "Excuse me."

Marie's eyes widened, but her mouth clamped shut.

Stella looked at the handsome doctor and apologized. "I'm sorry—again."

"Twice in one week. I should report you. There's got to be a rule against running over staff," said Dr. Novack as he brushed his dark-brown hair out of his eyes.

Stella remembered the hair, and Marie did, too. She found her voice and tried to explain.

"We didn't see you coming, Dr. Novack. Our capping ceremony is less than an hour away, and we have to—"

"Are you telling me that you weren't racing to the bedside of a patient? What are your names and who is your supervisor? I need to know, because if this happens again, I'm going to report you."

Marie looked at the floor, but Stella looked directly at the doctor and watched him break into a smile.

Reaching out his hand, he said, "I'm Pete Novack. We've got to stop meeting like this."

"Stella Goss." She wasn't sure if the rules allowed her to shake a doctor's hand, but she shook it anyway.

When the handshake went a bit too long, Marie thought it best to say something. "Thanks for understanding, Dr. Novack, but now we really have to go."

"Of course," he said as he released Stella's hand. "Enjoy your capping ceremony."

Dr. Novack turned and walked away as Stella and Marie headed in the opposite direction.

Glancing at her friend, Marie whispered, "He seems to like hand-to-hand contact."

Stella was silent. Her mind was flying to a place it shouldn't have been going.

* * *

Stella's class lined up at the back of Lenox Hill Hospital's auditorium. When the string quartet began to play, Marie looked back at Stella and gave her a quick wave, then the two lines of student nurses, all dressed in those crisp blue-and-white uniforms, started to move forward.

Stella marched down the aisle with her eyes front and center, and she didn't turn her head when Sal Leone called her name, but she knew he was there. In fact, he was the first one she spotted when she entered the hall. He was tall and she was expecting him, but she wasn't expecting Simon Miller. They were standing in the same row as her mother and Penny. As she passed them, she kept her eyes focused on the stage, where the superintendent of nurses and the hospital's chief physician were waiting. As soon as the music stopped, everyone sat down. After a dramatic pause, Dr. Isaac Zimmerman stepped to the podium, and every nurse in the hall stood up until he motioned them to sit.

"Congratulations, nurses! You are about to embark on a noble path. Tonight, your teachers will place a white cap on each of you and acknowledge that you have earned a great honor: the privilege to care for the sick and the dying. Do this with all your heart and all your strength, and you will reach a level of fulfillment that few men and women ever know."

Sitting in the audience, Mary Rose dabbed her moist eyes with a white linen handkerchief that Stella's father had given her many years before. Stella was seated in the second row and she pulled a similar white handkerchief from her sleeve and dabbed her eyes in the same way. A few minutes later, after another stirring speech—this time from the superintendent—a graduate nurse began to read the names of the young nurses seated at the front of the hall. Row by row, they stood and walked to the stage to receive their starched-to-perfection caps.

Stella looked around the hall and savored the moment. This time-honored tradition confirmed her entry into nursing, and the cap was the ticket she needed to step onto a ward and care for patients. If she persevered, she would receive a second cap trimmed with a blue velvet ribbon in the fall of her senior year. At the end of her third and final year, she would receive her nursing school's distinctive cap, a puff of white organdy shaped like a vanilla cupcake. As she waited, she tried to imagine wearing that hard-won cap with the *black* velvet ribbon.

When Stella arrived at center stage, she bowed her head to let a graduate nurse pin her cap firmly in place. As soon as it felt secure, Stella lifted her head and squared her shoulders. At that moment, she felt a shiver run down her spine. For the first time, she could see her future.

CHAPTER 15

February 2019

The snow and wind had been waging war against the rocky coast for hours. When I asked Google what the temperature was outside, it answered "One degree Fahrenheit" in a pleasing female voice. I bit my lip and shook my head. Artificial intelligence was oblivious. Only a computer could give a weather report of one degree without howling. As the southernmost tip of the St. George Peninsula reached white-out conditions, my hands kept flying over the keys of my laptop. The rhythmic sound was oddly soothing, and the fact that I could see Marshall Point Lighthouse through the window helped a lot. If thousands of sailors over 187 years could trust that light to bring them safely home, I could sit at my desk and stay calm through a blizzard. I was determined not to panic, but I was worried we would lose power and freeze to death before anyone found us in the upstairs apartment over the closed-for-the-winter museum. I was also worried that I might lose 38,000 words of my manuscript, so

I kept hitting save and wondered when I had last backed up to the Cloud.

Peering over my shoulder, Jake asked, "How's it coming?"

As he tickled me, I lifted my shoulders and giggled but didn't answer. When he started to massage my neck, I stopped typing, reached back, and covered his hands with mine.

"Well, this massage really helps. Today, more than ever, I feel the saving grace of that lighthouse out there."

Jake spun my chair around, bent down, and kissed me lightly on the lips. "My sweet Anna Rose, have you forgotten what day it is?"

I stood up and wrapped my arms around his neck. "Of course not. I was just waiting for my Valentine to remember first."

"Oh, really?"

"Yes, really. Close your eyes."

"Aye-aye, ma'am," he said with a salute.

Reaching under the bed, I pulled out an acoustic guitar. "Okay, you can open those baby blues now."

Jake opened his eyes. "What's this? You shouldn't have—"

"I had to," I said handing it to him. "I found it on eBay and it was a great deal. Besides, you told me yours was wrecked when you deployed to Iraq; I've never heard you play."

"Well, if I can tune her, I'll play you something that fits today."

"A love song?"

"No, a ballad called 'The Sinking of the Reuben James,'" he replied, strumming a few chords. "She was torpedoed and sunk on October 31, 1941, by a German U-boat, making her the first U.S. ship sunk by hostile fire in World War Two."

Shaking my head, I asked, "How does that tragic loss connect with Valentine's Day?"

"It doesn't; it connects to the lighthouse that is standing guard outside—and it reminds us of all the sailors lost at sea. Woody Guthrie wrote the lyrics and music in 1942. It's a classic."

He started to sing.

Have you heard of a ship called the good Reuben James
manned by hard fighting men both of honor and fame?
She flew the Stars and Stripes of the land of the free
But tonight she's in her grave on the bottom of the sea.
Tell me what were their names, tell me what were their names.
Did you have a friend on the good Reuben James?...

He stopped and I applauded. "Play it again, Jake!"

Putting the guitar down, he grinned and said, "Wait here."

When he returned, his hands were behind his back.

"Right or left?"

"Hmm, I choose right."

Jake nodded and pulled out his hand, revealing a box of Bixby dark-chocolate, sea-salted caramels from Rockland.

I grabbed the heart-shaped box and gushed, "This is a *sinful* gift, but it's worth every calorie, and I'm not sharing."

"Well, you're not made of stone, so I knew you'd like chocolate, but I'm not sure how you'll react to the surprise in my left hand."

Reaching behind his back, I teased, "You'll never know unless you let me see it."

At first, he blocked my move, then he caved and presented me with a paperback book.

"What's this?" I asked turning it over. I read the title, *Nellie, the Lighthouse Dog.*

"I thought you'd be interested in this because the action takes place here at the lighthouse. The hero is a little wire-haired fox terrier called Nellie," said Jake with a hint of embarrassment. "You probably think it's silly."

Shaking my head, I replied, "No, no, I don't think it's silly. I think it's a treasure—just like you."

I opened the book to the title page and read out loud: "'Text copyright 1993 by Jane Scarpino; Illustrations copyright 1993 by Robert Ensor. Published by Windswept House.'"

I looked up at Jake and sighed. "So, I'm not the first author to be inspired by Marshall Point."

"True," said Jake as he held me in his arms. "But you're the only one I love, and we're perfect for this place. Look at Moose sleeping over there in his bed. Jane and Robert would approve, right? Every lighthouse needs a dog, and we've got a Great Pyrenees."

We kissed until we ran out of air. I took a step back. "Wait a minute. Don't you want to see the other gift I have for you?"

Jake grinned. "Of course I do."

"Then follow me." I took Jake's hand, turned off the lamp, and guided him to the goose-down covers of our wrought-iron bed.

* * *

The next morning the sun rose at 6:39. I woke to see its lavender light already skimming over the ocean and river that met in front of our window. As I peered down at the sparkling amethyst harbor, I knew it was going to be a great writing day because for the first time, I saw the title of my novel in my mind's eye. When I crawled back into bed to snuggle with Jake, I wanted to wake him up so I could tell him.

He rolled to his side and I kissed him softly on the nose.

"What time is it?" he mumbled.

"A little past seven."

"Oh, that's too early," he groaned.

Tossing back the covers, I raised my voice, "No, it's not too early. I can hear the snow plow coming up the road, so they'll be plowing us out in no time. You've got a meeting in Rockland."

He rolled onto his back, pulled the covers over his head and refused to face the day.

"I don't want to go."

"You have to go. You're the chief engineer, remember?"

Jake sat up and rubbed his eyes. "Okay, I remember. Today I have to approve the plans for the station's new barn and organize the demolition of the old one."

"That's right, honey, you're a very important man. I'll let Moose out and make the coffee while you jump in the shower."

Jake swung his feet to the floor, sat on the edge of the bed, and grinned with his eyes still closed.

"How about jumping in with me?"

I stood in front of him and placed my hands on his shoulders.

"No, but I'll make you some scrambled eggs and share some good news if you can be ready in time."

"How much time do I have?"

"About fifteen minutes," I said as I gave him a peck on the cheek.

Closing his eyes, he replied, "Oh, that seems stingy."

And as I walked to the kitchen, I quipped back, "If you're fast, you might get more than breakfast."

Jake instantly stood and headed for the shower.

Ten minutes later, he came into the kitchen and poured himself a cup of coffee while I put two plates of scram-

141

bled eggs and buttered toast on the small table in our tiny kitchen. I brought over two glasses and we sat down to start the day.

"Good morning," Jake grinned. "Where's the orange juice?"

I raised an eyebrow and answered with a heavy dose of saccharin, "Of course, I forgot it. Let me get it."

"No, I'll get it," he said as he kissed my cheek. "After all, you made the sun shine this morning."

I laughed. "No, I made breakfast, but thank God it's going to be sunny all day long. We're supposed to see twenty degrees by noon."

"I'm glad you have hope. I'm not sure I could work through the winter without your optimism."

I raised my glass of orange juice. "Let's drink to warmer days."

We clinked our glasses and Jake asked me about my good news.

"Well, speaking of the morning light, the sunrise this morning inspired my title. What do you think of *The Keeper's House*?"

"Excellent."

That reply made me smile like a student who had just received an *A*.

"I'm glad we moved here, Jake. The sound, the smell, and the views add poetry to my prose. Marshall Point keeps my words flowing and I'm grateful."

From across the table, Jake studied my face. "Moving here was a leap of faith. I was worried that living at the tip of a peninsula in an old keeper's house might scare you away."

"Oh, sweetheart, don't you know? I'm fearless when I'm with you."

Jake raised his glass and said, "To love," then cocked his head and asked me how I felt about taking down a barn.

Playfully, I clinked his glass and grinned.

"You can't put the new one up until you take the old one down, but I'd wait until the temps hit a balmy forty degrees. Will Garrett be at the meeting this morning?"

"Yes, he's flying into Knox County Airport with a team from Keepers of Maine, Inc. He wants to discuss the improvements we've contracted to do for the station, and he wants to scout out a few other lighthouses up the coast that may need some work as well."

"He's always looking for the next big project, isn't he?"

Jake merely nodded. "Yep. I better get going. You know how he likes everyone to be on time."

I pursed my lips and stood to clear the table. "He's the boss," I said quietly.

Pushing back his chair, Jake replied, "So true. So true."

* * *

An hour after Jake left for Rockland, my phone rang, and I had to stop writing to answer. It was my former boss, Warren Dunlap.

"Hello, Anna, how's life at the lighthouse?"

"It's fabulous, Warren. How's life in Manhattan and L.A. and all the airports in between?"

I could hear Warren laugh and knew he appreciated my humor. After working on a few projects together, we liked to banter.

"I have no complaints, but Coastline Studios is missing you and so am I. When will that novel be finished, and when can we turn it into a screenplay?"

"Funny you should ask," I shot back. "I'm pushing 50,000 words, so I'm more than halfway there. Of course, it's only my first draft, and my agent hasn't seen it yet."

"She'll love it, and you'll be ready to send it to the publisher after three or four drafts—tops."

"Thanks for the vote of confidence."

He chuckled. "I believe you're going to hit another homerun. What can I say? I believe in winning streaks."

"Thanks, Warren! Now what can I do for you today?"

"Well, I want to know who your publisher is and how I can buy the rights for the screenplay."

There was a long pause.

"Hello, Anna? Are you there?"

"Yes, I'm here...Are you serious?

"Anna, this is Warren Dunlap. I'm always serious."

I pushed my hair out of my eyes and silently thanked God that I wasn't on a Facetime call. I took a deep breath and dove into business.

"I've signed with Manhattan Publishing."

"Okay, that's good. They're one of the best. Can I ask if they offered to buy the film rights?"

"No, not yet, but I think you should be talking to my agent about this. To be honest, right now I'm feeling some pressure to deliver a best seller. They gave me a sweet advance."

Warren laughed. "Of course you are, but not because of the money. You're part of a dying breed—you're a commercial writer with the soul of an artist. Keep writing, Anna. I'll talk with your agent. Maggie O'Shea, right?"

"Yes. I gave you her contact info, right?"

"Got it. I have to go, but I'll be in touch."

I said goodbye, but Warren was already off the line. His world moved at lightning speed. As I looked out the window at the elevated walkway covered with snow and leading to the door of the lighthouse, I wondered if I could survive another round of Hollywood. Then I thought of all the artists who had found a muse on the coast of Maine and realized I wasn't alone. I was surrounded by Andrew and Jamie Wyeth, Edward Hopper, Mary Ellen Chase, Stephen King, and Elizabeth Strout. Sitting by the window on the second floor of the keeper's house, I heard their voices.

I set my phone down on the desk and started to write.

* * *

Wolcott Marr was part of a legacy. On July 1, 1895, when he reported for duty at Hendricks Head, he was continuing a twenty-nine-year family tradition. Wolcott arrived at the lighthouse with his wife and their three children to replace his father as the lightkeeper. That night when he made his first entry in the logbook, he was surprised to hear his children misbehaving. He wondered if they were missing their former home, and it occurred to him that, as a child, he had been spared the heartache of moving from one lighthouse to another. He had been born and married in the same room, and now he was home again. Since his children were not as blessed, he decided to help his wife put them to bed.

"Hush!" he said as he entered the children's room. "I'm going to tell you a story that your grandparents used to tell me and my brothers and sisters. It's about a little baby girl who survived a shipwreck near this light because of her parents' quick thinking and the grace of God."

All three children put their heads on their feather pillows and listened quietly.

"There was a horrific March gale, and the lightkeeper and his wife could see a wrecked vessel at the mouth of the Sheepscot. The vessel was so close that they could see the sailors hanging on to the rigging. They looked like they were freezing. As night fell, the keeper saw a bundle floating on the water, so he took a fishhook to snatch it and haul it to shore. The keeper and his wife soon discovered that the bundle was two featherbeds tied together. When they cut the ropes, they found a box, and when they opened the box..."

"What did they find?" squealed the Marr children.

Wolcott smiled. "They found a baby girl alive and crying. They also found a note that was written by her mother's hand."

"What did it say?" asked the youngest Marr.

"May God protect this little one and you," whispered Wolcott, and then he kissed each of his children on the forehead and pulled up their covers.

"Daddy, who was the lightkeeper?" asked the oldest.

Wolcott turned in the doorway and answered, "Your grandfather. Now go to sleep. Tomorrow you may find something precious lost at sea."

* * *

The phone rang and I answered in a fog. "Hello?"

"Hi, it's me. Do you want me to pick up something at the market?" asked Jake.

"No."

"Are you okay?"

I came back from the writer's edge.

"Yes, I was just on a roll. I mean, the storyline is taking off and the pages are multiplying. It's been a good day so far."

"Great," said Jake. "It's going to be a good night, too. Garrett's invited us to dinner at Primo, Rockland's finest, so put on some fancy clothes."

"Okay, but I have to shower first. What time is it?"

Jake chuckled. "Anna, dear, it's time to get out of your pajamas."

CHAPTER 16

June 1939

S tella started her new rotation on the children's ward, and she was nervous. She couldn't fathom a child being gravely ill; nor could she understand how God would let a child suffer, but she knew that as a nurse she would witness that unbelievable heartache. She was so anxious that she woke before the rising bell. In her sparsely furnished room, she got out of bed and went to her writing table to make an entry in her diary. When she opened the leather-bound journal, the letter she had tucked inside for safekeeping slipped out, and she decided to read it for the umpteenth time. The letter was handwritten, and it was dated September 30, 1938.

Dearest Stella,

By the time you read these words, you will have received your prize, your first nursing cap. I will be there when they pin it on your head and I suspect my presence will surprise you.

Believe me when I tell you that I did not plan to witness the time-honored ceremony that would take you where I cannot follow. I'll be there because your mother invited me. I have met the source of your Irish beauty, and, as you know, Mary Rose is a force that will not be denied.

When your mother called me, she told me that your father had died when you were seventeen years old, and you have been missing him for over a decade. Stella, my belle, I'm twenty years older than you, and I've come to realize that you probably see me as a father, and I was foolish to hope for anything more. Mary Rose told me that your dad was an old salt, a dashing sea captain who fell in love with her after losing his first love and first child. I cannot imagine the anguish of losing a child. He must have been an incredibly strong man to survive such a loss and to remain loving. You are proof of his courage and are his finest legacy.

Since your father was a mariner, he probably kept a journal. I think you should, too. Record your passages in this red leather book, and remember you are loved and adored by your family and by me. You are about to embark on the most important voyage of your life. As Captain Thomas Goss would say, I wish you fair winds and following seas.

Stella, my darling, I have always admired your beauty and now I admire your strength as well. At the darkest hour of someone's life, you will bring them light. I wish you Godspeed, and if you ever need a safe harbor, I'll be here.

With all my heart,
Simon

Stella folded the letter carefully and tucked it back where she would always keep it. She flipped through the journal to the first blank page and wrote three commands: *Be brave. Be caring. Remain loving.*

* * *

An hour later, the elevator doors opened onto the children's floor, and Stella stepped out to face the nurses' station. She touched her cap, smoothed her apron, and walked up to the graduate nurse standing at the counter.

"Good morning. I'm supposed to start my rotation—"

"Nurse! Room 614 STAT!" barked a doctor running down the hall.

The nurse flew after the doctor and left Stella standing alone, but not for long.

A doctor with an RN two steps behind him came out of a patient's room and approached the station. Stella didn't know the nurse, but she recognized the doctor right away. She blinked and waited, but he passed her by without a glimmer of recognition. He put his clipboard down on the counter and immediately started to write a note on a patient's chart. For a moment, Stella felt lost, but the graduate nurse came to her rescue.

"Hello. It's the first of the month, so you must be Stella Goss, our student nurse for June, right?"

"Yes, that's right," said Stella as she extended her hand.

"I'm the nurse in charge, Heidi Gunther, and that's Dr. Peter Novack standing behind you. He's from the adult side, the dark side, but today he's helping us out because several of our patients have heart conditions."

Glancing over her shoulder, Stella's eyes brightened.

Without turning his head, the doctor said good morning as if they had never met, and Stella felt the sting.

Nurse Gunther chuckled. "Like I said, Dr. Novack is with us today because he's good with hearts, and we have a newborn with blue baby syndrome. We also have a five-year-old with a congenital heart defect."

Dr. Novack stood up and attempted a smile, but he apparently wasn't in the mood.

"I'm glad I could be of service, but now I have to get back to the adult side of medicine. I'll be back to check on the blue hearts before lunch." He handed Nurse Gunther the clipboard and said, "Follow my orders with care."

Keeping her eyes on the chart, the nurse nodded. "Of course, doctor."

As soon as the elevator doors closed, Nurse Gunther turned to Stella and said, "Would you like to meet the oldest heart patient on the ward?"

Lifting her chin, Stella replied, "Yes."

When they stepped into Room 601, Stella froze. A little girl with strawberry-blond hair was lying in a wrought-iron bed. Her eyes were closed and an oxygen mask covered her mouth and nose.

"What's her name?" whispered Stella.

"Lily," answered the RN with a slight quiver in her voice.

Stella was rendered speechless as her thoughts turned to her half-sister, Lily, who had died aboard their father's ship in 1887, twenty-one years before Stella was born. A sudden chill traveled down her spine, but she managed to control every muscle in her face.

"Are you all right, Stella?" asked Nurse Gunther.

"Yes, I'm sorry...She reminds me of someone I lost, but this Lily has a chance, right?"

"We hope so. She's sleeping now. We'll come back when she's awake."

Stella nodded. "I'll be ready then."

Placing her hand on Stella's shoulder, Nurse Gunther said, "You'll be ready. Caring for sick children is especially difficult. It isn't for everyone, but it does get easier."

* * *

By eleven o'clock, Stella had visited all the patients assigned to her care—some of them more than once. She had taken their temperatures, recorded their blood pressure, fluffed their pillows, listened to their breathing, and dispensed their medicine according to doctor's orders. On one occasion, in Room 601, she even sang "On the Good Ship Lollipop," a Shirley Temple favorite, because she wanted to brighten Lily's day. When she left the room for the third time that morning, she wiped her eyes with her handkerchief and bowed her head.

Suddenly she heard a familiar voice.

"Nurses are not allowed to cry, especially on the children's ward. This is the bright side, remember?"

She raised her head and opened her eyes to see Pete Novack.

"I wasn't crying, and I try to obey all the rules that are fair."

Pete looked down at her flushed face and his cool eyes melted.

"Rules are seldom fair. You're a student nurse, and I'm an attending physician. We're against the rules; that's why I couldn't act like I knew you this morning."

Stella looked away and muttered, "I know, but I was hurt when you didn't look back."

He glanced up and down the hall. Seeing no one, he pulled her into an empty room and closed the door.

"Ah, Stella, feelings are not allowed. It's rule number one."

Stella bit her lip and said, "I know. A student nurse cannot *fraternize* with an attending physician. I guess I'm just a rule breaker."

He let himself smile. "I guess we're both rule breakers, but it's time to be good. A lot of people depend on us."

He opened the door. "Go to lunch, Stella. Maybe you'll see Marie in the cafeteria, and the two of you can laugh over how foolish the staff can be."

"I doubt I'll find Marie in the cafeteria. Even if I do, I don't think we'll laugh about this. I'm afraid it will be a long time before I laugh again."

"I hope that's not true, because I miss it already."

"You're right, doctor. It's time to take a break."

She left the room, and Dr. Novack followed a few seconds later.

* * *

After checking the line and circling the tables in the cafeteria twice, Stella left without buying lunch or seeing Marie. She went directly to the atrium to find an available pay phone and dialed NSS, praying that her cousin would answer.

"Miss McGowan speaking. Good afternoon. This is National Screen Service. How can I direct your call?"

"Hi, Penny, it's Stella."

"Well, this is a surprise. Is everything okay?"

"No, nothing is okay," replied Stella.

"Where are you, Stella? Are you at the hospital?"

"Yes, I started on the children's ward today. Right now, I'm supposed to be at lunch."

"What happened?"

"I met a little girl named Lily," Stella said in a hushed voice.

There was an awkward pause followed by Penny's gentle response.

"Oh, I see."

The operator cut in. "Please insert five cents to continue this call."

Stella put another nickel in the slot.

"Could I meet you for dinner at the West Side Diner?"

"Yes, I can meet you there at five thirty."

Penny waited for her cousin to say goodbye, but all she heard was her weeping.

"Oh, Stella, keep your chin up. Your father would be so proud of you. Whatever is weighing you down, we'll talk about it tonight. I have to go. My board is lighting up. 'Bye."

Stella hung up the receiver and stepped from the phone booth, wiping her eyes with the handkerchief her mother had given her when she left home. It bore her father's initials, and Stella was never without it since moving to the city. She looked at her watch. It was almost noon. She walked to the hospital gift shop to buy a box of Loft's candies, the perfect lunch. In less than a month, she would take her exams and complete her first year of nursing school. She bit into a chocolate-covered caramel and imagined her summer vacation in Maine, then she straightened her cap and returned to work.

* * *

Stella arrived at the West Side Diner five minutes early and slid into the last booth with a sense of relief. It felt good to be back in her old neighborhood—far from the hospital, the supervising nurses, the physicians and their almighty rules. A middle-aged waitress, wearing a yellow apron over a brown-and-white checked uniform, came over and handed her a menu.

Stella smiled. "I'm waiting for someone, but I'll take a Coca-Cola, please."

The waitress nodded and walked away. Looking at the menu, Stella considered her choices.

"Hi, sorry I'm running late," said Penny as she slid into the seat across from Stella.

"You're not late; I'm early."

"I can see from here that you're not too happy. What's going on, Stella? You seem troubled."

Stella looked out the window onto the busy street. A yellow cab pulled up to the curb, and a gray-haired man in a perfectly tailored gray suit opened the door for a young woman dressed to the nines.

"No, just sad and maybe a little homesick."

"You're doing so well. Is this about the little girl, Lily? Does she remind you of your father's sorrow, your sister who died so young?"

"Maybe...yes."

Penny looked at her cousin and responded gently. "Our fathers were 'live Yankees.' They went to sea, and they risked everything for the voyage. They returned with great stories and a clear understanding of how vast and unforgiving the ocean can be, but they survived, Stella. They survived long enough to have us."

Stella nodded. "True, but they left us before we had a chance to really know them. They left us when we still needed them."

Penny folded her hands on her lap and said, "Tell me about Lily."

"She's a sweet little girl with the most amazing strawberry-blond hair. She has a congenital heart defect. I'm devastated because I know that medicine can't fix it."

Leaning forward, Penny said, "Not yet, but maybe someday they'll find a cure. That's why you're training to be a nurse, right? I'm sure you gave Lily hope today."

"I tried," said Stella as her eyes filled with tears.

"What else? Something tells me Lily's broken heart reminded you of your own. Let's face it, Stella, you haven't been lucky in love. You're smart, hard-driving, and incredibly talented in so many ways, but you have rotten luck when it comes to men."

Stella wiped her cheeks with her napkin and lifted her chin to take the punch.

"That losing streak continues."

Penny frowned. "So, the handsome doctor doesn't want to be friends?"

Stella shot back, "It's against the rules."

"When have you ever followed the rules?"

Pushing a strand of hair away from her face, Stella answered, "I'm starting today."

Penny sat back. "Okay. What's your new strategy for staying out of trouble?"

Stella laughed for the first time all day. "On the first of July, I'm going home for thirty days of vacation. I'm going to try to restart my heart, and I'm going to spend time with my mom, who I miss a lot."

The waitress returned to the table. "Are you ready?"

Penny picked up the only menu on the table, looked at the waitress's name tag and said, "Gladys, could you give us a minute?"

"Take all the time you need," said Gladys as she walked away in a huff.

The two cousins lowered their heads to hide their amusement. At that moment, Stella knew she would survive her worst day of training. After nine months of studying and working at a big New York City hospital, she had learned that laughter was still the best medicine for a broken heart.

"First, let's decide on what we're having for dinner, then we can talk about you and Sal."

"Well, I'm having the burger with a tossed salad. Sal asked me to go with him on his next trip to Boston, Portsmouth, and Old Orchard Beach."

Stella's eyes widened. "And what did you say?"

"I said…not until you put a ring on my finger."

Penny lifted her left hand to reveal her half-carat diamond, and Stella gushed.

"It's gorgeous! How did I miss that sparkle?"

With a grin, Penny replied, "I'm pretty sure you missed it because I was hiding it under the table."

"Well, you shouldn't have," said Stella. She reached across the table and took her cousin's hand to inspect the ring.

"It's perfect, Penny. I'm happy that at least one of us is lucky in love."

Gladys returned. "Have you two decided yet?"

Penny looked up and smiled.

"Yes. I'll have a burger, medium, with fries and a tossed salad with Italian dressing."

Smiling politely, Stella handed Gladys her menu and said, "I'll have the same."

"Anything else?"

"By any chance, could you tell me where the nearest phone booth is?"

"Sure. When you step outside, turn right. It's a block and a half away."

"Thanks, Gladys."

"You're welcome."

Once Gladys had left, Penny asked, "So who are you going to call?"

"I'm going to call Simon."

"Why?"

"I'm going to ask him if he knows a famous singer or dancer who would be willing to visit a little girl in the hospital."

* * *

Three days later, Stella walked onto the children's floor and was alarmed to see a small group of visitors and staff gathered outside Room 601. She rushed to the door and was relieved to find Ruby Keeler, the star of *42nd Street*, tap dancing in front of Lily.

Nurse Gunther came up behind her and said, "A bird told me you're responsible for this show."

"And who would that bird be?" asked Stella.

"I'm not going to say; I'm only going to commend you. Look at Lily's eyes! You've given our little patient something to dream about. Sometimes the best we can offer is hope."

She looked at her supervisor with bright eyes. "Yes, we're in the business of hope."

CHAPTER 17

May 2019

I was writing from my nest overlooking Port Clyde Harbor, but the museum and its gift shop were now open for business, and the constant stream of people was making it hard to concentrate.

"Crap!" I cried as I pushed away from my desk and closed my laptop. This wasn't working. What had I been thinking when I promised my agent and publisher a first draft by spring? Now Warren Dunlap had scheduled a meeting with Martin Gormley of Manhattan Publishing and Maggie O'Shea of the Greenwich Village Literary Agency for the seventh of June. I looked at my laptop and shuddered. I was supposed to deliver my novel, *The Keeper's House*, in thirty-three days. I looked at the calendar on the wall with its lighthouse of the month and threw up my hands.

"It's Cinco de Mayo," I said out loud. "I'm never going to finish this."

As the child of a Spanish teacher, I knew that the fifth of May was the day a band of *campesinos* in Puebla,

Mexico, had beaten a French army, but today I couldn't write a single page of historical fiction. I was doomed to disappoint.

"Hey, who are you talking to in there?" shouted Jake from the bathroom.

"The ghost of Marshall Point," I answered wryly.

"What? I can't hear you."

"Of course not. The tourists have arrived."

"Wait a minute," said Jake. "I'll be right there."

As soon as he stepped into the room, I continued whining.

"I wish I could write like the Irish author Josephine Leslie. In 1945, she wrote *The Ghost and Mrs. Muir* under the pseudonym R.A. Dick; a few years later it was made into a movie with Gene Tierney and Rex Harrison, and in the 1960s, it was made into a television sitcom with Hope Lange and Edward Mulhare. I call that a romance wrapped in history and laced with humor."

Shaken by my crazy rant, Jake posed a question.

"Are you trying to write a ghost story?"

I fell back on the bed, mumbling, "Oh, God, I'm losing my mind."

To ease my pain, Jake jumped on top of me, then reluctantly rolled away.

"I wish I didn't have a crew out there trying to reproduce a nineteenth-century barn."

I managed to laugh. "I know…and you mean that literally."

He bent down and kissed the tip of my nose.

"I'm sorry about all the noise. Maybe moving into a keeper's house with a tourist attraction on the ground floor wasn't the best idea."

"Maybe, but I said yes to living here. I guess we're both fools."

He threw up his hands and shrugged. "Well, it's not April Fools' Day, it's Cinco de Mayo, so after work let's talk about Plan B, okay?"

I looked at his smile and wanted to have his positive attitude, but I didn't. "Don't worry. I'm not leaving you, but I hope Plan B involves a ticket to Montevideo and a pseudonym so I can flee the country if I don't meet my deadline, my seafaring love story doesn't deliver a *New York Times* best seller, and the chance for a screenplay disappears."

"If that was an attempt to ease my mind, you've failed. I'm seriously worried about you. It's noon, and you haven't eaten a thing since six a.m. Grab a granola bar and come out to the barn with me."

I sat up and dangled my legs over the side of the bed, but I didn't stand up. Instead, I shook my head. "No, I have to finish this chapter. I can see the road, but the signs are blurry."

Jake went into the kitchen and came back with a granola bar. He tossed it at me and barked, "I'm not taking no for an answer! If you're writing a seafaring romance, talk to my crew. They're a bunch of salty sailors."

I had to cry uncle. "Okay, I guess it's bring-your-fiancé-to-work day somewhere."

Jake laughed. "Yes, it is. Don't worry. My guys will tell you lots of stories, and the details will spark your imagination. They may even put you in a *romantic* mood."

I followed Jake down the narrow staircase, and as he opened the door to the museum, I heard a woman say, "Are you the lighthouse keeper?"

Jake said no in a rather gruff voice, and the woman replied, "Well, that's a shame. With those broad shoulders, you could be right out of central casting."

"He's from Wiscasset," I said, stepping out from behind him.

The visitor blushed. "I could tell he was homegrown. Aren't you a lucky girl."

"Thank you," I said. "I'm very lucky."

I took Jake's hand and led him through the house's summer kitchen and out the back door. Once we stepped outside, my dark mood lifted—sunshine makes everything seem possible—and I knew I would finish the chapter and the book. With the sun on my face, I could almost hear the words.

* * *

As Jake and I walked up the slope to the construction site twenty yards away, I had a chance to view the progress he and his crew had made in what seemed like no time at all. I was duly impressed.

"Jake, that barn is going to look exactly like the old one when it was new. I think you've mastered the art of reproduction. You're probably going to finish ahead of schedule. If that's the case, why is your crew working on a Sunday?"

"In construction, finishing ahead of schedule is money in the bank, and my goal is to put a lot of money in the bank. If I do, the KOMI execs will be happy."

"You mean Garrett will be happy."

Jake cocked an eyebrow.

"Especially Garrett."

He waved to his foreman, who was perched up in the rafters. The wiry, white-haired man with a full beard was busy whistling a tune and hammering a nail until he spotted us.

"Hey, Jake, who's the pretty lady?"

Jake shouted back, "She's Anna, my soon-to-be wife, but you knew that already so watch where you're hammering. I need you to keep all ten fingers until this job is done."

"I haven't lost one yet...Ouch! Just kidding."

"Funny, Mitch. Now, tell the crew it's time for a break, and come on down."

As soon as Mitch climbed down, the others followed. A minute later, we were surrounded by four men wearing tool belts. Three were clearly seasoned carpenters, but one looked like an apprentice because he was too young to shave.

"There's some Gatorade in the cooler," Jake said. "We finally have some nice weather so let's enjoy it for five minutes."

"Wow! A whole five minutes," said Mitch. "You're in a good mood today."

I chimed in, "Jake is always in a good mood."

Mitch rubbed his chin. "No offense, Anna, but you don't work with him."

Jake placed his hand over his heart and feigned injury.

"I brought my author in residence over to talk with you and the crew about local history," he said with a grin.

Mitch shrugged, but the twinkle in his eye was disarming. I felt I could speak my mind with this "old salt" and not be judged too harshly.

"It's true. I've hit a wall and need some inspiration. Can you tell me some stories about Tenants Harbor and Port Clyde? I want to hear all about the fishermen and lighthouse keepers who made this peninsula such a gem."

"Well, if the boss gives us an extra five minutes, the crew and I will share a few secrets that will keep you writing for days—maybe weeks. Who knows how far our stories will take you?"

"Tell away! You know I'm just a girl who loves ships and boats...and a man who needs to live near the sea."

Surrounded by all those burly men, I blushed.

We all sat down at a weathered picnic table on a knoll that was just beginning to turn green. Before the storytelling started, we took a moment to enjoy the view. The waters of the St. George and the Atlantic shimmered in the sun while cresting waves broke into white foam.

Mitch began his story in a fitting tone—low and rough.

"Joseph Gray was the keeper at Marshall Point in the 1920s. He witnessed the steamer *Pelias* strike a ledge as it tried to enter the harbor in light snow. Alone at his station, unable to help, he watched ten crewmen pile into a small boat that soon capsized, and every member of the steamer's crew drowned. Gray later explained the unforgettable horror of their loss: If the crew had remained on their vessel, they would have been saved. The steamer didn't sink that day; it remained hung up on the ledge for years."

Mitch paused to clear his throat then continued. "As a keeper, Gray probably didn't believe in ghosts, but if you're a believer, and I am, the crew of the *Pelias* is still trying to come home."

A silence came over our wide-eyed band of listeners. The youngest, Nathaniel, asked if there was time for one more story. The boss tossed back an answer. "If you have one, tell it quick," said Jake.

Nathaniel didn't waste time.

"Have you ever seen a blue lobster?"

I shook my head.

"Well, I have. I saw one last September in Belfast at the United Farmers Market."

The rest of the crew chuckled and Mitch spoke for the group. "Here he goes again. He's going to tell us how he met this amazing woman, Captain Maddie Sawyer, at the market."

With a grimace, Nathaniel went on. "Well, she is a key part of this story because there aren't many women who own their own boat, trap lobsters for a living, and are only twenty-seven years old. Captain Maddie is almost as rare as a blue lobster—"

"Nathaniel," interrupted Mitch, "you're wading into Moby-Dick waters because blue lobsters are one in two million, and you already know two lobsterwomen, Maddie and her sister, Kate."

Jake elbowed Mitch and said, "Let him tell his story. This is a three-minute warning."

With a glint in his eye, Nathaniel said, "Well, Captain Maddie sells lobster rolls and oysters at the market every Saturday, and last fall, a sapphire-blue lobster weighing a little over a pound and estimated to be ten years old, showed up in her tank. People lined up to see it, and even the press was there. It was featured on the news."

Based on Nathaniel's excitement, I could only assume that Captain Maddie was a knockout. I smiled to indicate my appreciation for the story and Nathaniel took that smile as a sign that he should continue.

"Do you know that Captain Maddie caught that blue lobster in Rockport Harbor and that she has been fishing since she was seven years old? She owned her first boat at fourteen and now she owns *Must Behave*, a twenty-eight-footer. She's a real beauty."

"The boat or the captain?" Jake teased.

Nathaniel lifted his chin, looked Jake in the eye, and quietly answered, "Why, both, sir. They're both beauties."

We all laughed together.

When our laughter finally subsided, Jake boomed, "Time to get back to work. We have a barn to build."

As I stood up, I added, "Thank you! I have a deadline to meet, and because of you, I just might meet it. Your stories have encouraged me to keep writing."

One by one, the men shook my hand as they went back to work. Mitch was the last one and shook my hand long and hard.

Clear as a bell, he said, "This was the best ten-minute break I ever had. Good luck with your novel, Anna. Don't forget to give it a happy ending. Fishermen and sailors survive on optimism."

I kissed him on the cheek and said, "I will."

* * *

Five minutes later, I was sitting at my desk with a stunning view of one of the most photographed doors on the coast of Maine, the historic door of the Marshall Point Lighthouse. I looked beyond the light to Monhegan Island, spread my hands over the keys, and began to type. I didn't stop until dusk, when I heard Jake rummaging in the kitchen and noticed my teacup was full. Since I didn't make any tea that afternoon, I assumed Jake had filled it for me, and I felt cherished. After hours of writing, I was filled with hope for the lobstermen *and* women of Maine, for the ships and boats that visit our harbors every day, and for the fate of our country and our planet. If I could write a compelling story about our courageous mariners and lightkeepers, maybe the naysayers who doubted our future would see that prosperity is still possible and peace is not limited to heaven. I checked my word count and knew that I would be ready for the June meeting with Maggie, Martin, and Warren in the Big Apple.

My head was spinning when I heard Jake's voice.

"Hey, Anna, dinner's ready. Can you take a break for chicken and rice...and me?"

I called back, "Yes, my dear," then I closed my laptop.

Today had been an excellent writing day. When I looked out the window and saw the Point's majestic lighthouse, I murmured, "Thank you," again.

CHAPTER 18

July 1939

On the second of July, a quiet Sunday, Sal parked his newly washed Chevrolet as close as he could to Grand Central, New York City's impressive rail terminal in midtown Manhattan, then hopped out and opened both curbside doors simultaneously. As soon as they opened, two sets of shapely legs swung to the curb and Sal whistled his approval.

"Thanks, honey," said Penny. "You're as fast as that new comic-book hero, Superman."

In a dulcet tone, Stella echoed Penny's sentiment. "Thank you, Sal. I don't know about Superman, but I think you look like a movie star."

Shaking his head, Sal mumbled, "The two of you are impossible. You don't look alike, but you sure act alike."

He opened the trunk of the car and pulled out Stella's overstuffed suitcase.

"What on earth did you pack? Who's going to help you get this off the train?"

"Sorry, but I'm going to be in Bath for a whole month."

Sal grinned. "Well, from the weight of that suitcase, you have a new outfit for each day of your stay. Mary Rose is going to have to pay someone to carry your bag to the car."

Stella rolled her eyes and Penny intervened.

"Don't worry, Sal. Just like Superman, Maine women are made of steel—or at least Yankee grit. Aunt Mary and Stella will figure out a way to get home without losing a suitcase filled with clothes that are bound to impress all the shopkeepers in Bath, including my former boss at Grant Department Store."

"Yes, dear," replied Sal.

Stella laughed. "Oh, Sal, you're going to make an excellent husband because you know all the right answers. Speaking of marriage, have you told my mother the news?"

Penny looked down at her stylish new pumps, but Sal looked directly at Stella as he weighed his words.

"No, we haven't mentioned our engagement, and we don't want you to say a word. We want to tell her in person, so we're planning to drive up to Maine on the sixteenth. Can you keep quiet till then?"

Tossing her head, she said, "Yes...I can try."

Not quite convinced, Sal lowered his voice. "Try hard, Stella. Penny and I are counting on you."

"All right," she said with a nod. "I understand. Now tell me where you plan to stop on your way up."

"We're going to make a two-day stop at Old Orchard Beach for business, not pleasure. Don Ameche, his wife, Honore, Loretta Young, and maybe that newcomer, Henry Fonda, will all be there to celebrate 20th Century Fox's new release, *The Story of Alexander Graham Bell*."

Penny jabbed him with her elbow, but he ignored the signal and continued talking about his favorite subject, the motion picture business.

"Ameche plays the title role. He's become one of Fox's most sought-after leading men. It's hard to believe that just four years ago he played a bit part in *Dante's Inferno*, but that's Hollywood."

Stella's expression went blank, and Sal noticed.

"I'm sorry. I talk too much, and I obviously love my job."

Glancing at his bride-to-be, he amended his statement.

"Of course, I love Penélope Solis McGowan more."

Not amused, Penélope pursed her lips and added her two cents. "Not a word, Stella. If your mom finds out I'm on the road with Sal, she won't be happy."

Stella touched her lips with her finger and whispered, "Mum's the word."

The two cousins, opposites in so many ways, linked arms and followed Sal and the heavy suitcase into Grand Central.

Minutes later, Stella boarded the train for New Haven, where she would change trains for Boston. There she would change again for Portland. It would be a long journey, but it was worth every rattle and bump to be home.

* * *

On that scorching summer day, the rails overheated, and more than a few trains were delayed for hours at stations up and down the coast. Stella's ride home was affected by the heat. She arrived at Union Station just after seven that evening. As she exited the train, she heard the man behind her say, "If there's a hell on earth, it's on the train from New York City to Portland, Maine." She wanted to turn and agree, but she didn't have the energy. Instead, she whispered "Amen" and dragged her suitcase onto the platform.

"Stella! Stella!"

She looked up and spotted Mary Rose twenty feet away. She smiled and, in a flash, let go of her bag and embraced her mother.

"Oh, Mom, I've missed you so."

Mary Rose returned her hug. "Welcome home, Stella belle. I've missed you, too."

She waited for a blaring whistle to stop, then she rushed to say, "Your carriage awaits—the car is just around the corner."

Stella laughed. "That's good because my suitcase weighs a ton."

"Nonsense. You're just tired," said Mary Rose as she reached for her daughter's bag.

"No," Stella replied. "I'm fairly certain someone slipped a whale into it during the trip, making it even heavier than it was this morning."

Mary Rose tried to lift the monster, but promptly failed.

Standing in the shadow of the station's clock tower, Stella saw her mother's cheeks turn from a delicate pink to a cherry red.

"You're tired and I'm sixty-seven years old. It will take the two of us to carry this bag, but we can do it."

"Of course, we're stronger together than apart."

Mary Rose nodded. "Okay, on a count of three: one, two...lift!"

Mother and daughter gritted their teeth and proceeded slowly to the exit. A few minutes later, they were cruising north headed for Bath and home. Stella relaxed, relishing the smooth ride of her mother's beloved 1937 Packard Six.

"I'm sorry my train was delayed. It'll be dusk before we get home, and I know you don't like driving after dark."

Mary Rose glanced at her daughter. "Maybe I do prefer the daylight, but I enjoy driving at any hour. Your dad felt that way, too."

Stella gazed out the window at the evergreens lining the road. "I've been thinking a lot about Dad over the last few months. I wish he was still with us."

The car turned quiet except for the hum of the Goodyear tires on the road.

Finally, Mary Rose spoke. "His love is still here. When you were a child, you sat in his lap and gave him the sweetest kisses. When you were a teenager, you confided in him. Stella, even though he died when you were seventeen, you knew him well and were lucky to have him in your life as long as you did."

"It wasn't long enough..."

"Yes, that's true. Penny lost her dad a year before your father died. My brother Daniel was the same age as Thomas. They rowed together at Bowdoin, and would have graduated together if Thomas hadn't left to go to sea. The truth is, Captain Thomas Goss and Captain Daniel McGowan lived big, bold lives and they didn't have regrets."

"They did have some, though. We all do, Mom."

"Of course, but they had a chance to know joy and sorrow, and they accepted both with grace. Do you remember when your Uncle Daniel died?"

"Yes, I remember."

"Your cousin was only fourteen. My brother wanted to live long enough to see his daughter celebrate her *Quinceañera* in her mother's Mexican tradition, but he didn't. The winds of fate are fickle."

"When we were sharing an apartment, Penny and I had a lot of time to talk about where we had come from and where we hoped to go. Penny told me that her mother's full name was Angélica Solis Velázquez de McGowan."

"Yes, and she was as beautiful as her name. She was only forty-six years old when she died of influenza. Penny was eight. Her passing hurt us all, but my brother never recovered."

171

"I remember Uncle Daniel well; I thought he always seemed happy."

"Your uncle was the consummate actor. In the quiet privacy of our porch, he used to tell me that his heart had gone missing and he didn't know why he was still alive. Six years after Angélica's death, he decided to return to sea. At the age of sixty-nine, he was too old to command, but he owned a few shares of Percy & Small's *Wyoming*, the great schooner that shuttled coal up and down the coast, so it wasn't too difficult to secure an invitation to accompany the crew on a passage from Norfolk, Virginia, to St. John, New Brunswick."

Stella looked at her mother. "I remember reading about the *Wyoming*."

"Then you know your uncle's fate, as well. The *Wyoming* was last seen off Nantucket battling the gales of a fierce nor'easter on March 12, 1924. All hands were lost. My brother's grief was buried at sea, but his love survived."

Mary Rose gripped the steering wheel and silence filled the car.

Stella spoke in a hushed, nurse-like voice. "It's a painful memory, but sometimes it's good to look back before stepping forward."

With her eyes on the road, Mary Rose nodded.

"Penélope Solis McGowan turned fifteen on September 8, 1925, and Bath, the City of Ships, celebrated her *Quinceañera* with an unforgettable fiesta."

Stella smiled. "I remember that party and all of its color: turquoise, fuchsia, yellow, and orange. I've never been to Mexico, but those colors were the brightest I'd ever seen."

Stella took a deep breath, then she let it go as if she were blowing out candles on a birthday cake.

"I'm sorry. I think I have a case of the blues. I've seen so much death and heartbreak at the hospital. Sometimes it's difficult to leave it on the ward and come home to family and life. You know what I mean."

Mary Rose struggled to find the right words.

"I'm not a nurse, but I've come to admire those who are. I admire you, Stella. I can only imagine how difficult your training must be...but I do know what loss feels like, and I have always chosen hope and love over despair. In the grips of sorrow, I believe love is the force that saves us."

"I think you would have made a great nurse, or doctor. You certainly know how to console me. And you know what?"

"What?"

"I'm fairly certain that Penny's fifteenth birthday party was the first *Quinceañera* in the history of Bath. I bet Uncle Daniel was singing "My Wild Irish Rose" up above."

* * *

A week later, Stella was sipping a tall glass of sweet tea on the side porch of the Goss family home on Washington Street. After ten months of working on busy hospital wards and eight years of working at National Screen Service in midtown Manhattan, she savored the peacefulness of her mother's screened-in porch. Reveling in the summer breeze off the Kennebec, she closed her eyes and pondered the fact that she was thirty-one years old and this was her first real vacation since leaving Colby College in December of 1929, one semester short of graduating with a degree. The stock market had crashed on the twenty-ninth of October and her family's savings had vanished. By the dawn of 1930, Mary Rose, already a widow, was struggling to pay the bills and Stella had to go to work.

When Stella opened her eyes, she drank in the beauty of her childhood home. Her mother's porch had always been her safe place. Sitting on a soft floral cushion in a white wicker chair, she surveyed her quiet place and smiled. At both ends of the porch, there were clay pots filled with cascading red geraniums set on wrought-iron tables with marble tops. In the center, there was a low, glass-topped table surrounded by four more wicker chairs. As Stella looked out beyond the garden to the shimmering water, she wrapped herself in memories as she also imagined her future.

"Stella belle, I think you're daydreaming again."

"You caught me. Dreaming seems to be my favorite pastime these days."

"Well, that's what summer vacation is for, and you've earned it," replied Mary Rose as she set down a plate of homemade ginger cookies.

"Mom, you have to stop baking. I think I've gained five pounds in seven days."

"Nonsense," said Mary Rose as she sat down in one of the oversized chairs. "Besides, you're much too thin. What do they feed you at that hospital?"

Stella looked at her mother's face and noticed the lines. There seemed to be more since last September. Suddenly, in the summer light, Stella realized that her mother was aging. Her once dark hair was almost white. Her feet were swollen and her hands were twisted, but her soft green eyes looked exactly the same, still enchanting and loving.

Stella reached for a cookie. "I can assure you they serve us nothing that resembles your home cooking."

"Speaking of cooking, what would you like for dinner tonight?"

"Oh, I don't know...something light. Maybe we could walk into town and have an ice cream soda at Hallet's, see a movie, and come home for tuna salad. What's playing at the Opera House?"

"*The Story of Alexander Graham Bell* with Don Ameche in the title role—it opened last week and the ticket lines have been long. Helene saw it and says it's the best movie she's seen all year. She said Loretta Young as Bell's deaf wife is amazing. I'd love to see it."

Stella sat back in her chair. She was surprised that her mother had mentioned Don Ameche and Loretta Young, the movie stars Penny was scheduled to meet in less than a week at Old Orchard Beach. Could it be true that her mother had a sixth sense? Did she know about Penny's plan to accompany Sal on his business trip, then come up to Bath and spring the news of their engagement? Her head said no, but her heart wasn't certain.

"Jeez, that's funny. I've wanted to see that movie. I'm a fan of Don Ameche, and Penny and I talked about seeing it in New York."

"I'll take that as a yes. I'll check the *Times* for the schedule. We can leave around four for Hallet's and go to the movies from there. Hopefully, the ticket line won't be too long."

Eager to spend the afternoon downtown, Stella stood up and headed for the doorway.

"Don't worry. I don't think it's possible for the line at the Opera House to be as long as the line at the Hollywood Theater on West 51st Street in Manhattan, and that's the line I usually stand in to see a new release."

Mary Rose shook her head. "I don't know about that. When this show opened last Friday, Ray Mitchell and another police officer had a hard time controlling the crowd; they wound up arresting Cal Johnson."

At the kitchen door, Stella stopped and stared at her mother. "Do you mean Ray, the guy I dated in high school?"

"Yes, Ray Mitchell is a sergeant on the police force, and he's still single. I don't think he ever got over you."

"Oh, Mom, don't say another word. That's ancient history."

Stella turned and walked up the back staircase, but Mary Rose refused to let her have the last word.

"It's still true," she said quietly.

* * *

When Stella stepped into A. Hallet & Company at 70 Front Street, she felt as if she had traveled back in time. There was no place like Hallet's drugstore, especially in Manhattan. It was the essence of a small-town shop and everyone's favorite meeting place. The counter ran the whole length of the store, with lots of items stacked above and below it. In front of the counter was a single row of metal tables topped with glass cubes that displayed expensive perfumes and other treasures, and short, round stools were tucked beneath each table. Stella smiled when she saw the One-Cent-Sale signs posted on the shelves above the counter, but her jaw dropped when she spied the new liquid carbonic, streamlined twelve-foot soda fountain.

She remembered the article her mother had sent her a few months ago from the *Bath Daily Times* celebrating the arrival of a stainless-steel fountain with all "the latest modern improvements." She had read the description with keen eyes because she used to work at Hallet's. Now that she was standing in front of Bath's new marvel, she had to run her hand over its rounded corners, the corners that wouldn't tear a clerk's clothing or fingers. When she saw the two sinks and the cold compartments, electrically lighted whenever a door was opened, she shook her head in amazement. She noticed the six built-in bowls for fruit toppings and the twelve new syrup pumps. When she saw the two draught arms that would hasten the drawing of soda during rush hour, she audibly sighed. She blinked her eyes and wished it had all been there when she had worked at the drugstore, when all it took to be happy was an ice cream soda.

"Why, if it isn't Miss Stella Goss, the north star of Washington Street!" exclaimed the gray-haired gentleman behind the counter.

"Hello, Mr. Pruett. The store looks terrific and so do you!"

Ed Pruett smiled from ear to ear. "Aw, shucks, you're going to make me blush. What do you think of our new deluxe soda fountain?"

"I think it's the *wonder* of Bath. I hear your ice cream soda is even better than before, but I have to test it to believe it."

"Well, I'm glad you stopped in, Stella." He glanced at her mother. "And it's always a pleasure to see you, Mary Rose. Your favorite table is waiting."

"Thank you, Ed," said Mary Rose with a beguiling smile.

Stella noticed the smile and quizzed her mother as soon as Mr. Pruett walked away.

"So, Mom, do you come here often? Mr. Pruett seemed very attentive."

"Don't be silly. Ed's just a friend. I'm too old to complicate my life."

"You're not old, and life is supposed to be complicated," said Stella matter-of-factly.

Mary Rose lifted her eyes and studied the tin ceiling, then she looked at Stella and said, "We're here to talk about *your* love life, not mine."

"Oh no, we're not; we're here for ice cream sodas and that's all."

Mary Rose smiled, "Okay, truce, but only if you let me treat."

"Deal! Make mine chocolate."

Stepping back to the counter, Mary Rose waited for Ed to look her way. When he did, she asked, "Can we have two chocolate sodas, please?"

Ed winked. "I'll put it on your tab."

Just then, Ray Mitchell walked through the door.

Stella spotted him right away. His hairline was receding, but his build was still athletic. By any standard, he was good-looking. Hoping he would buy a candy bar and leave, she sat down quickly and studied the bottle of Chanel No. 5 displayed beneath the glass.

Maybe coming home wasn't a good idea. Her first year of training had taken its toll. She often felt alone in a crowded room, and she knew her emotions were raw. Her thoughts turned to Dr. Novack, Lily, Nurse Conley, and Simon Miller. Was she on the right path? Could she handle all the losses she would encounter as a nurse?

A deep baritone voice interrupted her train of thought.

"It's been too long. How are you, Stella?"

Speechless, Stella looked up at Ray and blushed. She remembered how he had broken his nose during a basketball game at the YMCA's court on Summer Street. The bump was still there.

Ray cleared his throat and added, "Bath has missed you."

"And I've missed Bath," replied Stella. "I'm training to be a nurse."

Ray was in uniform and clearly on duty, but he pulled out a stool and sat down.

"I've heard. As you can see, I'm on the force. How do you like nursing?"

"Lenox Hill Hospital feels like a city within a city. It's not an easy place, and the training is hard—emotionally."

"I bet it is. Police work can be that way, too. Speaking of work, I'm due back at the station in five minutes, so I best be going."

He stood up and tucked the stool back under the table.

"It's good to see you, Stella. How long will you be in Bath?

"I'm on break for three more weeks."

"Maybe we could see a movie or have a drink at the Sedgwick some evening and catch up."

Stella twisted her hands in her lap. "That sounds nice. Our number hasn't changed. You can call me."

"Great! I'll do that."

Mary Rose approached the table with two ice cream sodas in her hands.

Ray smiled. "Have a good afternoon, ladies. Nice to see you so happy, Mrs. Goss."

Mary Rose nodded. "It's always good to be with family, but Ray, 'Mrs. Goss' sounds too formal. You're all grown up so call me Mary Rose."

"I'll try," said Ray. He turned and strode away.

* * *

Under the front staircase was a tall walnut table tucked into a little alcove that could have been used as a hallway closet, but instead served as a communication center. Stella called it the family phone booth because that's where they kept a desk-top phone, the only telephone in the house. Since the girls had left for New York City, it hardly ever rang, but now that Stella was back for a visit, it was ringing every day. Whenever it rang, Mary Rose was the first one to pick up and say, "Hello! Mary Goss speaking." For her, answering the phone was like accepting a gift, and on the sixteenth of July she received a special gift: a call from Penélope.

"Hello, Aunt Mary, it's Penny."

"Well, hello, how are you? Is everything all right?"

"Yes, everything is great," gushed Penny. "I'm in Bath at the Sedgwick Hotel."

"Oh, my goodness, what are you doing at a hotel? Why aren't you ringing the doorbell?"

"Well, I'm not alone. I'm with Sal, and we'd like to stop by and share some news."

When the phone fell silent, Penny held her breath. After a long pause, she heard her aunt's calm voice and started to breathe again.

"Please do. Stella and I are both here. I'll make some lemonade. Can you come over now?"

Penny giggled like a schoolgirl. "Oh, yes, we'll drive over. Walking would take twice as long."

"See you soon!"

Ten minutes later the doorbell rang—a sound as delightful as the ring of a telephone—and Mary Rose opened the door as Stella flew down the stairs.

Penny and Sal were dressed in their Sunday clothes. Sal was wearing dark sunglasses, tan-colored pants, and a short-sleeved white shirt. Penny was in a red-and-white polka-dot dress with red pumps and a wide-brimmed red hat.

"That was fast," said Mary Rose as she gave Penny a peck on the cheek.

"I'll say," echoed Stella as she rushed through the door to hug Sal, then Penny.

Mary Rose cleared her throat. "Well, don't just stand there roasting on the front steps. It's cooler inside than out today, and I suspect we have a lot to talk about."

Penny took Sal's hand, and together they stepped into the grand old house. When her hands touched the delicate, harpsichord-like bannister, tears began to well in her eyes. Until that moment, she hadn't realized how much she had missed home.

* * *

An hour later, Stella was in the kitchen filling a pitcher with ice and lemonade when she heard a knock. She hurried to the entryway and saw Ray Mitchell standing on the other side of the screen door.

"Hello, Ray. What a nice surprise to see you twice in one day. Come in."

"I hope you don't mind my stopping by," he said. "I thought I'd take a chance you were home..." He shifted his weight. "Would you like to go to the movies with me tomorrow night?"

With smiling eyes, Stella said, "Well, that depends. What movie did you have in mind?"

"*Stagecoach*. It's playing at the Opera House."

"I hear that's a great film with a lot of action and a wonderful cast. According to the critics, Claire Trevor and John Wayne are completely believable."

His eyes widened. "I'm glad you like westerns! Can I pick you up at seven?"

"Yes, it's a date. And Ray, I'm glad you took a chance."

As soon as Ray left, Stella returned to the kitchen and found Penny waiting.

"Was that Ray Mitchell's voice I just heard?"

"Yes."

"Imagine that!"

Stella laughed. "Oh, that's exactly what I'm doing."

CHAPTER 19

June 2019

O nce again, on a Sunday evening, I found myself sitting on a plane waiting to take off from the Portland Jetport, but at least I wasn't traveling alone. Jake was sitting next to me. At the last minute, he'd decided to take a few days off and accompany me on a business trip. The timing was perfect. His crew had just finished the lion's share of the work at Marshall Point. The tasks left to do were minimal, and their Mount Desert project wasn't scheduled to begin until the sixth of July. Our plan was to fly into LaGuardia, cab over to the Empire Hotel on West 63rd Street, and enjoy two whole days together in the Big Apple before I had to meet with the trifecta—Maggie, Martin, and Warren—on Wednesday morning at Manhattan Publishing. The first draft of *The Keeper's House* was stowed away at my feet, packed in my coveted seabag. I'd packed it in that bag because I thought it would bring me luck. It was made from the same material as the sails of a tall ship and appliquéd with dark-blue anchors that reminded me of the U.S.

Navy, my father, and my grandfather. Call me superstitious, but even though I had already sent a PDF, I was determined to carry a paper copy of my manuscript into Martin Gormley's office. As the plane lifted off the runway, I grabbed Jake's hand. Could I possibly be one landing away from a dream come true?

I glanced at the middle-aged woman sitting in the aisle seat, and noticed she was reading a murder mystery by one of my favorite Maine authors, Bruce Cole, and I had to smile. Maine seemed to produce and attract authors of every genre, but mysteries reigned. If only I had written a murder mystery or a modern-day thriller, I might have felt more confident about my novel's success. Lately, terror was a lot more appealing than historical fiction, especially historical fiction with a romantic twist. While I was terrified to meet with a leading publisher, I was also determined to fight the good fight.

I whispered in Jake's ear, "You're going to love the Empire Hotel."

He turned his face toward mine, gave me a kiss on the nose, and said, "I know I'll love it because I love you."

My voice turned wistful.

"It's close to the Juilliard School in Lincoln Center. I think Lincoln Center Plaza is the coolest place in New York City."

Jake cocked an eyebrow. "Wait. I thought Central Park was your sweet spot."

I paused and grinned like a child who couldn't make up her mind between a lollipop and a candy bar.

"Yes and no. In springtime, when you walk through the gates of Central Park, it's like entering a fairy-tale garden. Rows and rows of yellow tulips sway in the breeze and say hello. Flowering trees, redbuds and dogwoods, beckon you to sit and enjoy the color. All that natural beauty pales in comparison to the glitter and shine of Lincoln Center for the Performing Arts—a sixteen-acre plaza with a magnificent fountain surrounded by towering buildings, and park-like flower beds on the Upper West Side. From morning till night, you can see every kind of performer crisscrossing the plaza."

"Even comedians?"

I pressed my lips together and jabbed him with my elbow.

"Just kidding. When we wake up tomorrow morning, let's grab a cup of coffee and a bagel and have breakfast with all the artists on the plaza."

I stretched over the armrest and encouraged another kiss.

"Getting back to flowerbeds, did I ever tell you that your eyes never fail to hold me?"

He kissed me, and I heard the woman in the aisle seat clear her throat, but I ignored her disapproval and kissed him back.

* * *

Less than two hours later, our yellow cab pulled in front of the hotel, and I could tell Jake was impressed. The multistory, redbrick building occupied a stretch of West 63rd Street that seemed more like a peninsula than a corner, offering a fabulous view of Lincoln Center. Perched on top of the building was a towering electric sign that was designed to light up the night sky with its name, Empire Hotel. As soon as we stepped out of the cab, we both looked up and admired the skyscape.

The taxi driver unloaded our bags and waited for his tip. Jake was generous, making the portly man flash a smile with a missing front tooth.

"Thank you, and welcome to the city where buildings go up, people go down, and the lights are always on unless there's a blackout."

Jake nodded. "So true! Where is the nearest subway?"

The cabbie pointed across the broad, busy street. "Over there, where people are going down the steps to the underground."

"Thank you," said Jake with a wave. "We'll be going there, too."

We turned and met Enrique, the bellboy waiting to help us with our luggage.

"Welcome to the Empire. Is this your first time staying with us?"

"It is for me," smiled Jake. "I'm from Maine."

I chimed in, "Not for me. I stayed here once with my parents. My grandfather was stationed at the Brooklyn Navy Yard and my mother was born in Brooklyn."

Enrique laughed. "So, you are both from out of town."

I slipped into Spanish. "Eres muy cómico, Enrique. Pienso que Brooklyn es el diamante de la ciudad. ¿No estás de acuerdo?"

Enrique's mouth dropped open; for a second, he lost his words. He clearly wasn't expecting to hear Spanish from such an Irish-looking girl, but I knew he approved when his face broke into a smile.

"No estoy de acuerdo, señorita. Prefiero Manhattan, pero me encanta la gente de Brooklyn."

Jake shook his head. "I wish I knew what you were saying, but since you're both still smiling, I'm not going to worry. I'm just going to check in at the desk while you two compare and contrast the boroughs. Don't forget to mention the Bronx, Queens, and my personal favorite, Staten Island. Did you know that in the late 1800s, Bath solicitors used to live on Staten Island while they sold Bath-built ships at the South Street Seaport in Manhattan?"

With a quizzical look, I said, "Yes, I think I knew that."

Rubbing his forehead, Enrique replied, "No, I didn't know...¿De dónde es usted?"

Jake raised an eyebrow; he looked lost.

"He's from Wiscasset, Maine, close to Bath, a little city famous for building nineteenth-century square-rigs, and three, four, and even six-masted schooners, not to mention twentieth-and twenty-first-century U.S. Navy destroyers."

Enrique shook his head. "No comprendo, señorita. Are you speaking English?"

We all laughed.

I winked. "Wait here while we get our keys, then we can discuss the Yankees and Red Sox on the way to the room."

"Sí, señorita," said Enrique with a winning smile. "I love the Yankees!"

Jake laughed. "I love the Red Sox!"

* * *

Holding hands, Jake and I passed through the hotel's glass doors and stepped into the sparkling lobby. The opulence was breathtaking, and Jake's reaction was immediate.

"I've never been to the Taj Mahal, but it must look something like this, right?"

From vaulted ceiling to marble floor, the lobby was bedazzled with black marble fountains, gold-framed mirrors, and jewel-like mosaics. The Empire Hotel was the essence of luxury.

"It's even more mesmerizing than I remember. Maybe that's because I'm viewing it as an adult, not a child. I think grownups appreciate hotels more than kids, don't you?"

Jake didn't answer. Suddenly, he was in a hurry. I watched as he quickly checked us in, then I listened as he told Enrique to bring our bags up to Room 610. Enrique nodded and said he would use the service elevator, but we should use the main elevators because they were nicer. He seemed to intrinsically understand that Jake was no longer interested in talking about baseball. His focus had shifted. On the elevator ride, I realized what was driving him and was grateful we were alone. He stopped the elevator somewhere between the third and fifth floors, and we indulged in some delicious fun.

When we finally arrived at our room, Enrique was waiting. Jake gave him a big tip, and Enrique grinned like a man who knew too much.

"Muchas gracias, señor. Enjoy your stay at the Empire. ¡Es fabuloso! ¿Verdad?"

Jake wasn't quite sure what *verdad* meant, but he understood *fabuloso* and Enrique's smile, so he said, "Sí, señor," and waved goodbye.

* * *

The next morning, we woke up in the king-size bed, wrapped in five-hundred-count sheets and surrounded by uber-soft pillows. We heard sirens blaring, horns honking, and the unmistakable sound of a garbage truck unloading a dumpster. At the top of the crescendo, a shrill whistle reached up to our sixth-floor windows and shook us awake.

"Someone must be hailing a cab right below us," Jake whispered in a dry voice.

"What time is it?" I asked in a daze. "And why is it so loud?"

"It's almost nine; I think it's noisy because millions of people live and work here, and apparently sleep isn't a priority."

I rolled over and said, "You're a genius. You've been here less than twenty-four hours, and you've already figured out what makes this city tick."

He kissed me and whispered back, "No, I haven't, but I'm hoping to find out with you."

I looked into his eyes and thanked God my meeting with the trifecta wasn't until Wednesday morning. I sat up, pulled his pillow out from behind his head and gave him a whack.

"Well, what are you waiting for? This is a Calvin and Hobbes moment. 'Let's go exploring!'"

Jake practically jumped out of bed. "Okay, who's Calvin and who's Hobbes?"

The pillow was still in my hand, and I threw it as I laughed.

"Don't be silly. It's obvious. You're Calvin and I'm Hobbes."

He reached down and pulled me into his arms. "No, you're not imaginary; you're real, and I'm the luckiest guy in the world."

He tickled me until I cried, "*Tío!* Stop! I have to shower and get dressed, and you do, too."

* * *

Thirty minutes later, we headed out the Empire's double doors, walked around the corner to a coffee shop, ordered two coffees and bagels to go, then headed for the fountain at the heart of Lincoln Center Plaza. We were not alone. The plaza was humming with people, and they all seemed to be dressed in black, gray, or dismal brown. My pink L.L. Bean sweater stuck out like a button-down shirt at a rock concert. I had forgotten how hard it was to keep clothes clean while navigating crowded sidewalks or riding in packed buses and trains. In the city, dark clothes were a practical choice, but shoes and boots were a fashion statement, and there was a wealth of footwear to admire on the plaza.

Within a minute of finding a vacant bench, I caught my first glimpse of Juilliard students on their way to class, and I assumed they were dancers because of the graceful way they moved and the overall tone of their bodies. As they passed, I audibly sighed and Jake noticed.

"If I lived in Manhattan," he said, "I think people-watching would become my favorite pastime."

"True…"

"What are you thinking about, Anna? All of a sudden you're quiet."

"Oh, I don't know. I suppose Lincoln Center has always been a dreamy place for me. I applied to Juilliard but wasn't accepted. Don't get me wrong; NYU was the right place for me, and I was thrilled to go there. In the end, it was a good choice, but I would have liked a nod from the Juilliard School. I made it to the final round."

"What final round? You've never talked about anything but writing."

"In high school, I aspired to be an actress and landed a few starring roles in the fall play and spring musical. At the end of my junior year, I decided to apply to several big theater schools, De Paul and Northwestern in Chicago, and Juilliard and the Tisch School of the Arts in New York. Juilliard was the only one that denied me. I think my parents were relieved, because they wanted me to have a more traditional education."

"I see. And the Tisch School led you to screenwriting?"

"Yes. It was a circuitous path, but there's always more than one way to get where you want to go. Today I feel as if I'm making progress."

Jake sipped his coffee then draped his free arm around my shoulders and tilted his head until it touched mine.

"Publishing this novel will not be your last stop, and Port Clyde isn't our final destination. I believe you and I are travelers, and we can't possibly see all the points in our future, but if we keep our eyes on the horizon, we'll enjoy the ride, and we'll find our way."

I tilted my head back and spoke to the sky. "¡Dios mío! You're a bona fide oxymoron, a poetic engineer, but that's why I'm so in love with you it hurts."

Jake took his arm away and grabbed the bag of bagels sitting on my lap.

"I never want to hurt you," he said. He reached into the bag and pulled out my lightly buttered bagel. "Here, you're probably just hungry. Have a bagel."

I laughed. "You're right. I'm always hungry when I'm around you."

I took the sesame bagel with cream cheese out of the brown bag and handed it to Jake. "You should eat, too. There's nothing finer than a New York bagel on a Monday morning at Lincoln Center. When we've finished our breakfast, let's try to buy tickets for tomorrow night's performance of *Jane Eyre* at the American Ballet Theater."

"A ballet? What happened to the classic American art form, the musical? Look!" Jake stood up and pointed to a huge poster outside the Vivian Beaumont Theatre.

"You must have laser vision. I can't see that far."

"It says, *My Fair Lady*."

"Really, Jake? Eliza Doolittle over Jane Eyre?"

"Yes, I'm in the mood for a romping chorus of 'Get Me to the Church on Time,' not a nineteenth-century psychological thriller about a troubled governess employed by the brooding Mr. Rochester."

When I heard Jake's response, I almost dropped my bagel. How could he remember so many details about English literature? Maybe he really was a genius. I wasn't surprised he preferred musicals to ballets, but I was stunned by how much we didn't know about each other.

"I had no idea you favored musicals over dark drama," I said with a hint of a smile. "Okay, you win. Let's try to get tickets to *My Fair Lady* because we're on a two-day spree in the theater district and it doesn't have to be terrifying."

Jake broke into a grin. "Sorry. I guess Charlotte Bronte's *Jane Eyre* reminds me of my high school English class, which was a nightmare."

He took my hand and pulled me off the bench. I stood on my tiptoes and brought my lips to his.

"Did I tell you I played the role of Eliza Doolittle in my high school musical?"

With his mouth lingering over mine, he whispered, "I'm not surprised. If I had known you then, I would have been in the front row."

He took my breath with a kiss. When our lips parted, I let my heels touch the ground and whispered back, "I'm glad you didn't know me in high school. If you had, you might not be with me today, and that would be too sad. Sometimes I feel as though I've been waiting for you forever."

* * *

On Wednesday morning, I woke up before the seven o'clock alarm, humming "I Could Have Danced All Night." Jake was still asleep, so I put on my yoga pants and long-sleeved T-shirt and tiptoed out the door for coffee and something from the neighborhood bakery. Today was game day and, being anxious about the meeting at Manhattan Publishing, I thought a made-in-Manhattan Danish would boost my confidence and sharpen my focus.

By the time I returned to the room, Jake was up and showered.

"You were operating like a stealth destroyer this morning. I didn't hear a sound. Where did you go?"

"I went to Bumble Bee and got an apple, an apricot, and a raspberry Danish and coffees to go. I couldn't sleep after seven. I guess I'm a little nervous."

As he grabbed the apple Danish, he chuckled, "You think?" He paused. "Wait a minute. Where's the apricot one?"

"Oh, I ate that on the elevator ride."

"Whoa! You really *are* nervous. A Danish before showering is not your style."

"Don't worry. In the words of Billy Joel, 'I'm in a New York state of mind,' but it's only temporary. I'm hopping in the shower right now. I'll be dressed in power-blue before you finish that Danish."

* * *

An hour later, Jake and I stood in the lobby deciding whether we should sit down for a full breakfast or hail a cab and grab something to eat closer to Manhattan Publishing. Since I was wearing a sleeveless dark-blue dress with a red belt and three-inch heels, I was definitely in a decision-making mode. I was also wearing red lipstick and pearl earrings, so Jake knew I was serious.

"I'd like to head downtown sooner rather than later. Manhattan Publishing is on Broadway in the heart of the Financial District. It's in a class-A landmark office building, so I'm sure it's surrounded by good restaurants. We should take the subway, but I'm afraid I'll sweat too much. Since the publisher's paying for this trip, let's take a cab."

Jake nodded. "I agree. Your meeting doesn't start until ten, right?"

"Yep."

"In that case, we'll have time for a leisurely breakfast. When you head up to the meeting, I'll find a café and answer some e-mails. I'm sure Garrett is gearing up for our Mount Desert project, and I don't want to be buried with documents when I get back Thursday night."

I smiled bravely. "I wish we could fly back together, but Maggie hinted that I would meet the editor assigned to my book today, and I'll probably have to meet with him on Thursday and maybe even again on Friday morning."

Jake reached for my hand. "No worries. You're going to be great. They're going to love *The Keeper's House*, and we'll both be enjoying the view at Marshall Point by Friday night or Saturday at the latest."

I chuckled, "You're such an optimist."

"Maybe, but my optimism won't hail us a cab as fast as you can in those red high heels. There's not a doorman in sight."

I tossed him a smile, walked to the curb, and raised my arm. In a New York minute, a yellow cab pulled up. As we climbed into the backseat, I teased him.

"You know, you could have texted an Uber or a Lyft."

He chided back, "Now where's the fun in that?"

Our driver launched into a closing argument. "You did the right thing. Uber and Lyft have stopped accepting new drivers in New York City. The city has imposed new rules to slow the growth of ride-hail companies and help traditional cabbies survive. Manhattan is cab-friendly, and taxis are here to stay."

Jake glanced at me and responded in a serious tone, "I'd take a taxi any day of the week here. Heck, the yellow cab is a New York icon. Truth be told, taxicab drivers know city streets better than anyone."

Our cabbie smiled with satisfaction. When we arrived at our destination, with time to spare, Jake tipped him well.

* * *

Maggie met us at 9:45 by the central elevators of 195 Broadway dressed in a white jacquard-dot coat and dress set and wearing stiletto heels. At five foot nine, her stature was imposing, making me glad she would be at my side on the twentieth floor.

"Hi, Maggie, how are you?"

"I'm glad to be here. How about you?"

"I'm excited. Before we go up though, I want to introduce you to my fiancé, Jake Summers. And Jake, this is Maggie O'Shea, my literary agent."

Jake flashed a smile. "It's a pleasure to meet you, Maggie, and now I'm off to the nearest café. The two of you look ready. In my opinion, the guys upstairs don't stand a chance."

"I hope your opinion is right. Anna told me you were a dream, and now I see why."

The elevator doors opened and six people piled out. I bit my lip. Everything—the city, the morning, the people—was moving fast, and I was being swept along. It was exciting and nerve-racking at the same time. I gave Jake a quick hug and stepped into the elevator. He mouthed, *I love you*; I answered with a quick wave, and the doors closed.

By a stroke of luck, Maggie and I were the only ones on the elevator, and we used the time to discuss our strategy.

With her eyes still fixed on the doors, Maggie said, "MP received a digital copy of your book last week, so Martin and one of his editors have probably reviewed it. They may have some criticism, but don't react. We wouldn't be here if they didn't like it."

As the elevator rose, my anxiety did, too. I glanced over at my gritty agent and said, "You're beginning to scare me. I'm going to listen, but I'm not going to remain silent. We're going to talk about my work. It's *personal*."

"No, Anna. Today it's business."

I wanted to stop the elevator and get off, but I kept breathing. The doors opened on the sixteenth floor and two gentlemen in light-gray suits stepped on and pressed the button for the twenty-seventh floor. I wondered what they did. Were they attorneys, financial advisors, actuaries, or the staff of another publishing house? Were the higher floors reserved for the most prominent firms? Suddenly, I felt lost in a confusing maze of profit and loss and didn't like the feeling.

The doors opened again. We had arrived on the twentieth floor, which was entirely occupied by Manhattan Publishing. It was our turn to exit the elevator.

Fortunately, Warren was on hand to greet us. He had arrived a few minutes early and was waiting for the receptionist to break free from an onslaught of phone calls to announce his arrival and direct him to the appropriate office. I was relieved to see him standing there and grateful for God's divine intervention.

"Hello, ladies! Fancy meeting you here, and I do mean *fancy*. This place is the Ritz...and you both look stunning."

I shook my head. "Oh stop! We're not in Hollywood anymore. This is New York."

He laughed and gave me a hug, and when I stepped away, I tilted my head toward Maggie.

"Warren, this is my agent, Maggie O'Shea; Maggie, this is my former boss, the head of Coastline Studios, Warren Dunlap."

Maggie and Warren shook hands, but before we could start a conversation, the receptionist informed us that Mr. Gormley was waiting for us in Suite A, so we all followed her instructions and walked down a long hallway to the meeting room next to the corner office.

Martin was already seated at the head of the conference table, but he stood as soon as we entered the room.

"Welcome to Manhattan Publishing!" he boomed as he walked toward me. He gripped my hand and pumped my arm. "You must be Anna. I've been looking forward to this meeting. I've been a fan of yours ever since I saw your documentary, *The Mariners of Long Reach*, when I took my family to the midcoast of Maine and visited the Maine Maritime Museum. They had a special showing, and my wife and I couldn't stop talking about it. My sons enjoyed it, too. In fact, one of them has applied to the Coast Guard Academy in New London. I think your film affected him."

Warren stepped forward. "Well, if you liked her documentary, you would have enjoyed reading her screenplays. Have you seen Coastline Studios' new release, *Captains of the Kennebec*? That's Anna's work, and so is *Daisy Longtree*."

"Yes, I'm aware, Mr. Dunlap. With your help, Anna has established herself as a rising star in the film industry, but today I'd like to discuss her debut novel. I suspect you're here to secure the screen rights, but let's not get ahead of ourselves."

He pointed toward an antique table in front of a wall of windows. "Would you like some Perrier, coffee, tea, or juice? Help yourselves and take a seat. As soon as our editor arrives, we can get started."

As I poured myself a glass of water and placed a scrumptious-looking croissant on a plate, I gazed at lower Manhattan and admired the resilience and majesty of the rebuilt World Trade Center. Now the tallest building in the country, One World Trade Center stood as a symbol of freedom, valor, and the power of love over evil. How could I possibly be afraid of failure in the shadow of that level of courage? I took my place at the table and waited for the appointed editor.

Even though I wasn't hungry, I lifted the croissant to my mouth and took a bite just as the editor entered the room. His youthful look astonished me. He had curly brown hair that fell over his brows, but not his eyes, and he was wearing a polo shirt with expensive designer jeans. As soon as he arrived, Martin stood to introduce him.

"Anna, Maggie, Warren, I'd like you to meet one of our best editors, Dan Leone. He's been with us for almost twelve years, has an excellent eye, and requested to work on this project because he's drawn to maritime history. He also has family ties to Maine."

I put the croissant down, swallowed hard, and glanced at Maggie. What did Martin mean by family ties? Maggie had read my screenplays, seen my films, and reviewed the first draft of my novel. She knew that my storylines were rooted in family history. By the look on her face, she'd felt the impact of Dan Leone as much as I had. Warren must have felt a gust of fate blow in as well, because he put his elbow on the table, rested his chin on his hand, and shot me a *Twilight Zone* look.

I forced myself to think. Why did the name Leone ring a bell? Could I have seen that name when I was researching Maine's maritime and my family's history? It wasn't a Bath name, but in the scores of shoe boxes filled with my grandmother's letters and personal papers, I might have seen it.

Martin's voice interrupted my train of thought.

"First, Anna, I want you to know that Manhattan Publishing would like to continue working with you, and we'd like to fast-track your book so we can have it ready for production by September and in stores by Christmas. We see the seeds of a best seller in your work."

"Seeds?" I asked with a quizzical look.

"Yes, *seeds*. We've got our work cut out for us, but Dan is ready to start this afternoon. If you can stay in the city until Saturday, the two of you can go over the book line by line and make the necessary changes."

"Necessary?"

"Let me rephrase that. Dan will make suggestions and you can make decisions, but keep in mind that Dan knows how to craft a best seller. Listen to what he has to say. I don't think you'll be disappointed."

Maggie weighed in. "If you're going to move this fast, we're going to need to modify the original contract. To get this novel ready for Christmas is no small task."

"We'll all be under pressure to get this done, but, as you know, timing is everything in business. Producing and selling books requires a well-oiled machine."

"Okay, but we'll need to see an amended contract, and our attorney will have to review it."

"Of course," said Martin as he stood and walked around the conference table to stand by me. "We'll have that ready this afternoon, but for now I'm delighted to present Ms. Malone with a check for submitting her novel on time and as promised to Manhattan Publishing."

I stood up and reached for the envelope with a steady hand, but my mind was doing cartwheels across the room.

"Tomorrow, Dan will probably tell me I'm too wordy, but right now there are only two expressions dancing in my head: *Wow* and *Thank you*."

"That will do," laughed Martin. "I think *The Keeper's House* is the first of many books MP will publish with you. In case you're wondering, I *love* the title and think we'll all agree it's a keeper."

Warren stood. "Okay, so now can we talk about the movie?"

I grinned, "Yes, Warren. Let's talk about the movie."

CHAPTER 20

September 1939

Stella woke to the morning bell. With her eyes tightly closed, she pulled the crisp white sheet over her head. Her second year of nursing school was about to begin and she silently wished for one more hour of sleep, but mornings at Lenox Hill were not for sleeping. It was the fifth of September, the day after Labor Day. Two days ago, France and Britain had declared war on Germany. Four days ago, Germany had invaded Poland, and thirty-six days ago, Stella had said goodbye once again to Maine, her mother, and her sweetheart Ray. The world was plunging into chaos, but the hospital was waking up to another well-defined day. Regardless of the terrifying headlines and alarming radio reports, the hospital's clock kept ticking, and a nurse's duty remained unchanged. For twenty-four hours every day, the ambulances kept arriving, the gurneys kept rolling, wheelchairs kept moving, mothers in labor kept panting, and newborn babies kept opening their eyes.

Peeking over the edge of her covers, Stella could see her starched white cap ready and waiting on the top of her bureau. It was time to go to work; it was time to keep breathing and believing that life would go on and goodness would prevail. She stretched before sliding her feet into her slippers. As she grabbed her towel, she sighed and felt immediately guilty. She was feeling sorry for herself, missing her private bathroom at home, when Jews in Germany, Austria, Holland, and Poland were disappearing in the night. How could she complain about having to wake up early on the Upper East Side of Manhattan?

As she shuffled down the hall to the bathroom, she heard a voice.

"Stella?"

She turned to see her best friend, Marie Capelotti, fully dressed. "Are you coming or going?" Stella asked with a yawn.

"I'm coming. I've been on duty since last night, but I'm not here to brag. I'm on break and came to tell you that you had a phone call just before eleven. As I was leaving for my shift, one of the graduate nurses came in to do a pop inspection, and she took the call downstairs. There's a message waiting for you at the desk."

"Thanks. I'll check after breakfast."

Marie shook her head. "I wouldn't wait. The nurse repeated the caller's name aloud: Simon Miller. Isn't that your old boss?"

Frowning, Stella replied, "Yes, that's him. I'll check as soon as I'm dressed."

She took a quick soak in the tub, and minutes later hurried downstairs with her apron tied at her waist and her cap pinned on her head. Scanning the board, she spotted a folded note with her name on it. She recognized the elegant handwriting and wondered why Marie hadn't mentioned that it was Nurse Conley who took the call. As she reached for the note, she prayed her supervisor hadn't recognized Simon's name, but that was unlikely. He had written her letter of recommendation and attended her capping ceremony; he was also a hard man to forget. Student nurses were not supposed to receive calls after nine at night. Nurse Conley would not tolerate any shenanigans, but Simon wasn't a rule breaker. She hadn't spoken to him in months. If he was calling after hours, something was seriously wrong. She held her breath and read the message: *Call Simon Miller at Murray Hill 5-2376 as soon as possible.*

Stella looked at her watch. She had to be on the maternity ward in less than thirty minutes. She paused in front of the nurses' dining room. Maybe she had time for a bowl of cornflakes and a cup of coffee before calling Simon back. No, she had to call him right away. She walked over to the phone on the wall near the front staircase and dialed the number.

The phone rang several times before Simon answered in a weary voice.

"Hello?"

"Good morning, Simon, it's me. I'm sorry to wake you, but I just got your message."

"You didn't wake me; I haven't slept a wink."

Stella's tone changed. "What's wrong?"

As he answered, Simon's voice began to shake. "David and Caleb want to learn how to fly and join the RAF because Britain needs pilots. They don't understand why Roosevelt remains unfazed by the fall of Poland and why we're not getting into the fight. I don't know how to keep my sons out of the war. I don't even know if I want to. Their mother was from Poland. Most of her family is still there. I tried to get them out over a year ago, but I failed. If Naomi weren't dead already, this would kill her—"

Sobs enveloped his words.

"Listen, Simon, there's nothing you can do to stop your sons from fighting. If I could, I would go with them. You need to sleep; you need to restore your spirit."

"I can't," he said as he calmed down.

"You have to try. You have to stay strong for your sons and for National Screen, too. So many people depend on you."

"I'm so tired."

"I know you are, Simon," she whispered. "Just sleep, then come to the hospital at noon; I'll wait for you in the cafeteria. I have an hour for lunch, and we'll spend it together."

"I'll try," he said with a heavy sigh.

"I'll be there waiting."

"Okay."

She heard a click and realized he had hung up.

Stella checked her watch again. She made a beeline over to the sideboard in the dining room and grabbed a banana then dashed out the front door toward the hospital. With minutes to spare, she walked calmly onto the maternity floor and reported for duty. She was ready for whatever the day would bring. She had to be.

* * *

By midmorning, the obstetrician on call had delivered four babies, all healthy and pink. The number of new admissions had slowed to a trickle. Stella stopped at the nurses' station to request a lunch break at noon, and the nurse in charge agreed without protest. The sun had replaced a full moon hours ago, and the sunshine had a calming effect on everyone, including the close-to-delivery mothers. The nurses on duty were convinced that false labors rarely happened on beautiful days, so they weren't anticipating the admission of too many first-time moms. Stella was as relaxed as she could be on a maternity ward until she turned around and spied Nurse Conley walking toward her. She wanted to flee, but knew there was no escape.

"Good morning, Nurse Goss. How is your day going?"

Stella cleared her throat and managed to smile. "It's going well."

"I'm glad to hear that."

Nurse Conley paused to study Stella's face then asked, "Did you see the message I left on the board last night?"

Stella nodded silently.

"I hope late-night calls from gentlemen aren't a common occurrence at the nurses' residence."

"No, I assure you they aren't. In fact, I've never received one until last night."

The head nurse knitted her brow. "Hmm, until last night. And how is Mr. Miller? I remember meeting him at the capping ceremony last year."

Stella blushed and stammered, "He's...not well at all. You see, he's a widower with two sons, and both of them want to fight with the RAF as soon as they can. He's lost family members in Poland, and he's quite distraught."

In a blink, Nurse Conley's whole demeanor changed.

"Oh, I see. I'm truly sorry to hear that. He must have needed a shoulder to lean on and a kind ear to listen. I detected more than a little pain in his voice."

"Yes, he couldn't sleep and was beside himself with grief."

Nurse Conley looked away. "I hope you offered him some comfort."

"I tried, but it was hard on the phone. I told him to sleep. I'm meeting him for lunch even though I don't know what to say."

Bringing her gaze back to Stella's young and eager face, Nurse Conley said, "I'm at least ten years older than you, so I hope you will accept my words the way they're intended. There's nothing you can say to Mr. Miller to ease his pain. You can only listen."

The head nurse turned and walked away.

* * *

A few hours later, Stella circled the tables in the cafeteria looking for Simon, but she didn't find him. She grabbed a tray and filled it with tuna salad sandwiches and two small bottles of Coca-Cola. She was betting Simon would keep his promise; he would come.

As she headed toward the cashier, Dr. Pete Novack came up beside her.

"That's a lot of food for one person," he said.

"It's for two."

"Oh, who are you having lunch with?"

Stella paid the cashier, picked up her tray, and looked directly at Pete. "Not with a doctor. That's not allowed, remember?"

She turned, spotted Simon, and walked toward him with her fully loaded tray and the certainty that Pete's eyes were following her all the way.

She chose a table in the middle of the bustling cafeteria, and as soon as Simon sat down, she offered him an open bottle of Coca-Cola. "I think you need a shot of sugar, Simon. Don't take this the wrong way, but you look awful."

Simon shook his head in wonder. "I don't know how I got here. I don't even know what day it is. The world is at war and I'm having lunch on Manhattan's Upper East Side. I told the driver to take me to Lenox Hill Hospital, and here I am having lunch with a beautiful nurse."

Stella reached across the table and touched Simon's hand. Her hazel eyes, more blue than green, said nothing and everything.

Simon poured his soul into Stella's open heart. The last letter he had received from his sister-in-law, Ruth, a native of Warsaw, had confirmed that the Nazis were exterminating Jews. She had called it "Hitler's evil solution." With the news that Poland had fallen, he knew that his wife's family and their Jewish friends and neighbors were lost. Now he feared for the Jews in Paris and throughout Europe. He desperately wanted to help, but he didn't know how.

"I couldn't convince Ruth to leave Poland. I couldn't save her or her children, but even if I can't save them all, I must try to save as many as I can. I was up most of the night crying and thinking. How can I get Jews into America? That's what I have to do."

Simon pounded the table with his clenched fist, causing the nurses at the next table to stop chattering long enough to glance at Stella and express their concern. She reassured them by mouthing, *It's okay.*

"We'll find a way," Stella said tenderly. "It's only a matter of time before we get into this war. Hitler will be stopped."

"We may be running out of time. I don't want my sons to fly for the RAF. I'd prefer they fly for the U.S. Army Air Corps and have the stars and stripes on their sleeves when they shoot the German Luftwaffe out of the sky. God forgive me, but I want those German pilots to see my sons' brown eyes from their cockpits and realize that some good Jewish boys from America sent them to their fiery graves."

Biting her lip, Stella struggled to find something helpful to say, but her mind went blank. Simon's rant had pushed her to a dark place. Like so many Americans, she was feeling torn. As a nurse, she was trained to preserve life, not destroy it. She didn't want anyone to die a fiery death, but Hitler was evil, and evil had to be destroyed.

As she opened her mouth to offer a comforting word, she spied Nurse Conley at the cashier and waved.

"Simon, there's someone I'd like you to meet. Will you excuse me for a moment?"

Stella didn't wait for an answer. She jumped up and caught her supervisor before she found a seat.

"Do you have a minute? I'd like you to speak with my friend, Simon Miller. He wants to help the Jews fleeing Europe. Maybe there's a way nurses can help."

"Where is he? I'd be happy to speak with him."

Glancing at Simon, she said, "He's right over there. I'll introduce you."

At the table, Stella pulled over a third chair.

"Simon, this is Nurse Conley, my supervisor. Nurse Conley, this is Simon Miller, my former boss. I thought you two should meet and have a chat. You've both helped me so much."

"It's a pleasure to meet you, Mr. Miller," said Nurse Conley as she placed her tray on the table. "I read your letter of recommendation for Stella. It was quite eloquent."

"Thank you, but please call me Simon," he said as he stood to shake her hand.

"All right, but only if you call me Theresa."

Simon nodded. "I think I can manage that, Theresa. Please join us."

Nurse Conley sat down and started talking fast. "Forgive me, but I'm on a short lunch break so I'm going to be direct. Stella told me you're Jewish and you still have family in Europe. I live in Brooklyn, and there's a group in my neighborhood organizing to help the Jews. Right now, they're focusing their effort on the children who were separated from their parents and are now seeking asylum in the United States. Would you be interested in attending a meeting?"

Simon sat up and looked directly into Theresa's mint-green eyes. "Yes, I'm definitely interested."

"Good. I'll make some inquiries about the day, place, and time of the next meeting and let Stella know."

"We don't have to communicate through Stella. Why not call me directly?"

Theresa took a bite of her pastrami sandwich and thought for a moment.

Finally, in a lilting voice, she replied, "But I don't have your number."

Stella's eyes widened. She had never heard Nurse Conley use that girlish tone that signals *stay, don't go.* She reached into her apron pocket to pull out a pen.

"I have a pen if you want to give Nurse Conley your number."

Simon pulled out his business card and reached for the pen with his left hand. He quickly wrote his home number on the back and handed it to Theresa.

Noticing the dark circles under Simon's eyes, Theresa took the card and put it in her pocket. "You're a lefty—that means you're smart and probably a good baseball player."

With a hint of a smile, Simon replied, "I'm fairly smart and exceptionally good at baseball. I played all through college."

"I bet you did," teased Theresa. "Well, I have to go, but I'll call you as soon as I know the details of the meeting, and I'll see you there."

"Are you Jewish?"

"No, but I'm a nurse and like to help others," said Theresa as she stood to leave.

Simon quickly stood to shake her hand again.

"You've already helped me, and I'm grateful."

Theresa responded with a warm and engaging smile. Stella was shocked. This was another first. She had never seen Nurse Conley smile that way, and it made her wonder, *Who is this woman?* Whoever she was, Stella liked her and felt fortunate to be her student.

CHAPTER 21

August 2019

I climbed through the window onto the roof of the front porch. Jake was still sleeping, but I was wide awake so it seemed like the perfect time to slip outside and let the mist touch my face. As I looked at Port Clyde's harbor in the raspberry-orange light of an early morning, I begged the summer to slow down. In fifteen days, August would slide into September, and I would be flying back to New York City for another meeting at Manhattan Publishing. At our June meeting, I had agreed to an aggressive timetable, and I was determined to make my deadlines. By the second of September, I had to clear all Dan's comments and corrections and be ready to choose the cover art and title. Even though Martin had complimented my working title, he'd told me it was best to present five titles to the creative team for consideration. Upon leaving his office, I wondered why the first title was rarely the chosen one.

Standing on the roof of the keeper's house at Marshall Point, I prayed I was ready for the December launch. I had never given birth, but I imagined the process of pub-

lishing a novel was much like having a baby. The fear
of publishing was beginning to interrupt my sleep, and
other worries were contributing to my insomnia, as
well. After this trip to New York, Jake and I would have
to decide whether or not to renew our lease. Without a
doubt, Marshall Point had inspired my work. How could
we leave one of the most charming places in Maine?
Perhaps we should stay, but the location wasn't ideal for
either of us. As a project engineer for KOMI, Jake was
overseeing jobs up and down the coast; as soon as I published my book, I would be traveling to bookstores near
and far. My practical side told me we should live closer
to the Portland Jetport, but my romantic side told me to
stay at the Point.

"Are you out on the roof again?" called a groggy voice
from inside.

I answered, "Good morning *Mr. Lightkeeper*. If you don't
get up soon, you're going to miss the sunrise altogether."

Without missing a beat, Jake volleyed back, "That's
okay. I prefer sitting under a crescent moon with you."

I climbed through the window and crawled back into
bed. Since the alarm wasn't set to go off for another hour,
we wrapped each other in the present and enjoyed some
early-morning love.

* * *

I was scrambling eggs when I heard a truck pull into
the parking lot. Jake was in the shower, so I gave him a
three-minute warning.

"Hey, Jake, I think Garrett just pulled in."

"What?"

"Your boss is—"

"Stall him!" he shouted.

I heard Jake's ringtone and answered, "Hello! Jake's
phone."

"Good morning, Anna, it's Garrett. I'm downstairs at the side door. Can you let me in?"

"That depends," I said in a hushed voice. "What's the password?"

Garrett chuckled. "*Jake is a good catch.*"

"Jake who?"

"You're kidding, right?"

When I didn't answer, Garrett continued, "Okay, I'll play—your soon-to-be-unemployed fiancé if you don't open this door."

I quickly replied, "Okay, I'll come down and let you in," and ended the call before dissolving into laughter.

A minute later, I opened the door. "Always a pleasure to see you."

"What took you so long?" asked Garrett.

"I was making breakfast. Would you care to join us?"

He shook his head. "Let me guess: Jake's not ready."

I looked directly into his dark eyes and told a harmless fib. "Of course, he's ready, but breakfast is the most important meal of the day, and you and Jake deserve a good start. Come on GL, take ten minutes and enjoy some home cooking."

Garrett didn't budge. He wasn't buying it.

Rubbing his chin, he said, "If I didn't know better, I'd say the two of you are feathering a nest like a couple of lovebirds. Have you set a date yet?"

I pursed my lips and threatened silence, but then decided to be candid. "No. Frankly, we're too busy to make plans. In case you're not aware, you're part of our chaos."

Garrett shrugged. "I'm aware, but Jake is phenomenal, and KOMI needs him. Look on the bright side: You're engaged to a rising star—but then again, so is he."

I sighed. "Thank you, Garrett. I needed to hear that this morning. Join us for a quick breakfast. A couple of eggs and a stack of blueberry pancakes will keep you sharp all day long."

Now Garrett's eyes melted.

"That's an offer I can't refuse."

I said, "Follow me!" and as I turned, I noticed the crinkling lines under his eyes that were oddly endearing.

* * *

After Jake and Garrett left to inspect KOMI's project on Mount Desert Island and visit a potential project on Isle au Haut, I cleaned up the kitchen and packed for my visit to Bath.

Ninety minutes later, I pulled into my parents' driveway and tooted the horn to announce my arrival. My mom opened the door and waved, making me feel at home, cherished, and suddenly queasy. I took a cleansing breath and got out of the car. My dad, who had been busy working in the yard, came around to the back of the Subaru and offered to carry my bag upstairs. I thanked him with a tired smile and followed him into the kitchen.

My mom gave me a quick hug. "Hey, there, Gypsy Rose, you look exhausted. How about a glass of sweet tea?"

"Yes, that sounds nice."

I stepped into the pantry and checked the calendar on the wall, the one they kept next to the shelf of coffee mugs for easy access. I flipped back to May, then quickly to June and July before returning to August with a wave of nausea. Today was the eighteenth of August, and my last period was the twentieth of May. What happened? I reminded myself to breathe and reviewed the events of the last few months. I had come down with strep in April, and the doctor had written a prescription for penicillin. At that time, I was struggling to finish my first draft for the June deadline and my meeting with the publisher. I wasn't paying attention to my *personal* calendar.

Without warning, I was gripped by fear, and a shiver ran down my spine. Through a fog, I heard Mom's voice.

"Anna, are you okay? You seem a little spooked."

I turned to see her sunny, reassuring face.

"I'm fine...I was just thinking how busy this summer has been."

"Well, I'm glad you were just lost in thought, because for a New York minute I thought you'd seen a ghost."

Even though I was feeling queasy, I had to laugh. "Frankly, Mom, finding a ghost in this hundred-and-ninety-six-year-old house wouldn't be that surprising."

"Oh, Anna, I don't think anything would surprise you."

I dropped my eyes and looked at the floor.

"I wouldn't say that," I said, bursting into tears.

At that moment, Dad walked into the kitchen and froze in place.

"What's going on? Why are you crying?"

"It's nothing. I'm just feeling overwhelmed with the final edits, the book cover, the bio, the summary, and..."

"And what?" asked my dad as he handed me his white hanky straight out of his pocket.

I dabbed my eyes and blew my nose.

"Our lease is up and we need to plan our wedding."

Mom added her two cents in a nice way. "I can help with the wedding plans, and don't worry about all the book stuff. Your editor sounds wonderful. What's his name?"

"Dan Leone," I said blowing my nose again. "He's great, but the final decisions are mine, and I'm beginning to feel the pressure."

My dad draped his arm around my shoulders and kissed the top of my head.

"Beginning? You've been stressed for months. Have a little faith, Anna."

I looked up and met my father's chocolate-brown eyes.

"I will, but right now I think I need to take a walk and clear my head. Route 1 was brutal today. I wish Port Clyde was a little closer to Bath."

Smiling, Mom put a positive spin on my battle with summer traffic. "It's never too far if you can get there by car."

"Right," I said as I closed the door and headed downtown.

As a high school student and even as a college student, I had never suffered from test anxiety. On the contrary, I had relished the challenge of an impossible test, but now, as I walked to Wilson's Drugstore, I was sweating with anxiety because a pregnancy test at age thirty-seven is a lot more terrifying than the SAT at seventeen.

* * *

Three days later, I once again sat outside my bedroom window on the roof of the keeper's house and let the amazing view of boats, birds, rocks, waves, and a solitary lighthouse console me. I was waiting for Jake. He was on his way home, and I was going to tell him the news after dinner. We could walk over to the General Store and grab a sandwich or fish and chips at the counter, then have an ice cream cone on the dock. In the middle of consuming a scoop of black raspberry, I'd tell him we were expecting, and he'd be shocked, but happy. I wasn't nervous, not really.

A truck pulled into the parking lot. It had to be Garrett's. I heard a door slam, then a couple of beeps as the truck drove away. Jake had called to tell me that Garrett wouldn't be staying for dinner because he had a meeting in Camden. I climbed back through the window, put on some lipstick and spritzed myself with L'eau de Issey because I knew Jake loved it, and I wanted to create an unforgettable evening.

When I heard Jake climbing the stairs, I called out, "Hi, honey!"

At the kitchen door, he dropped his bag, and said, "Phew! It feels good to be home!"

I rushed into his arms. When he kissed my neck, I had to bite my lip to keep from telling him my secret, the one I had been keeping for over forty-eight hours.

"I missed you."

"I missed you, too," I whispered as I buried my face in his neck. "Let's *only* travel together from now on."

He lifted my chin and kissed me. As our lips parted, he wistfully said, "If *only* that were possible."

I stepped back and looked at him with wonder.

"*Anything* is possible, but I truly believe you and I work too hard. Let's take tonight off and have dinner by the dock."

"You're a genius. Why didn't I think of that?"

I winked and gave him an excuse: "Because you just got home and you probably wanted a home-cooked meal."

He gave me a peck on the cheek and headed for the bedroom.

"Give me a minute to wash up and change. I want to look my best when I go out with the fairest woman on the peninsula."

Rolling my eyes, I half shouted, "You're a master of hyperbole!"

He didn't respond, and I was happy in the moment— the last word was mine.

* * *

It was the perfect August night, so we sat outside and enjoyed our haddock and fries at a table on the deck. The harbor was humming with lobstermen, tourists, artists, sailors, and all kinds of skippers. Looking across the table at Jake's sunburned nose and handsome face, I felt like I was in the middle of an Old Spice commercial. How did I wind up here? How do I tell my husband-to-be that he's about to become a father?

At the height of the season, we lingered as long as we could at our table, but a line of hungry people were waiting, so we left a big tip and went over to the ice cream stand. Armed with two scoops of our favorite flavor, we found a spot at the edge of the dock and sat down to enjoy the violet sunset and our just dessert. After a few licks, I looked out on the water and calmly posed a question.

"So, Jake, what project will you be working on next year at KOMI?"

While savoring his cone, Jake pondered the question.

"I'm not sure, but Garrett's looking into buying the keeper's house on Isle au Haut. Like Marshall Point, the lighthouse on the island is owned by the town, but the keeper's house is privately owned and has been operating as an inn for a long time. It went on the market last year, and Garrett is interested. The property needs a lot of work. If he makes a deal, that could be my big project. Why do you ask?"

Keeping my eyes on the water and my hand on my cone, I stammered, "Well, we haven't set the date for the wedding, and in February or March…we're going to have a baby."

Jake coughed and sprayed ice cream into the hot summer night.

"We're going to have a baby?" he asked, searching my face for an answer.

In a soft voice, I said, "Yes, we have a baby on the way, and I need to know how that makes you feel."

"How it makes me feel? I'm out of my mind in love with you *and* our baby!"

My whole face lit up. "I was hoping you'd say that."

Jake tossed the remainder of his cone into the water, put his arm around me, and squeezed. "It's true. I'll always love you. I want children with you, and I want to marry you as soon as possible."

I tossed my cone into the water and kissed him harder than I'd ever kissed him before.

We stood up and faced each other; I placed my hands on his warm cheeks and together we glowed.

"I don't think we can get married this month or even next month," I said, "but early October is a definite possibility."

Jake raised his arms in a winning Rocky Balboa pose and shouted into the wind, "I love October!"

Holding hands, we looked toward the ocean and counted our blessings, one wave at a time.

CHAPTER 22

September 1940

Penny and Sal were holding hands as they walked up the granite steps of Saint Mary's Church at 838 High Street. They were ten minutes early and unusually quiet before their meeting with the pastor to discuss their upcoming wedding.

"You're going to like Father Foley," said Penny as she paused on the top step. "When I was young, I dreaded his long sermons, but I realized he had a good heart. He used to walk around town with his pockets filled with dimes, giving them away to everyone in need."

Sal looked at Penny with a discerning eye. "I have two comments. First, you're still young, and second, ten cents is hardly enough to help anyone."

She tilted her head and spoke deliberately. "Thanks for thinking I'm still young, but thirty is on the verge of old. As for the dimes, back then, ten cents would get you into the movies and you could stay for a double feature. And for some people, a ticket to the movies could be a saving grace."

He laughed with a hint of nervousness. "Well, if Father Foley gives us a dime today, I'm going to save it for our honeymoon, throw it into the water at Niagara Falls, and make a wish for you and me."

Penny stood on her tiptoes to kiss his smooth olive cheek.

"You're beginning to sound as corny as my aunt," she chuckled.

Sal shook his head. "No, Mary Rose is one of a kind."

Penny smiled as she placed her hand on the church's beautifully carved door and pushed, but as soon as the door was opened halfway, she paused. Her mind flooded with memories, and she couldn't move. She was about to enter the holy place where she had received Baptism and First Communion with both of her parents present. Later, when she received the sacrament of Confirmation, only her father was with her. Suddenly she felt closer to her faith and to her parents than she had in years and wanted to hold on to that feeling for as long as possible.

She glanced next door at the Convent of Our Lady of Mercy, and her thoughts turned to Sister Isadore, her fifth-grade teacher. Sister Izzy, as the children liked to call her, had a passion for local history, and Penny had caught that passion in 1920. Because of her teacher's spark, Penny had developed an affinity for historic places and key facts. For instance, she remembered the City of Bath was originally called Long Reach and could be described as a slim needle. One mile wide and five miles long, Bath stretched along the western bank of the Kennebec River and consisted of a series of granite-supported ridges that ran parallel to the Kennebec and rose like steps from the water's edge.

Standing in front of the white church with its towering steeple, three arched doorways, and sparkling stained-glass windows, Penny's eyes filled with gratitude for Bath and for all the people who had cared for her as a child. She was home, and her heart was remembering the good and the bad. When she was in the third grade, her mother died. By the time she entered the fifth grade, she was struggling in school, but Sister Izzy wouldn't let anyone fail. Her enthusiasm for learning was contagious. Looking back, Penny thought her fifth-grade teacher must have been an angel sent by God at her mother's request.

In addition to Sister Izzy's kindness, Penny would always remember her lessons pertaining to Bath. Her most dramatic one was about the burning of the South Church. In 1854, after an angry mob—incited by the Know-Nothing Party—had burned down the church that the Catholics were renting, Oliver Moses, a pillar of the community and a professed Universalist, vowed to right the wrong. He invited the Catholics to worship in his home, and then he raised funds to build the first Catholic church in the City of Bath.

Before entering the church, Penny thanked God for leaders like Oliver Moses and Franklin D. Roosevelt—leaders willing to help people regardless of their background—and prayed for peace.

"I'd give you a penny for your thoughts, but that seems like a play on words unless I call you Penélope."

Penny laughed, but she remained on the church's front doorstep. Instead of entering, she turned around to admire the view. The shade of the graceful elms, the soft hues of hydrangeas, and the vivid color of marigolds scattered across the front yards made it feel good to be home. She was happy to be at Saint Mary's door with Salvatore Dominic Leone at her side.

"Good morning. I'm sorry I'm late," shouted Father Foley from the sidewalk. "I had a last-minute phone call at the rectory."

Penny waved and called back, "Don't worry, Father. You're not late; we're early."

* * *

On Friday afternoon, the train pulled into Depot Square at four thirty and most of the bridal party and wedding guests from New York City arrived in force. Ray was waiting for Stella with open arms, and Sal was waiting for everyone else with hands ready to carry their luggage. Both men had driven to the station in separate cars so they could help transport everyone except Stella to the Sedgwick Hotel. It was a short trip up to the corner of High and Centre Streets, so unless the guests had brought an excessive amount of baggage, Sal was confident they would get everyone settled without a hitch. Later, they would meet for a casual dinner at one of the nicer downtown bars.

Simon Miller was the first to step off the train, and Sal recognized him right away. As he rushed to shake his hand, a middle-aged woman stepped forward and smiled hello as well, and Sal was instantly dumbfounded. Penny had told him that Simon was bringing a guest, but she hadn't mentioned that the guest would be Theresa Conley.

Observing Sal's surprise, Simon cleared the air.

"I've brought a friend. I hope you don't mind."

"Not at all," stammered Sal. "Penny mentioned you were bringing someone."

Theresa shook Sal's hand. "I recognize you, but I don't think we've been formally introduced. I'm Theresa Conley, a nurse at Lenox Hill."

Sal grinned. "Yes, and unless I'm mistaken, you're the *top* nurse, right?"

Theresa laughed. "You could say that, but *head* nurse or *chief* nurse might be a more accurate term."

"Okay, Chief, can I help you with that bag?" asked Sal.

As Sal reached for the bag, Stella approached the group.

"Hi, Sal, are you ready to say 'I do'?"

She kissed him on the cheek, and he gave her a one-armed hug.

"Oh yeah," he said, "I'm so ready."

"Don't be too anxious," chided Stella as she scanned the platform. "Penny is nervous enough for both of you."

"You're absolutely right."

"Well, now that we've clarified the situation, I see my wedding date over there, so I'm going to give him a proper hello."

Ray, of course, had spotted her as well, and before she could take five steps, he was putting his arms around her.

"Have you missed me?" he asked in a low voice.

She kissed him and then whispered in his ear, "Does that answer your question?"

He grinned like he was seventeen all over again. "Yes, yes it does."

He took her bag. "I've got my car waiting."

A chorus of voices called out, "Hey, what about us?"

It was Penny's friends from the office, Alice O'Connor, Evelyn May, and Carole Schaeffer.

Stella looked over her shoulder and shouted, "Hurry up! If you can all squeeze in the backseat, Ray can drop you at the Sedgwick."

Sal chimed in. "No need for squeezing. Alice, why don't you come with me? You can sit in back with Theresa. Evelyn and Carole can go with Ray and Stella."

"Is that everyone?" asked Ray.

"That's everyone who took the train," said Sal. "My family is on the road. Some are driving from Staten Island and others are coming from Lubec. The New Yorkers will arrive late tonight and the Mainers will arrive in time for the wedding, but no telling at what hour."

In a lilting voice, Stella sang, "They're coming from everywhere just to hear you say 'I do'!"

As he walked to his car, Sal crooned, "And I will because I do, do, *do* love Penélope."

The chorus responded, "Of course, you do!"

* * *

Sitting on the swing on the side porch, Stella and Penny watched the sun come up over the Kennebec. It was the fourteenth of September. Neither cousin could sleep because one of them was getting married—and because the German Luftwaffe had been bombing London for seven consecutive days.

"I'm happy and scared at the same time," said Penny.

Stella shivered as she pulled up the soft green quilt covering their legs and hugged it to her chest. She rocked the swing and fixed her eyes on the red sky.

"What do the sailors say?" she asked in a quiet voice.

Penny replied, "Red sky at morning, sailors take warning."

"Well, I don't believe it. Today, the world is going to be okay. It's your wedding day."

"But we're not okay, Stella. If FDR declares war on Germany, and he should, Sal is going to enlist and so are Ray and thousands of others. We're on the brink of—"

"Stop! We can't predict tomorrow. The future is promised to no one, but today belongs to you and Sal."

Penny raised her hands to her face and said, "Yes, and I have to look ravishing in three hours and forty-five minutes. Do you think I'll be able to hide the fact that I barely slept last night?"

Stella jumped off the swing.

"Yes, I have lots of makeup. Come with me!"

* * *

A handsome black Cadillac with Helene Milhomme's son at the wheel pulled up to the curb a few minutes after ten. The bride was appropriately late, and all the doors of Saint Mary's were wide open. From the backseat, Penny could see her bridal party waiting at the back of the church.

As soon as she stepped out of the car, Stella, the maid of honor, rushed out to help her.

"Penélope Solis McGowan, you look radiant. If I didn't know better, I'd say you slept at least eight hours last night."

"Very funny," said Penny, shaking her head.

Stella fussed with Penny's veil until the lace fell perfectly on her shoulders. Then, stating the obvious truth, she said, "You're beautiful."

"If you say so, but I wish I looked like you."

Stella laughed. "You know, we're exactly the same height."

Penny reached for her cousin's hand. "I miss my dad. I wish he were here to walk me down the aisle."

"He's here, Penny. We just can't see him."

Stella pulled a blue handkerchief from the sleeve of her sea-green dress and gave it to her cousin.

"Wrap this around your bouquet and don't cry. Keep your eyes on the altar and Sal."

* * *

As soon as they heard the processional song, guests on both sides of the aisle stood and looked toward the bride, but first came the bridesmaids on the arms of the groomsmen: Alice and Vinny, Evelyn and Dominic, Carole and Ray. Then came Stella with her hair swept up and her long silk gown cinched at the waist. She looked like a porcelain doll. When she smiled, everyone in the church sighed. Sal, waiting at the altar with his brother Nick, only had eyes for Penélope. As soon as he saw her luminous face, he beamed. In their presence, Mary Rose began to cry. She reached for her handkerchief, but it wasn't there so she simply let the happy tears flow.

Carrying a bouquet of pink orchids laced with baby's breath, Penélope walked down the aisle with her eyes on Sal. When she approached the front of the church, she glanced left at her Aunt Mary and her dear friends then right at Sal's family sitting in the front row. Having no siblings, and knowing only one cousin, Penny had always longed for a big family. She was happy that Sal had five siblings, and she was eager to add them to her family circle.

Sal reached for her hand and she reached for his. They stepped onto the altar, and Father Foley began celebrating the mass. Their family and friends let the prayers, the music, and the sacrament envelop them. Penny remained calm throughout the ceremony and even giggled once. When Sal's brother Michael sang "Ave Maria," she trembled and Sal put his arm around her. She unwrapped the blue handkerchief from the bottom of her bouquet and wiped away a tear.

As soon as Penny and Sal said "I do" and the rings were on, Father Foley said, "I now pronounce you man and wife. You may kiss the bride."

With his arm around her waist, Sal pulled Penny up until her feet were off the floor and kissed her.

* * *

As guests of the bride, Simon was sitting next to Theresa on the left side of the church. Theresa was clearly delighted, but Simon wasn't smiling. In fact, as the music began to play, his expression became more somber. Even though he was Jewish, not Catholic, the candles and the music made him feel God's presence intensely, and he was moved to pray. In June, against his wishes, his sons had joined the Royal Air Force. Today in this peaceful church, he fixed his eyes on one of the stained-glass windows and fervently prayed that Hitler would be stopped and his sons would come home. Surrounded by love, his eyes filled with hope. He took Theresa's hand and kissed it. Taken aback, she blushed, then kissed his hand in return and smiled. In this holy place, like the bride and groom, they chose to place their trust in love.

CHAPTER 23

September 2019

My stomach was queasy and my head was spinning. From deep inside a tunnel, I heard a voice calling my name.

"Anna...are you, all right? Here, drink some water."

When I opened my eyes, I saw Dan's worried face twelve inches above my own.

"Are you okay?" he asked earnestly.

I sat up, reached for the glass of water in his hand, and nodded.

After a long swallow, I smiled sheepishly and murmured, "I'm pregnant."

Helping me to my feet, he stammered, "You're... pregnant?"

"Yes, I'm quite sure, and I'm sorry I scared you, but I haven't been feeling at all like myself these days. I guess this morning's decision-making session was a bit too much."

Dan's face lit up.

"Congratulations! And I'm the one who should be sorry. All this talk about the color of the paper, the size of the book, the cover design, and the need for endorsements is enough to make anyone nauseous."

I shook my head. "No, you're just doing your job, but I have a whopping case of morning sickness, and I'm too fuzzy to make these decisions."

"Don't worry about it. I think we both need a cup of coffee or, even better, some herbal tea. Does that sound good?"

"Oh, yes, herbal tea sounds like the perfect remedy for everything that ails me."

Dan chuckled. "Great! I know a place." Then he winked. "It's called Café Loco and it's right around the corner."

* * *

Fifteen minutes later, seated in a cozy faux-leather booth, I ordered a cup of ginger tea, and Dan ordered a café con leche with an apple Danish. Considering its prime location, Café Loco was inexpensive and cheerful, and I felt instantly at home.

"Is it okay to ask when the baby is due?"

I giggled. "Our best guess is the end of February or beginning of March."

"Have you told the boss?"

"If by *boss* you mean Martin Gormley, no I haven't. In fact, outside of my family, you're the first to know."

"I'm honored."

"Well, you should be. Thank you for receiving the news so well. I do plan to tell Martin, Maggie, and Warren this afternoon. Coastline Studios wants me to start working on the screenplay as soon as we launch."

Dan frowned.

"What's wrong? Aren't you in favor of turning a novel into a film?"

"It's not that…I love movies, but I've been waiting for the right time to give you my final comment on your manuscript."

Our pink-haired waitress suddenly appeared with our order. I waited for her to ask "Anything else?" before I replied no.

"I'm all ears. What's your final note?"

Dan cleared his throat while I stirred my tea.

"You know that section where you describe the first tenants of the keeper's quarters—the photographer and his wife—at Marshall Point?"

"Yes."

"Well, I was drawn to their story. They lived at a lighthouse station for fourteen years, observed how the natural world affects our lives, and chronicled their adventure with award-winning photographs."

I nodded knowingly. "Marshall Point is an amazing place; that's why it functions like a character in my novel."

"Yes, I see that, but I think you should step into your own fiction—like Gabo."

My cup of tea hit the table so hard it splashed. I dabbed the placemat with my napkin and asked the obvious question: "Like Gabriel García Márquez?"

"Yes, the father of magical realism from Aracataca, Colombia," said Dan. "In 1982, Gabo won the Nobel Prize for *One Hundred Years of Solitude*, the sweeping story of the Buendía family."

Altogether mystified, I threw up my hands and shot Dan a puzzled look. He responded with a belly laugh.

"How do you know so much about the greatest Spanish-speaking author since Miguel de Cervantes?"

Dan flashed a wicked smile.

"My father told me his maternal grandmother was born in Mexico and arrived at Manhattan's South Street Seaport on a sailing ship in 1909. Because of my father's

Latin-American roots, he studied Spanish in school and learned to speak it fairly well. I'm not fluent, but I can defend myself *en la lengua de mi bisabuela*. In New York, Spanish comes in handy."

"Who knew," I laughed, "but how do you connect me to Gabriel García Márquez?"

"You follow the thread of history by telling a family's story, and that brings history closer to home. Like Gabo, you have a strong sense of place, but unlike him, you let your cities and towns keep their names. For instance, you describe Portland, Bath, St. George, and Port Clyde as coastal communities in Maine. Gabo describes Macondo, a fictional village, in the jungle of an unnamed Latin-American country. Readers assume the village is Aracataca, Colombia, but Gabo—the magical realist—prefers to mix reality with fantasy."

Completely baffled, all I could do was blink and fire another question. "What's your point?"

Leaning forward, Dan said, "My point is that you and Gabo bring places to life, but Gabo enters his own fiction and plays tricks with reality. I'm suggesting you step inside *The Keeper's House* and add a little magic."

"Be specific," I said with an edge.

"You and Jake have been living at Marshall Point for a year. I suspect living at the Point has affected you as powerfully as it affected the first couple who rented the space. Take a risk and enter the story. Show how living on the coast has changed you, and don't be afraid to exaggerate."

I stared at my editor's Roman nose and wide mouth while listening to his words as if they were clues to a hidden treasure.

"I'm familiar with *Cien años de soledad*—my mother taught Spanish for thirty years and kept her hard-cover copy on a shelf in the family room. Me defiendo en español, but neither my style nor my spirit are conducive to magical realism."

"I understand—"

"No, I don't think you do. My writing is infused with truth. Perhaps I romanticize the truth, but I prefer Disney magic to Gabo magic. Gabriel García Márquez believed all of history was a myth. I believe all of history stems from a seed of truth. In other words, while I paint the beach, Gabo paints the jungle. My view is brighter than his. We don't share the same outlook."

Dan winced. "I'm sorry. I've clearly hit a nerve. Let me try to explain. Your novel already weaves present and past together in a magical way. I'm suggesting you add an element of magical realism. Include your time in the lightkeeper's house, and share how living at Marshall Point, surrounded by the natural world, affected you. If you do that, I'm convinced your family love story will be unforgettable."

I leaned back and winked.

"Oh, the natural world *has* affected me. Estoy embarazada—I'm pregnant."

We laughed and kept laughing until our waitress showed up with the check. I reached for it, but Dan was faster.

"This one is on me" he said.

"Okay, but I want you to join Jake and me for dinner at John's Pizzeria this evening. It's the best pizza in the city."

"I think I've heard of it. I live here, remember?"

Smiling, I said, "Yes, I remember, and I want you to meet us at John's. I'd like to talk more about how you became an editor and how your *bisabuela* arrived in New York. Maybe her ship was built in Bath. I have this strange feeling we're connected in some 'magical' way."

Dan chuckled. "You don't give up, do you?" Then, looking at his watch, he said, "We're supposed to be meeting the trifecta in five minutes."

"We may be late, but it's okay because this tea break was just what I needed. I've decided I'm going to listen to you. My editor knows best, right?"

He grinned, and I suddenly realized why he seemed so familiar. I had seen that same grin on a similar face in an old photo album when I was rummaging through my parents' attic.

* * *

Martin, Maggie, and Warren were all seated at the conference table when I rushed into the room flushed and out of breath. Dan was right behind me, but he wasn't sweating. On the contrary, his demeanor was cool and calm, the professional I *wanted* to be.

"I'm sorry we're late. The elevator was slow."

Warren Dunlap, my west-coast boss, laughed. "Oh, it's the old elevator excuse."

My beautiful agent pulled out a chair. "Sit next to me, Anna. I can protect you from these brutes; I know how to dodge bullets."

"Thanks, Maggie," I said as I sat down beside her. "I may need some assistance; I'm feeling vulnerable today."

Frowning, Warren said, "I don't believe it. You have nerves of steel and multiple super powers."

Dan sat down next to Warren and weighed in with, "I think I saw two of those powers this morning."

I swallowed hard and put on a brave face.

"Thank you, everyone, but before we discuss the schedule for the publication, launch, promotion, and distribution of *The Keeper's House*, I have some news to share."

The room went silent.

"Jake and I are expecting our first child in March."

The room erupted in hoots and hollers, and there were even a few tears. It wasn't the reaction I was expecting, but I kept talking.

"Of course, you're all invited to the wedding next month. We're going to have the ceremony at a small chapel in Newcastle, Maine, that happens to have a Paul Revere bell. We're inviting fifty guests, and you're among them because we consider you part of the family."

Maggie reached for the box of tissues on a side table; Martin took off his glasses and beamed; and Warren walked around the table and kissed me on the cheek.

"A baby!" he shouted. "That's the best news I've heard all day. Count me as a *yes* for the wedding. As soon as you set the date, I'll put it on my calendar."

"We've already set the date. Go ahead and mark the nineteenth of October. It's going to be a beautiful day in the Pine Tree State."

"I'll be there!" exclaimed Martin. "I want you to know that MP will work with you to create a schedule you can handle as we prepare to launch your novel."

"I think that's a good segue to the first item on our agenda," said Maggie, "but first I have to shout *hooray!* I'm so happy for you and Jake."

The *hooray* was my tipping point. I started to cry, and we all reached for the tissue box at once.

Dabbing her eyes, Maggie said, "I think this is the best business meeting I've ever attended."

I smiled through my tears and nodded. "Now we have to get down to business and talk about my book."

Martin cleared his throat. "I agree. How does the seventeenth of November look for a launch here in New York?"

When I heard November 17th, I realized my novel would have to be press-ready by October 17th, two days before my wedding, and I thought I was going to faint, but Dan came to my rescue once again.

"Martin, I'm afraid that's too soon. This morning I asked Anna to make one more change, and she agreed. It's a transformative change. I think she needs more time."

Martin leveled his gaze and furrowed his brow.

"What do you think, Anna?"

"Dan's right. If you can give me a little more time, I can add a touch of magical realism to one of my storylines."

"I'd like to say yes, but you know how important timing is for a new title and author. September through December are prime months if you want to catch the holiday shoppers."

Everyone around the table nodded their agreement, including me.

"I understand, but could you give me two weeks? I think I can make the change and be ready by the first of December."

Martin placed his hands on the table and smiled.

"It's hard to deny you anything and easy to grant you two weeks, so be happy, eat healthy, get married, and be brilliant. My marketing team will get ready for a double launch, December first in New York, and December seventh in Maine, but in order to do that, your book has to be ready to print no later than the first of November. Can you meet that deadline?"

I felt nauseous, but I said yes.

Martin stood up and suggested we all meet after dinner at the Tavern on the Green to celebrate with champagne and a bottle of Pellegrino for the mother-to-be. At that moment, I thanked God for Dan's persistence and Martin's good sense.

* * *

At 4:30, I texted Jake that Dan and I were headed over to John's on 44th Street, and I would put my name in for a table. He immediately texted back that he'd be there by 5:00 p.m. and was bringing Garrett and Oliver with him. He also let me know in cryptic fashion that our *muffin in the oven* was still a secret. I didn't respond, and my sensitive editor noticed the pause.

"Is everything okay?" he asked as he hailed a cab.

"Yes," I said as I slipped my phone back in my pocket. "Why?"

"Your thumbs stopped moving. There was a pregnant pause—no pun intended."

I jabbed him with my elbow and said, "You're so funny. Jake hasn't told his boss we're expecting, but I just told the entire MP team and invited them to our wedding. Obviously, we're not on the same page. Now I'm worried because he's asked Garrett and another KOMI exec to join us for pizza."

As we climbed into a cab, Dan posed another question.

"What are they all doing in the city? I thought Jake worked for a Maine-based company."

"He does, but KOMI has acquired a five-acre island off the coast of St. George, which can only be accessed by boat and includes a private compound with a library. Of course, the buildings and dock need renovation."

"Sounds expensive," Dan chuckled.

"Yes, it's expensive, but it's also the sacred mission of Keepers of Maine, Inc., and since they specialize in saving lighthouses and island compounds, there's a maritime engineering firm in Manhattan that would like to do business with them. When Garrett heard that Jake was going to be with me in New York, he decided to schedule a meeting."

Stepping out of the taxi at Times Square, Dan tossed back the remark of the day: "Good use of time and place."

* * *

Fifteen minutes after we arrived at the restaurant, I received a message on my cell phone that our table was ready. As Dan and I walked to the hostess's station, Jake, Garrett, and Oliver walked through the door. I waved and Garrett spotted me right away.

By the time the hostess said, "Follow me," the three KOMI men were at my side.

"Perfect timing, gentlemen," I said.

Jake gave me a one-arm hug and laughed. "We'd walk five hundred miles to eat one of John's thin-crust pizzas from one of those old brick ovens."

"And to see you, dear," added Garrett.

I caught Dan rolling his eyes and I shook my head. I would never understand why men act like boys when they gather together. Maybe Gabo was right. History is a myth shaped by the storytellers. The moment we sat down, Dan smiled at Oliver and they seemed to make an immediate connection.

CHAPTER 24

June 1941

With magnolias blooming all around, Stella and Marie stood in the hospital courtyard waiting to graduate. They were not alone. Twenty-eight classmates were standing with them, making as much noise as a flock of nightingales. Nurse Conley, a former softball coach, had to put two fingers in her mouth and whistle to get their attention. Fortunately, the tactic worked. A hush fell over the nurses, and every young woman in white looked toward their chief nurse.

"It's time to process into the lecture hall for your last assembly as students. In a few minutes, you'll be pinned and recite the Nightingale Pledge. It has been an honor and a privilege to teach you in the classroom and to work with you on the wards of Lenox Hill Hospital. You're becoming registered nurses at a critical time in history. No one knows what the future holds, but many of us feel that we're moving toward war. Whatever lies ahead, I'm confident you're ready. Be brave. Remember, you are highly trained professionals in the noble field of medicine."

Nurse Conley paused to study the earnest faces of the young women waiting to enter the hospital to take their oath of service. She smiled and continued.

"I'm proud of each and every one of you. Nurses, line up in alphabetical order and let's finish what you started three years ago."

Without further ado, the Class of 1941 fell into a single line. They were silent, but their faces were jubilant as they eagerly awaited the cap with a black ribbon, the coveted RN stripe.

* * *

An hour later, Stella and Marie were back in the courtyard, surrounded by family and friends, wearing their pins and caps and kissing everyone who wished them well.

When Dr. Novack approached Marie, she took his hand, and kissed him on the lips without thinking twice. When the kiss finally ended, Marie stepped back, feigned surprise, and asked for forgiveness.

"I'm so sorry, doctor. I didn't realize it was you."

Pete laughed. "If that's the way you greet a stranger, I wonder how you say hello to a friend."

"If you stay a little longer, you may find out."

At that moment, Stella and her sweetheart from Bath, Ray Mitchell, came over to join them.

"Congratulations!" said Ray. "You look like you should be carrying a lantern with that fancy white cap on your head,"

Marie gave Ray a gentle kiss on the cheek, and Pete noticed the qualitative difference.

"Thanks, Ray. Lenox Hill certainly has a distinctive cap."

Stella chimed in, "It's distinctive, all right. I feel like I'm wearing a cupcake trimmed with a black ribbon."

Turning to face Pete, Marie winked and said, "It's the ribbon that makes us special."

Noticing the wink and the extra lilt in her friend's voice, Stella glanced at Pete and caught him grinning like a sophomore who had just kissed the captain of the cheerleading squad. At that moment, she decided to offer an invitation.

"Marie, we're going out to lunch with my family. Simon and Nurse Conley are coming, too. Sal made reservations at Tavern on the Green, and requested the Elm Tree Room. Would you and your parents care to join us?"

"Oh, I've been wanting to eat there. I've heard they built that room around one of Central Park's classic American elm trees. Since my parents don't know the city well, I'm sure they don't have reservations or even a plan. Let me ask them; I'll beg them to say yes."

Dr. Novack, always so dashing, looked oddly uncomfortable.

"Doctor," Stella said demurely, "I hope you can join us, too."

"I think that's the best invitation I've had in a *long* time, but I'm on duty this afternoon."

Marie refused to take no for an answer. "Your shift doesn't start until three. We could catch a cab together, and you'd be back in plenty of time. If that doesn't convince you, I bet my dad will insist on picking up the check."

Witnessing true hospital drama for the first time, Ray had to add his two cents. "Be careful, Dr. Novack. There's no such thing as a free lunch."

Pete smirked at Ray, then pivoted toward Marie and flashed a smile.

"You're right. We can take a cab over to Central Park West and meet everyone there in twenty minutes."

Stella looked around the courtyard and shook her head. "What a memorable day. Next week, we'll be back on the wards saying, 'Yes, doctor; of course, doctor; right away, doctor,' but today, the nurses are in charge."

Everyone laughed, including Pete. With their plan for the evening set, the couples moved to separate corners to discuss their futures. The rumor around the hospital was that Dr. Novack had already taken an oath to serve in the Army Medical Corps. If that was true, the time to celebrate was running out.

* * *

Even though it was only noon, the twinkle lights were on at the Tavern on the Green, and the Goss party of eleven was seated at a banquet table in the elegant Elm Tree Room.

"Isn't this place the perfect garden?" asked Mary Rose rhetorically.

She motioned to the waiter. When he stepped to her side, she ordered daiquiris for the table. As soon as the drinks arrived, she proposed a toast.

"Let's raise our glasses and celebrate our graduate nurses, Marie and Stella. We're proud of you, and we wish you both rewarding careers. I can't speak for the Capelottis, but for the Goss family, today is historic. Stella is our first RN."

"Oh, to be the first," said Marie. "I'm just one of a long line. Right, Mom?"

Mrs. Capelotti laughed. "To my knowledge, dear, you're the fourth, and I was thrilled to pin you."

Simon interrupted the banter with a serious question. "What's your plan, Marie, now that you're a graduate nurse?"

For a fleeting moment, the table fell silent.

"I plan to continue nursing at Lenox Hill until President Roosevelt decides we're going to help save Europe, then I'm going to join the Army Nurse Corps."

Simon turned his sad eyes toward Stella. "Is that your plan, as well?"

"Yes and no. I plan to stay at Lenox Hill until we enter the war, then I'll join the Navy. It seems like the best choice for me. After all, I'm from Bath, a shipbuilding city."

Ray put his arm around her and swallowed hard. She sensed he had something on his mind, but now was not the time for whatever it was.

Mrs. Capelotti raised her glass. "I'd like to make a toast to our nurses, as well. May they bring comfort to many, be steadfast and strong, and carry God's love wherever they go."

"Hear, hear!" echoed all the guests.

Marie looked across the table at her cherished friend and nodded. Stella wiped away a tear and smiled back.

* * *

Ten days later, Penny called Stella at the nurses' residence.

"You're not going to believe this, but Sal bought a movie theater in Greenport!"

"No! He didn't!"

"Yes, he did. One of his buddies at National Screen is from there, and he told Sal that a circa 1915 theater was destroyed by a hurricane in 1938. Because it was so important to Greenport, it was rebuilt the next year. To make a long story short, the theater went up for sale a few months ago."

Stella reacted with silence as she tried to grasp the full meaning of her cousin's news.

"You're moving to the North Fork of Long Island? Isn't that far away?"

"It's not that far and there's a train, but yes, we're moving. Sal quit his job at National Screen and is going to manage the theater and help his friend, Fred De Vries, manage his family farm. Fred quit his job at NSS a few months ago to take over the farm from his dad. He plans to grow grapes and thinks a winery could do well on Long Island."

"I'm sorry, Penny, but this is a lot of serious news to absorb on the first day of summer. Is Sal sure he wants to leave the city and a good-paying job?"

"Yes, he's sure, and I'm supporting his decision. He's tired of traveling all over New England, partying with wild and crazy movie stars, and leaving me at home."

"I suppose I understand, but I'm going to miss the two of you terribly."

"I'm going to miss you, too, but I'm pregnant, and—"

"What? You're pregnant? Why didn't you tell me sooner?"

"Well, I wanted to be sure."

"How are you going to handle all this change way out there in Greenport? How far is it from here?"

Penny's voice began to shake. "It's a hundred miles from Manhattan." She started to cry.

"Don't cry. I'm going to call Mom. Maybe she can help you. She's living alone in that big house in Maine. Maybe it's time to circle the wagons."

With a quivering voice, Penny replied, "Oh, that would be an answer to my prayers. I'd feel so much better if Aunt Mary would come and stay with us. I'm scared, Stella. No, I'm terrified. We're making this big move, but I know Sal intends to join the Army if we go to war. A baby won't change his mind."

"You're not going to be alone, Penny. I'll make sure of that. We'll decide on a plan, and we'll stick to it. Your baby will be born in a beautiful place by the sea. It's good news!"

"I hope so. Thanks, Stella."

"For what? I'll call you after I talk with mother bee, but I already know what she's going to say."

"Okay, 'bye."

"We'll talk soon. Try not to worry. It's not good for the baby. 'Bye."

As soon as Stella hung up, she called her mother. On the third ring, Mary Rose picked up.

"Good morning."

"Hi, Mom."

"What's wrong?"

"What makes you think something's wrong?"

"The fact that you're calling me before noon."

Stella sighed. "Well, it's serious business, but it's not bad news. In fact, it's a blessing."

Mary Rose gasped. "You're pregnant."

"Mom, for heaven's sake, don't say that. I'm not pregnant, but Penny is."

"Oh, my goodness, that's wonderful!"

"It is, but Penny is more than a little worried. Sal has quit his job and bought a movie theater in Greenport, a little village on the east end of Long Island."

Stella's words were flying, and Mary Rose was struggling to grasp all the details.

"Slow down, darlin'. I'm listening, but you're talking as if your house was on fire."

Stella took a breath and tried to calm herself.

"I don't own a house, but I do believe the world is on fire, and I'm certain the threat of war isn't helping anyone's nerves. Penny is afraid Sal is going to enlist as soon as FDR commits to helping Churchill."

Over the phone, Stella heard her mother sigh as if they were in the same room.

"We're all worried, but Penny shouldn't be afraid. She won't be alone. I'll go and stay as long as I'm needed."

"I was hoping you'd say that. Can you call Penny today?"

"Of course, but first tell me how you're doing."

Stella laughed. "Oh, that's another long story. I'm okay, but Ray told me yesterday that he enlisted in the Army. He couldn't wait. He wants to be on the front line as soon as he can."

"I'm sorry, Stella. The two of you have grown so close."

"Yes, yes we have. He asked me to marry him, but he wants us to wait…"

Mary Rose finished her sentence, "In case he doesn't come back."

"More or less…How sobering is that?"

"And what did you say?"

"I said I'd wait."

"You gave him the right answer. I'll pray for him, and all the others. I'm going to call Penny now. I love you, Stella."

"Thanks, Mom. I love you, too."

CHAPTER 25

December 2019

If someone mentions Sundays in New York, my mind flips to Prospect Park or Cobble Hill Park, two places in Brooklyn my grandpa used to take me to when I was a child. Those green parks and Grandpa's classic brownstone are etched in my mind. That's why I didn't hesitate when my publisher suggested I launch my debut novel in New York City on a Sunday afternoon. In fact, I promptly wrote *Cobble Hill Bookstore, Cobble Hill, NY,* on a green Post-it note and gave it to him at the end of our September meeting. I think my decisiveness surprised him because he didn't say a word. He simply read the Post-it and nodded his approval.

A few days later, Martin Gormley called my agent and said he had never been to the Cobble Hill Bookstore on the corner of Smith and Canal, but he had just made an appointment to meet with the owners, Max and Emily Gallo. He wanted to see for himself their stacks of books, reading nooks, armchairs, and fat cushions. Of course, Maggie assured him it was a fabulous place. Since its grand opening in 2017, the bookstore had become a Brooklyn treasure. Typically, when people entered, they wanted to stay for a while, and when they had to go, they left with a bag full of books.

By the end of the call, Martin had changed his mind. He told Maggie he was going to call the Gallos back to tell them he was stopping by that afternoon. He couldn't wait one more day to see the little hilltop bookshop that had captured so many hearts, especially the heart of his newest author and her agent.

As I stepped off the subway and climbed the stairs toward daylight, my brain flooded with memories of those summer days I'd spent with Grandpa Donovan in Brooklyn. My mom and dad used to take Joe, Frank, and me to Grandpa's house every summer for a week-long visit. Some of my best memories had been created there. On our way home, my brothers and I would argue about what our favorite part of the family vacation had been: walking across the Brooklyn Bridge, touring the Navy Yard, visiting the South Street Seaport, listening to Grandpa's stories, watching baseball games on TV, or visiting our favorite parks—Central, Prospect, and Cobble Hill. It was a silly debate, but Mom and Dad loved listening to us because they knew that memories were the main point of a family vacation, and we were making a virtual scrapbook with our words.

New York City has five boroughs, but in terms of my family history, Brooklyn is the most important. My mom lost her mother to lupus in Brooklyn, found a way through grief in Brooklyn, forged a bond with her father in Brooklyn, and developed a deep respect for the United States Navy in Brooklyn.

Suddenly, as Jake and I approached the corner of Smith and Canal Streets, I felt a quickening and rubbed my baby bump without even thinking. It was the first of

December, and I was filled with life and ready to launch my first novel. There was no place else I was supposed to be.

Standing in front of the Cobble Hill Bookstore and peering through its glass door, I could see six rows of chairs, all occupied, and a podium with a banner that said, "*The Keeper's House*—a maritime story by Anna Malone Summers." In addition to the thirty-six people sitting in chairs, there were people standing in the back of the shop, as well.

I gasped, "Oh, my God. That's a lot of people." I turned and looked Jake in the eye. "Do I look very pregnant or just a little pregnant?"

Jake didn't laugh. Instead, he put his hands on my shoulders and in a reassuring voice said, "All those people are waiting for you. They want to meet you, and you look terrific."

I nodded, and my husband opened the door. I was six months pregnant and hoping they wouldn't ask the two most obvious questions. How long have you been married? When is the baby due? Thank God, no one asked those personal questions. Instead, they laughed at my jokes, listened when I read a short excerpt, sighed at a few of my emotional remarks, and best of all, they applauded at the end of my thirty-minute talk. They even lined up and asked me to sign a copy of my baby, no pun intended. Every time one of them spelled their name slowly and deliberately, so I could write it on the title page above mine with good wishes, I was reminded of how personal books are to the author *and* the reader.

As I was about to sign the next-to-last book of the afternoon, Baby Summers kicked like a soccer player. I automatically rubbed my belly in an attempt to soothe him or her. (As a writer, I value suspense.) Of course, the last woman in line noticed. When she stepped forward, her arthritic hand placed a copy of my book on the table.

"You look radiant, my dear. May God bless you and your baby."

I stared at a face I thought I knew.

"Thank you," I said with a ghost of a smile. "What's your name?"

"Celia," she said. "It's an old name, but I believe it's having a comeback."

I blinked. "I think you're right. It's a beautiful name."

I gripped my pen, and I tried to write in a slow and steady hand:

For Celia,
Keep home in your heart!
With warm wishes,
Anna Malone Summers

* * *

As we left the bookstore, I asked Jake if we could walk over the Brooklyn Bridge and admire Roebling's masterpiece with our feet on the ground, the best way to enjoy it. He rubbed his chin and closed his eyes. I read that as a firm *no*.

"Why not?" I asked.

"I may be from Wiscasset, but this isn't my first trip to New York City. I happen to know Brooklyn covers about seventy square miles. It's not the largest or the smallest borough, but the bridge is almost two miles from here and that's too far to walk, especially in your condition."

I was tempted to step on his foot, but instead I just smirked.

"What does that mean?"

He answered in a hushed voice, "You're pregnant."

"Really?" I asked wryly.

"Come on, Anna. You must be tired. You've been on your feet all day, and everyone knows the city is *exhausting*."

"Well, I'm not *everyone*, but you're right. It's a long walk from Cobble Hill to the Brooklyn Bridge—that's what cabs are for."

I saw the hurt in his eyes and stopped.

"I'm sorry, honey. I'm a bit tired, but I'd like to walk over the bridge. It's a balmy fifty-five degrees and we're dressed for winter in Maine, so let's take a cab over to the bridge, then walk to clear our heads and think about tomorrow."

"What's tomorrow?"

"It's the day we're going to make a decision about our living arrangements, remember? We've been renting the apartment month-to-month since our lease ran out, and I think we need to decide whether or not we should buy a house."

"Tomorrow? But next Saturday you're going to launch your book at the Cushing Public Library, the library near the Olson Farm that inspired *Christina's World*, one of your favorite paintings. In a few days, you'll be surrounded by the places that shaped your story—Thomaston, St. George, Port Clyde, Tenants Harbor, South Cushing, and Maple Juice Cove."

He put his arms around me and I rested my head on his dark-blue jacket. With his face in my hair, he whispered, "Anna, my love, slow down. Enjoy the journey."

"I'm trying. I just need some fresh air to clear my head."

He pulled up his collar and shrugged. "Okay, let's head over to the bridge, but let's delay our decision about Marshall Point."

I raised my arm to hail a cab. As I got into the backseat, a strange feeling came over me. My thoughts turned to Celia Gannett, one of the key women in *The Mariners of Long Reach*, my documentary film about Bath. My grandmother Stella Rose used to call her Aunt Celia because she played such an important role in her life. When I was working on my documentary, I'd found letters, newspaper clippings, and diaries packed in an old steamer trunk in my parents' attic. Most of those mementos belonged to my grandmother, but some went as far back as my great-grandmother. Several diary entries and an obituary showed that Celia and I were connected by love, not blood, but that didn't diminish her profound effect on me. Over time, she had become my muse.

* * *

A week later, Jake and I decided to spend a few days with my parents in Bath to recover from the chaos of two book-launching events in one week, and to begin our quest to find a house in or near Bath. With Baby Summers due at the beginning of March, we were anxious to find a home with easy access to the water and central to KOMI projects along the coast. On Sunday, the fourteenth of December, Jake scheduled a lunch in Brunswick with Garrett to finalize their plans for Ram Island. I went along. En route to the restaurant at Cabot Mill, we took a side trip to Harpswell to consider the peninsula as a place to live. As we drove along Basin Point Road, I spotted a big white sign with *Sunrise Farm* painted in gold. Beneath it was a realtor's sign.

"Stop!" I shouted. "Look at that farmhouse on the hill."

Jake hit the brakes, pulled to the side of the road, put the Jeep in park, and barked, "Anna, if there was any traffic on the road, we would have been rear-ended!"

"But there isn't any traffic this time of year," I said hopping out of the Jeep. "It's December and no one's here except deer and mice."

Jake came up behind me. Together, we looked up at the white house perched on top of the snow-covered hill.

With its two dormers and an inviting red door, we saw its potential.

"This place is sleeping," I said quietly, "but I bet it would be awesome to wake it up."

"It's quaint," he whispered back. "Maybe it's a diamond in the rough."

Jake and I turned around. My eyes scanned the hill sloping toward the water, and I knew I was HOME. I think Jake felt the same way because he put his arm around my waist and pulled me close.

"Let's call the realtor," he said as he pulled his phone out of his coat pocket.

"Yes! Let's find out about its condition."

He entered the realtor's name and number into his contacts list and deliberately tucked his phone back into his pocket.

"Let's start with the asking price, but I'm afraid this call is going to have to wait until after lunch. If we want to buy a house, we should keep my boss happy and show up on time."

I reached down, grabbed a handful of snow, and tossed it like confetti.

"This is going to happen...I can feel it."

He chuckled, "In your toes?"

I replied with a snowball to his gut, and he answered the volley with a snowball to my shoulder. I cried, "*Tío!*" and he said, "What?"

"Uncle!"

"Okay, but try to remember I'm not as multilingual as you."

"I've noticed," I said with a grin, "but I'll keep you just the same."

It started to snow, and we walked down the hill like two turtle doves about to make a nest.

* * *

We arrived at the Cabot Mill shortly after one. Garrett had called ahead and reserved a table overlooking the Androscoggin River and was already seated, but he jumped up to greet us.

Giving me a quick hug, he smiled, "You're glowing, Anna."

"Thanks. I'm feeling well, and I'm happy my book has been launched not once, but twice."

We sat down and Jake couldn't resist the urge to brag. "She's too modest to say it, but she hit homeruns in Brooklyn, New York, *and* Cushing, Maine. That's not easy."

Raising his water glass, Garrett made a toast. "May your joy keep flowing and your blessings keep coming."

As we clinked our glasses, Jake proposed a second toast. "May Keepers of Maine, Inc., continue to find coastal treasures in time to save them."

Garrett grinned and immediately looked ten years younger. "Have I told you lately that I'm glad I hired you?"

"No, but that's okay. I'm used to tough bosses, like sergeant majors."

Sitting back, Garrett replied, "I'm going to take that as a compliment." He turned toward Anna. "I've heard from a reliable source that *The Keeper's House* is generating a lot of buzz. You may have a best seller on your hands."

I glanced at Jake, then looked at Garrett. "Forgive me for asking, but how do you know all this insider information?"

He leaned back and laughed. "I'm dating your agent."

"Maggie?"

At that moment, our server appeared.

"Are you ready to order?"

Garrett shook his head no.

"Can you give us another minute?"

"Of course."

As soon as she stepped away, Garrett answered my question. "Yes, Maggie. I've been seeing her for months and that's unusual for me. Of course, there's a speed-bump—geography."

Jake shot me a look, then shrugged. "I had no idea."

"Way to keep a secret, gentlemen."

Our server returned with her tablet.

"Have we made any decisions?"

Garrett looked across the table. "How about three Belgian Whites?

Jake nodded, but I shook my head. "I'm okay with water."

"Make that two Belgian Whites and a bottle of Perrier," said Garrett.

"I'll get your drinks. When I come back, I'll take your lunch order, okay?"

Garrett replied, "Yes, thank you." As soon as she walked away, he looked at me and lowered his voice. "I'm sorry. For a moment, I forgot you're expecting."

"Don't worry," I said with a wink. "I'm *fully* aware. Besides, you've got Maggie on your mind."

At last, when the drinks arrived, we were ready to order, and no one was happier than our server. As she picked up our menus, Garrett thanked her for being patient, then turned his laser focus on Jake and me.

"What are the two of you planning for the holidays?"

Jake and I locked eyes. He nodded, and I gushed.

"We're looking for a home to buy. This morning we drove by a small farmhouse on a beautiful piece of land just where Basin Point Road curves around the cove."

"On Harpswell Neck?"

"Yes, do you know Basin Cove?"

"As a matter of fact, I do. Are you talking about Sunrise Farm?"

"Yes," said Jake, "the house is at the top of the hill on the west side of the road."

Garrett grinned. "Yep, that's the place. It belongs to an old friend of mine. He's a widower, too, but he's at least ten years older than me. He wants to move to South Carolina to be near his only daughter. She's a physician and has no interest in the farm."

"Do you know how much he wants for it?" asked Jake.

"No, but I can find out. Have you walked through the house yet?"

My eye twitched, perhaps with nerves, but I looked directly at Garrett and smiled.

"I suppose we should, but I doubt we'll be disappointed."

He raised his eyebrows and placed his hands on the table.

"You're probably right, but play it safe. Make an appointment with the realtor and *look* at the house. If you still love it after you see it in broad daylight with all its fine features and rusty faults, I'll call my friend and put in a good word."

I gasped, "You must be Santa Claus."

Garrett blinked his dark-brown eyes. "No, but I know Charlie Van Cleve. He's a reasonable man, and he's old enough to have a soft spot for a couple about to have a baby. I'm sure we can make this happen if you want it."

CHAPTER 26

January 1942

The phone at the end of the hall was ringing, and Stella woke up in darkness except for the moonlight slipping through the blinds. Moaning, she reached for the alarm clock and opened one eye to check the time. When she realized it was three thirty, she bolted out of bed, but she wasn't the only one on the floor to respond to the sound of the telephone. Her hall-mates reacted the same way. They got up and ran toward the phone anticipating bad news because they were nurses and thirty days ago President Roosevelt had declared war on Japan, Germany, and Italy. Even though they were trained for triage, they were afraid. Their world was in jeopardy—everyone and everything they loved was at risk.

On December 7, 1941, over two thousand sailors, including 1,177 aboard the USS *Arizona*, had died at Pearl Harbor along with hundreds of Marines, soldiers, and civilians. In the wake of that Sunday-morning attack, Americans had found their greatest common denominator, their resolve to protect certain unalienable rights: life, liberty, and the pursuit of happiness. The Axis powers were threatening freedom around the world, and now Americans were determined to stop them.

Marie's room was the closest to the phone, so she was the first to reach it.

"Nurses' residence, Lenox Hill Hospital, Nurse Capelotti speaking."

"Oh, Marie, thank God it's you."

"Mrs. Goss?" asked Marie.

"Yes, I know it's late...or early...but I need to speak with Stella."

Marie looked up and saw Stella standing a few feet away.

"Of course, Mrs. Goss. She's right here. I'll put her on," said Marie in a hushed voice.

She held up the receiver and motioned Stella to come to the phone. By this time, most of the nurses were in the hallway, and they were all anxious to learn the reason for the dead-of-night wake-up call.

As Stella put the receiver to her ear, she looked at her friend for reassurance, and Marie mouthed, *It's your mom.*

"Hello."

"I'm sorry to be calling at this hour," said a shaky voice.

"It's okay, Mom. What's wrong?"

"I'm at Eastern Long Island Hospital with Penny and Sal. The babies are coming."

"*Babies*? Is Penny having twins?"

"Yes, we believe so. Her doctor picked up two heartbeats at her last appointment."

"She never mentioned she was having *twins*."

"She saw the doctor on Monday, the eighth of December, and everyone was reeling from the news of Pearl Harbor. She didn't tell me about the twins until her water broke at one this morning."

"Jesus, Mary, and Joseph! Penny isn't due until February."

"I know, but we're at the hospital now, and there's a delivery room here."

"One delivery room? How big is the hospital? Are they prepared for twins?" asked Stella in one breath.

The line went quiet.

"Mom? Are you there?"

"Stella, we're practically at Orient Point. We're not in the city, and this is the only hospital for miles. It doesn't really matter if they're prepared or not. The babies are coming and there is no place else to go."

Every nurse on the floor was up and listening to Stella's side of the call, and they were all worried. Most of them knew Penny and Sal. A small community hospital would not have been their choice for a first-time mom delivering twins.

"What aren't you telling me? I feel like there's another shoe about to drop."

"Penny's blood pressure is high. If the babies don't come soon, they're going to deliver them by C-section."

Stella swallowed. "If only I had a car...but I'll get there as fast as I can. I'll take a cab to Penn Station and catch the earliest train to Port Jefferson or as far east as I can go. Tell Penny I'm coming."

As soon as Stella hung up the phone, a handful of nurses rushed to her side and offered to cover her shifts for as long as necessary, but Marie took charge.

"Don't worry, Stella. We've got you covered. Go pack and I'll call a taxi."

"Thank you! You're a lifesaver."

She turned to face her hall-mates. "Thank you, everyone. When you get an early-morning phone call, it's good to be surrounded by sisters. Please pray for my cousin, Penélope, and her precious babies. Now try to get some sleep. I'll call with an update later today."

On that final note, she rushed back to her room to pack and write a quick note to her supervisor. She hated to leave the hospital with one less pair of hands. Many nurses had already left to join the war effort, but this was a family emergency. Since the attack on Pearl Harbor, time was spinning faster and faster, but Stella, Marie, and some of the other graduate nurses at Lenox Hill had made a pact to wait at least thirty days before enlisting in the Army or Navy Nurse Corps; they wanted to weigh their options, examine their consciences, and make the right decisions.

* * *

On the long train ride out to the North Fork, Stella had a lot of time to think and worry about everyone and everyplace she loved. Above all else, she thought about Ray, who was waiting to be deployed to Europe or North Africa. She took a thin white envelope from her handbag. It was folded in half and she unfolded it as if it were made of glass. She pulled out the slip of paper and read the words scrawled in pencil.

My Darling Stella,

I'm writing to you from a bunk in my barracks after lights out, which is another way of saying my battalion has been busy, and that's why I haven't written in a while. Tonight, I'm writing to you by flashlight. How's that for romantic? We'll be shipping out soon. I know you're too smart not to worry, but I wish you wouldn't. I can't say where we're going because I don't know. (The U.S. Army only tells us what we need to know.) But even in the dark, I'm certain I'll be far away from you for months. Some guys like to say we'll be back as soon as we win the war

and it won't take us long. I think those guys are full of bull. War
is hell and only the lucky ones survive. I hope I'm lucky because I
have you to come home to.

Pray for me. Pray that I come back so we can get married
and have half a dozen kids, three boys and three girls. Right
now, my only regret is that I didn't marry you before enlisting.
At the time, it seemed like the right thing to do. I wanted
to marry you at Saint Mary's right after Penny and Sal said "I
do," but I didn't want to marry you and then go off to war as if
nothing bad ever happens on a battlefield. Okay, this is getting
too grim. It's time to turn off the flashlight. I just want you to
know I'm going to fight like hell so I can spend time with you.

Funny, I never considered myself lucky until I met you. When
you told me you loved me, I was the happiest I've ever been in my
whole life. Sometimes my buddies catch me smiling and they ask
me what I'm smiling about, but I don't say a word. The truth is,
I'm thinking of you and I don't want to share you with anyone.

I love you, Stella. I hope my luck holds out until I'm home
again sleeping beside you. In the meantime, try not to worry too
much. My sergeant thinks I'm the best shot in our platoon. The
lieutenant must agree because he put me in for a promotion. As
of eleven hours ago, yours truly is a corporal.

Love,
Ray

When the conductor came by to tell her they were pulling into Greenport, the end of the line, she folded Ray's
letter and put it back in her purse for safekeeping. Stella
noticed the train car was less than full. There were only
three other passengers. She wondered if Greenport was

like a lot of coastal towns in Maine—noisy as a flock of birds in summer, but quiet as a mouse in winter.

* * *

Neither Sal nor Mary Rose was willing to leave the hospital, so they'd asked Ida Jones, the neighbor, to pick Stella up at the station. Ida arrived five minutes early and waited for the train with a photograph and a detailed description of Stella: curly, chin-length, strawberry-blond hair, five foot two, wearing a navy-blue coat with a red beret. Ida recognized her the moment she stepped off the train and called out her name.

A few minutes later, they were speeding along a country road toward the hospital in Ida's 1928 Model A coupe, a car that kept on running despite hard times. As Ida rounded the umpteenth curve at forty miles per hour, Stella began to regret the doughnut she had eaten on the train, but she was glad to be sharing a ride with a friend of the family.

"I've only known Penny and Sal for a short time, but I adore them," Ida half shouted over the noise of the tires.

"I can't imagine anyone not loving them," replied Stella wistfully as she gazed at barren potato fields through the dusty window of Ida's Ford.

Ida glanced at Stella and sensed her growing fear.

"Don't worry, dear. Penny is young and strong, and the doctors here are Columbia and Bellevue trained. The Cesarean section went well. Baby one is breathing beautifully and baby two is fighting. Penny is—"

Stella started to cry.

"I'm a nurse, Ida. I can fill in the rest...If at all possible, drive faster."

Ida fixed her pale-blue eyes on the road, pressed the gas pedal a little harder, and didn't say another word until she pulled up to the hospital's main entrance. Stella stepped onto the curb.

"Room 232, second floor, west wing, but you'll have to check in at the reception—"

Stella slammed the car door and ran.

* * *

It was just after seven thirty when the elevator doors opened. Sal and Mary Rose were sitting in a small waiting area a few feet away. They both appeared to be dozing, but as Stella approached, they opened their eyes.

"You're here!" cried Mary Rose.

Standing up, Sal quickly added, "She's all right, Stella. She turned the corner about thirty minutes ago."

"Oh, thank God!"

Sal put his arms around her. "I think she knew you were coming and wanted to be ready."

Mary Rose gave her a hug, too.

"When can I see her? How are the twins?"

Sal smiled. "Our baby girl arrived a few minutes before our baby boy. Rosemary at four point seven pounds was crying on delivery; Marco at four point five pounds needed a little encouragement, but both seem to be doing all right at the moment, and the doctors are hopeful."

Mary Rose grabbed Stella's hand. "I've been praying nonstop since midnight."

Stella kissed her mother's cheek and whispered, "Me, too, Mom, and I believe God is listening."

At that moment, a nurse pushed through the double doors. She walked directly toward them and said matter-of-factly, "The doctor says Mrs. Leone can have visitors now, but the rule is two at a time."

She looked at the three of them and winked. "Not counting the father, of course, so all of you can follow me."

CHAPTER 27

March 2020

I looked up and saw a Maine Bicentennial calendar hanging on the wall next to a clock. I put my elbow on the table and rested my chin in the palm of my hand. It was high noon on the fourth of March, and we still didn't have the keys to our circa 1910 farmhouse. How many documents did it take to make a house your own? Our attorney, Alex Paulin, had come to us highly recommended by Doris Van der Waag, my friend and mentor. We liked him a lot, but he didn't prepare us for how long our real estate closing would take, and I was running out of patience.

Alex must have sensed my frustration because he offered a little encouragement.

"We're almost done."

I shot him a don't-patronize-a-pregnant-woman look, and he immediately fell silent.

The seller, Charlie Van Cleve, sat back in his chair and raised his pen.

"Done! You're the luckiest people in Harpswell. Heck, you're the luckiest people on the planet. The two of you are going to make beautiful memories at the cove. I know you will, because that's what my wife and I did."

Jake and I hurried to finish. We signed the last page of the last document and raised our pens as well. Jake stood, reached across the table, and shook Charlie's hand.

"I promise we'll take good care of your farm."

"It's yours now," he said with a twinkle in his eye. "A lot of living went on in that house, and a lot of loving, too."

I walked around the table and gave Charlie a hug.

Grinning from ear to ear, he looked at Jake and said, "Hold on to this one. She's a keeper."

He reached into his pocket, pulled out a skeleton key, and placed it in the palm of my hand.

"There's a cedar chest in the master bedroom. This key will open it. The chest was in the house when I bought it some forty years ago. I was told its contents go with the house, so now they belong to you."

Speechless, I stared at the key, then with a childlike voice I asked, "What's in the chest?"

Charlie chuckled, "Oh, my dear, I love mysteries. Don't you?"

Our attorney cleared his throat. "Now, Mr. Van Cleve, don't scare the new owners before they move in."

Coming to my side and taking my hand, Jake said, "We love a good mystery and can't wait to find the treasure at Sunrise Farm."

Charlie winked. "I'm glad we agree, and since we do, I'll leave you with a clue. The shape of Basin Cove resembles a Spanish guitar."

* * *

An hour later, Jake carried me, heavy with child, over the threshold of our farmhouse, and our dog rushed in behind us. Once inside the door, my Herculean husband let my swollen feet touch the hardwood floor, and we admired our antique home in silent awe. Moose, our Great Pyrenees, barked hello and ran upstairs to check out all the rooms. Standing in the entryway, we could see the afternoon sun shining through the kitchen window, and Jake reached out to touch my pregnant belly.

"We're home, Anna, and our baby is going to grow up here. As a matter of fact, I can feel him kicking right now."

"*She*'s kicking, all right, and I'm so anxious to move in and set up the nursery that it hurts, and I mean that literally."

Laughing, Jake spun me around.

"My only regret is that we didn't give the OB permission to tell us the sex of our baby after she ordered the ultrasound. If we had, we would know what color to paint the nursery, blue for Patrick or lavender for Patricia."

I raised my hand and objected vehemently. "Oh, honey, babies rarely come on their due dates, so I don't think I'll be delivering on Saint Patrick's Day, which means we don't have to name our baby Patrick or Patricia."

"But wouldn't that make your mother happy?"

"And since when do you aim to please Ellie Malone?"

Kissing my lips, Jake murmured, "Since I married you, my dear."

I tilted my head and laughed. "Let's stop playing the name game until we set up the nursery."

"Who are you kidding? You've probably decided on a boy's name *and* a girl's name already."

"Maybe," I said with a half smile, "but right now we have to unload the car and get ready for the move-in crew."

"Okay, boss, but as soon as we're settled, we're going to come up with a short list of names and deliberate together. Agreed?"

As I walked back to the Jeep, I tossed a "Yes" over my shoulder.

* * *

On March 18, 2020, two hundred years and three days after Maine was voted into statehood, Celia Rose Summers was born in Brunswick. After seventeen hours of hard labor, I was exhausted and elated, and Jake was over the moon. With Celia swaddled tightly in her bassinet and Jake dozing in a chair, I opened my eyes and realized we had made our first memory as a family.

Jake opened a sleepy eye.

"Good evening, Mama," he said in a hushed voice. "How are you feeling?"

"Like my body has been torn in two and miraculously put together again," I said dryly. "Can I have some water?"

"Oh, you can have more than that. You can have cranberry or apple juice. What's your preference?"

"Water, please, and I'd like to hold Celia Rose."

"Of course," he said.

A few minutes later, a silver-haired nurse popped into the room to check on us.

"How's the pain, dear?" she asked as she took my temperature.

"It's not so bad when I'm holding Celia."

"What a pretty name," she said as she updated my chart. "I don't hear it too often. Is she a namesake?"

I brought my face close to Celia's and cooed.

"I suppose it's a family name. At least it belonged to someone close to the family. My grandmother kept a diary, and I read every entry for a documentary I was working on. Anyway, she talked about her Aunt Celia, the sister of her father's first wife."

The nurse looked at me and said, "Wow! That sounds like a modern-day soap opera."

I chuckled then winced with pain. "I know. Truth inspires fiction and is, quite often, less believable."

Boosting me up with pillows, she replied, "Isn't that the truth," then she took Celia and loosened her swaddle. "Let's see if we can get this little stinker to latch onto your breast."

Jake popped out of his chair and stood opposite the nurse at the other side of my bed. "I think six pounds and seven ounces is a respectable weight, and I just checked her diaper. For the record, Celia Rose is not a stinker. She smells as sweet as she looks."

The nurse glanced at me and then at Jake, threw back her head, and laughed.

"The dad is always right. Celia Rose is a sweet baby, and I think she smells like a rose."

With her hand on the back of Celia's head, she positioned the baby's open mouth perfectly over my nipple, and I felt the latch like magic born of pain.

* * *

Twenty-four hours later, the three of us were finally home. Celia was sleeping in our bedroom in the cradle my dad had made. Jake was still floating on air, and I was waiting for him to crash. He had slept in that awful hospital chair for two straight nights, and I knew he was running on empty.

"Honey," I whispered as we tiptoed away from the cradle, "let's have a cup of tea in the kitchen. We can watch Celia on the monitor, then maybe you can catch a nap on the couch."

As soon as we closed the bedroom door, Jake whispered, "I don't need a nap, but you should rest while the baby sleeps. You have to keep up your strength."

With the monitor in my left hand, I used my right to shoo him into Celia's nursery across the hall so we could talk above a whisper.

"You make it sound like I'm getting ready for battle. Truth be told, I think we both need to rest. If we don't, we'll probably come down with irritable-parent syndrome."

Digging his hands into his khaki pockets, Jake looked at the floor. "You're right, but I can't sleep. I'm too wound up."

My eyes fell on the old chest we had carried into the nursery to make room for the cradle at the foot of our bed. On move-in day, we'd decided to keep it locked until we brought our baby home. Now Celia was asleep in her cradle, and it was time to discover our farm's hidden treasure. Touching the handle, I said, "We should open it."

"Yes, who knows? Maybe it's just what we need to rest easy. Where's that key, the one Charlie gave us at the closing?"

I closed my eyes, ran my fingers through my tangled hair, and visualized the skeleton key. "It's in the junk drawer in the kitchen."

"Of course," said Jake. "We're in the house for only fifteen days, and we already have a junk drawer."

I whispered, "Let's hurry, but tread lightly. We don't want to wake the baby."

Jake shook his head and headed toward the stairs.

Following him, I watched his big, rough hand slide down the maple bannister, and I felt the warmth that comes from an old and storied house.

When we returned, Jake fit the old key into the lock, and voila, the chest opened to reveal its contents: a rolled-up print tied with a purple ribbon, an exquisite hand-sewn quilt, a well-read book of poetry by Emily Dickinson, a dove-white tablecloth with twelve matching napkins, two silver candlesticks desperately in need of polishing, a map of Casco Bay dated 1851, and at the bottom of it all, a first edition of Harriet Beecher Stowe's *The Pearl of Orr's Island.*

Jake whistled.

"Shhh, not so loud, but ditto."

Jake picked up the print, which he had unpacked first and set aside, and put two fingers on the ribbon.

"Can I have a drum roll please?"

"No," I chided, "pull the ribbon and don't be silly."

As soon as he unrolled the print, I recognized *The Old Guitarist*, and I gasped, "It's personalized."

I bent down and read the note aloud.

Rosita,
De sol a sol, eres la flor más bonita.
Te envío un besito,
Pablo Picasso

As I stood, Jake bent down and carefully studied the signature. He looked at me and I said, "¡Dios mío!"

"What does it mean?" asked Jake almost reverently.

I read the painter's words aloud. "'Rosie, from sunrise to sunset, you are the prettiest flower. I am sending you a little kiss, Pablo Picasso.'"

"And what does *Dios mío* mean? It seems to be your go-to expression."

"You're right. I say it when I'm shocked; I say it when I don't know what to say. It means *My God!* in Spanish."

Jake looked at the print...looked at me...and whispered, "¡Dios mío!"

I shook my head and laughed. "I think we've found a treasure within a treasure, and 'Gracias a Dios' is the best response."

"Okay," grinned Jake. "That, too."

Out of the blue, Celia let out a wail and we both ran to her cradle with Jake getting there first. He picked her up, rocked her in his arms, and started to sing.

Sweet lullabies and goodnight kisses
Bring nightingales and sunlit wishes.

Oh, Celia Rose,
You have ten toes
And a button nose.
How love grows!

When you wake,
The robin sings.
When you sleep,
Dreams have wings

Sweet lullabies and goodnight kisses
Bring nightingales and sunlit wishes.

Dance on the sand
And sail on the sea.
Take my hand
And be with me.

One day you'll find
A river to cross,
And I won't mind.
Love's never a loss.

Sweet lullabies and goodnight kisses
Bring nightingales and sunlit wishes.

As I watched Celia drift back to sleep, I knew Jake would
be playing her song on his guitar for many years to come.
He'd written the music and lyrics the day she was born.

CHAPTER 28

December 1942

Ten months after joining the Navy, Lieutenant Junior Grade Stella Goss entered the wardroom of the hospital ship USS *Solace* for a cup of coffee, her third since midnight. It was 0500 hours. She had been on duty for twenty-two hours straight, and the only patient she could remember with any clarity was a lieutenant commander who had needed a plasma transfusion at 2340 hours yesterday. Every bed on the ship was occupied by a sailor or Marine injured during the fight for Guadalcanal. The newest arrivals had been pulled out of the Coral Sea in the wee hours of the morning on the first of December.

According to scuttlebutt, American Task Force 67—four heavy cruisers, one light cruiser, and five destroyers—had departed Espiritu Santo, New Hebrides, at 1800 hours on the twenty-ninth of November in search of Admiral Tanaka's "Tokyo Express," and they found it shortly before midnight off the shores of Guadalcanal in a stretch of water the sailors were calling "Ironbottom Sound" because so many ships had been sunk there. On a moonless night, the American warships had surprised the enemy. They opened fire and wreaked havoc on eight destroyers, four transports, and two cruisers for seven straight minutes before the opposing column launched their torpedoes aimed at the flashes from the American guns. When the fish hit, flames lit up the water and sky. By dawn, it was clear the Japanese had sunk the USS *Northampton* and severely crippled the USS *Minneapolis*, *New Orleans*, and *Pensacola*. Only the *Honolulu* sailed away unscathed.

From listening to wounded sailors, Stella had gleaned that the Battle of Tassafaronga was a victory for the U.S. Navy. Task Force 67 had stopped the Japanese column from reaching Guadalcanal. Despite their injuries, the survivors from the "Fighting Nora" were feisty, and the doctors and nurses on the *Solace* were working round the clock to save their lives, hasten their recovery, and keep their spirits high.

Stella bowed her head over her steaming mug of coffee and breathed deeply. She knew the aroma of Maxwell House would not erase the memory of burnt flesh, but for a moment, the scent brought her home. She reached into her pocket and pulled out a folded letter on tissue-thin paper.

Dearest Stella,

I don't have much time, but I want this letter to reach you so you know I'm thinking of you and loving you. Uncle Sam has been keeping my buddies and me busy. It's hot and dusty here, and I'm missing home. From where I'm crouched, a few feet of Maine snow sounds pretty good, especially if that snow is near my dad's camp at Rangeley Lake. Right now, I'm dreaming I'm there with you. Wouldn't that be swell?

Wherever this finds you, I hope you're safe. My lieutenant is calling, so I have to go. Did I tell you I was promoted to sergeant? You still outrank me, but I don't mind a bit. I'm happy to salute you, Lieutenant Gross, and I hope to do just that and more when I see you.

Until then, sail safe.

Love,

Ray

"By any chance, is that another love letter you're reading?" asked Lt. Muriel Lonergan.

Stella looked up in a daze. When she realized the sweeter-than-candy voice belonged to her bunkmate, she tried to smile.

"Yes, it's a letter from Ray, but it's already a month old. I haven't heard from him lately."

Muriel shrugged. "North Africa is a world away, and the U.S. Army has trouble reaching the U.S. Navy sometimes. Don't worry. You'll get another letter soon."

"I hope so. The last time I slept, I had a terrible nightmare."

"When was that?" asked her friend grimly.

Stella frowned. "I can't recall. Don't ask such hard questions."

The two overworked and completely spent nurses laughed uncontrollably until Commander Betty Morris entered the wardroom.

Snapping to attention, they said "Good morning, ma'am" in unison.

The commander's eyes swept the room.

"Good morning, lieutenants. I'm glad to see you caught a break, but now it's time to get back to work." She checked her watch. "You have a little less than two hours till the end of your shift. You can rest then."

"Yes, ma'am," they answered.

The exhausted lieutenants placed their coffee mugs in a basin filled with dishes waiting to be washed and returned to duty.

* * *

Back on the ward, Stella noticed one of her young petty officers from the *Northampton* was awake and restless. She checked the chart at the foot of his bed.

"Close your eyes, Luke. Try to rest. It's too early for breakfast and too soon for morphine. How's the pain?"

"Not too bad," replied the twenty-one-year-old from Rockford, Ohio, "but I'm thirsty as hell."

"I bet. Fire has that effect. Let me get you some nice cold water."

"And don't forget the straw," he said holding up his bandaged hands. "I can't do much with these two mitts."

When Stella returned, she adjusted his pillows and held the straw to his lips.

After taking a long draw of water, his head fell back on the pillows. "Thank you, nurse. If it's not too much trouble, I have another request. I'd like to dictate a letter to my folks. Do you have a minute?"

"For you? I have at least ten." She pulled a pen out of her pocket, then turned and reached for a pad of paper on the metal table next to the bed. "All right, I'm ready."

"Let's do this," said Luke with a quiver in his voice.

Dear Mom and Dad,

I had to take a two-hour swim the other night. The water was warm, not cold. I'm not exaggerating when I tell you I was swimming in a ring of fire. Before I jumped, I had a grandstand view of the battle. The good news is we stopped the "Tokyo Express." We kept those Japanese transports, loaded with troops and supplies, from reaching Guadalcanal. I was at my station on the mainmast, standing on an eight-foot platform sixty feet above the deck, when the first torpedo hit directly below me. My hands and legs are burned, and we lost the Nora, but I'm okay. The doctors and nurses tell me Uncle Sam will patch me up. Don't worry. I'm lucky.

Remember that article you sent me about the Great White Ship? Well, I'm on her right now. That New York reporter was right when he said, "Every blue jacket knows if he's lifted onto the Solace, he's one of the lucky ones." Did you know the Solace was the only ship not fired upon at Pearl Harbor? I don't know why she was spared, maybe her red crosses saved her, but she was able to send out motor launches loaded with stretcher parties to evacuate the wounded from the battleships Arizona, West Virginia, and Oklahoma. She really is a floating miracle. One year later, she's still saving sailors. She saved me! Tell Ginny the fire didn't touch my handsome face. I miss you and the farm, but I don't regret signing up. We're going to win this war.

Your loving son,
Luke

"How should I address the letter?"

"You can send it to Mr. and Mrs. Dennis Everett, Six Linden Lane, Rockland, Ohio."

She folded it carefully and tucked it into her pocket. "Mission accomplished! Now you can rest easy, Petty Officer Everett."

Luke wasn't listening. His eyes were closed and he was snoring.

* * *

Stella looked at her watch and realized her shift was finally coming to an end, but she had one more patient to check, the lieutenant commander. Picking up his chart, she noticed his last dose of morphine had been six hours ago. He was still dozing, but not peacefully. She read the doctor's note, then studied Francis Donovan's face. He seemed too young for his rank, but the war was promoting men quickly. Despite his injuries, he looked more like a leading man in a motion picture than a wounded naval officer. With thick, jet-black hair and eyebrows to match, he reminded her of Tyrone Power in *The Mark of Zorro*, a movie she had seen with Marie when they were in nursing school.

Stella blinked in order to focus. She couldn't let her thoughts wander. Thirty injured men were assigned to her care. She had to steel herself against frivolous feelings and useless emotion. She reread the doctor's note: *Change dressings every 6 hours. Watch for infection. Prognosis good.*

Stella noted the time. She needed to check the commander's vitals and change his dressings, so she pulled a cart loaded with bandages, iodine, and salve toward the head of the bed. She touched his shoulder to let him know she was there. She hated to wake him, but the doctor's orders were clear.

"Commander Donovan, I have to take your temperature," she said in a soft and steady voice.

The commander, however, didn't respond calmly. He opened his eyes, sat up with a jolt, and yelled, "Seal the hatch! Seal it!"

Stella's hand flew to the syringe on the nearby cart. On the verge of giving him a sedative, something made her stop and put the needle down. She placed her hands on his shoulders and told him where he was.

"You're safe, Commander. You're aboard the USS *Solace* along with other men from your ship."

He looked into Stella's hazel eyes and whispered, "I watched her burn; the *Nora Maru* slipped into a black hole."

"*Nora Maru*?"

"That's what the radiomen called her," he said with a wince.

"Commander, you have some serious burns—"

"How many men did we lose?"

"I only know what I hear, and I hear the *Fletcher*, the *Drayton*, and a few PT boats picked up over 700 survivors from the *Northampton*. Your cruiser took two torpedoes, and the crew did everything they could, but the fire was too big to beat."

Donovan shook his head. "We should have saved her. I ordered two sailors to seal one of the hatches. They refused. They said there were still men below. I pulled my pistol and told them it was an order. The ship was sinking and we had to seal the hatch to give the men time to get off."

"What did the sailors do?"

With tears in his eyes, Donovan answered, "They sealed it, and we heard the screams."

"It's not your fault, Commander. The enemy torpedoed the ship, not you. By sealing that hatch you bought time for the crew to abandon ship before she rolled. One of my patients was on the salvage crew that stayed with the captain. He told me the order to abandon ship came at 0115 hours. The captain and salvage crew stayed with her till 0240. She sank twenty-four minutes later."

Donovan closed his eyes and fell silent again.

"Let me take your temperature, check your blood pressure, and change your bandages. How's your pain?"

He opened his eyes, and Stella noted the change. Before, they were deep blue. Now they were as dark as sapphires.

"I can't feel a thing," he said. "Change the bandages, but I don't need morphine. Save it."

As Stella gently unrolled one of Donovan's soiled bandages from his left leg, she glanced up at his clenched jaw and said firmly, "Okay, Commander, but I'll have to talk with the doctor about the morphine. He'll make that call. You know, he thinks you'll make a full recovery."

"Good! I want to get back on a ship and kick those A-holes back to Tokyo!"

"Yes, sir. I hear you loud and clear."

* * *

As the USS *Solace* approached New Caledonia, Stella stood at the bedside of Lt. Commander Donovan while Colonel William Bedell, U.S. Army Medical Corps, told him some good news.

"You're healing, Commander. I don't expect your stay in New Caledonia to be long. You'll be able to return to duty without being evacuated to a long-term facility. You're lucky."

For the first time, the stoic commander smiled, and Stella had to restrain herself from sighing audibly.

"Call me Donovan, doc; everybody does. And thanks for giving me the best news I could ask for."

The colonel laughed. "Okay, Donovan. I'm glad I could make somebody feel good today. Now listen to your nurse. Do what she tells you to do, and you'll be back on a cruiser in no time."

"Yes, sir."

"Call me Will," the doctor said as he shook Donovan's hand. "You're a good man, Commander, and I'm happy to be sending you back to the fleet. We need men like you at the helm. I hear they're making you a full commander. Congratulations!"

Donovan flashed another smile and this time Colonel Bedell heard a sigh. He immediately looked at Stella.

"Well, Lieutenant Goss, I know I'm leaving the commander here in good hands. Carry on."

The doctor winked and strode away.

Feeling herself blush, Stella touched her cheek with the palm of her hand, then quickly straightened her cap to conceal the telltale sign. A moment later, she looked down at her patient and realized he was watching her.

"Would you like to sit up, Commander? I can bring you some lunch."

"Only if you agree to stay and eat half of my sandwich."

"Sorry, sir, but that is strictly against regulations," quipped Stella with a grin.

"Oh, you're no fun, Nurse Goss. Please tell me your first name to celebrate my promotion."

"Well, if that's an order, I'll have to tell you."

"In that case, it's definitely an order."

"Stella," she said.

"Stella," he repeated. "It suits you. I like it, and I like you, too."

Feigning disapproval, Stella held up her hand as if to say STOP.

"Let's not go there, Commander. Fraternization is not allowed."

Donovan frowned and dropped his guard.

"But if it *was* allowed, would you be interested?"

Now Stella felt her cheeks turn red, and completely embarrassed, she looked away.

"I have a fella with the First Infantry. They're headed for Morocco or North Africa. I mean, I don't know for sure, but that's what I gather from reading between the lines."

Now it was the commander's turn to look away.

"I'm sorry. I didn't see a ring so I had to try. You're beautiful...so beautiful I think you've brought me back...I mean you're the best medicine a Navy guy could ask for."

Their eyes met.

"Thank you, Commander. You know I wish you fair winds—"

"And following seas," said Donovan. "Yeah, I know you do."

"All right, then. I'll get you that lunch, and I'll bring you some extra pillows, too."

When Stella turned to walk away, Donovan asked one more question.

"After I'm discharged from the hospital and I return to duty, would you mind if I wrote to you? You don't have to write back. Think of it as a thank you note. Sometimes it just helps to have someone to write to."

Stella responded, "Of course, Donovan. You can write to me."

CHAPTER 29

May 2020

As someone who has always been aware of changing tides and the flow of events that blend generations, I woke on Celia's christening day to a house filled with sunshine. Jake was already up; he was probably tending the chickens and collecting eggs. I looked out the window to see the first blooms of the season, tulips and daffodils, and hoped Celia would sleep a little longer so I could cut some for the breakfast table. We were beginning to enjoy the perks of living on a small farm. When I went downstairs, I found my dad frying bacon and my mom sliding a tray of cinnamon buns into the oven. They had decided to sleep over the night before, and I was grateful they were here to help.

A few hours later, our friends and family gathered at Saint Katharine Drexel's Chapel on Mountain Road. I had to smile when I saw the Ray-Ban sunglasses, blue blazers, crisp khakis, floral dresses, and Pashmina shawls. Everyone looked like they were ready for a cover shoot, and I was humbled by their presence. Holding hands, looping arms, or single and smiling, we all entered the chapel. As Father Gerard prepared to baptize our sweet Celia Rose, sunshine streamed through the arching windows and drenched us with its glow.

"I baptize you in the name of the Father, the Son, and the Holy Spirit."

Celia was cooing in her daddy's arms when the water spilled over her head. Instantly, she closed her eyes and wailed. I was standing next to Jake and reached over to touch her white eyelet gown; her godparents, my brother Joe and my dear friend Maggie, tried to soothe her as well. All our guests, including my six-year-old niece, Stella, formed a circle around the font and said a prayer for the newest member of our family. As soon as Father Gerard completed the baptism, Jake brought Celia to his chest and covered her head with kisses. All together, we beamed our thanks for one of God's greatest blessings, a child.

* * *

We caravanned back to Sunrise Farm because some of our guests weren't familiar with Harpswell. Jake and I didn't want a carload of New Yorkers to miss a turn and wind up at the wrong cove. It was the right decision, and we all arrived at the house in good order.

When we met the catering crew from Mike and Marty's at the back door, I said "Thank God" out loud. We had toyed with the idea of a barbeque, but then we came to our senses and decided to hire a team of professionals to prepare, deliver, and serve pulled pork, rolls, coleslaw, fruit salad, cornbread, and cupcakes, rain or shine. Like the caravan, it was the right decision.

As soon as we pulled into the driveway, I told Jake I was going upstairs to change, nurse, and hopefully put Celia down for her afternoon nap. Fully aware that our party girl was off her schedule, I considered the siesta a long shot, but I had to try. We knew from our RSVPs that we'd have more people at the house than at the church, so I wanted to be ready to show our home at its best. In other words, I was dreaming that my baby would sleep for an hour or two so I could be the perfect hostess. Of course, that didn't happen. Instead, Celia fussed and I rocked her for over fifteen minutes. Just when I was about to give up, the door to the nursery slowly opened and my favorite editor, Dan Leone, tiptoed in with a big gold envelope in one hand and a pink toy whale in the other.

"Hi," he whispered, "can I join the two of you?"

"Enter at your own risk," I chuckled with a smile.

"I brought Celia a cuddly friend. Her name is Mirabella, not Moby-Dick."

I laughed without making a sound, but couldn't stop my shoulders from shaking.

"Don't be funny. If I start laughing, Celia will never go to sleep. What's in the envelope? It's awfully big for a christening card."

After he placed the toy whale in Celia's crib, he put the envelope on top of her changing table and turned to face me.

"The envelope is for you; the whale is for Celia Rose," he said sitting down on the rug with his legs crossed like a yoga instructor.

"I'm sorry I didn't go to the ceremony. I don't do church."

I looked down at Celia. Her eyes were closed, her mouth was as pink as a rosebud, and her thumbs were tucked into her little fists. She was finally asleep.

"Don't worry. We love you just the way you are," I said in a hushed voice.

"Is that a Mr. Rogers line?"

I tried not to laugh. "Yes, I think it is."

Dan's poker face broke into a boyish grin. "I've been tracing my grandmother's roots, and I found a box of letters and diaries at my parents' house in Greenport. Most of them date back to the 1930s and '40s. One of the diaries had a photograph tucked inside that I thought you should see. Two young nurses are standing in front of Lenox Hill Hospital with a third young woman dressed in a dark-blue skirt and a polka-dotted blouse."

"Oh, *Dios mío*, I have to see it."

I stood up, put Celia in her crib, and opened the envelope. The graduation photo was on top of a short stack of letters and photos tied with a yellow ribbon, and I recognized Stella Donovan right away.

"The strawberry-blonde is definitely my grandmother because my mom looks just like her," I said with a girlish giggle.

I quickly flipped through the letters. They were all addressed to Mrs. Penélope Leone, 16 Pancake Lane, Greenport, New York. I sat down and studied the top photo. When I turned it over and read the inscription, my hand started to shake. I read it aloud:

Lenox Hill Hospital
Graduation Day
June 20, 1941
Stella Goss, RN, Marie Capelotti, RN, and Penny Leone

"Dan, this is amazing."

"Yes, these documents confirm that our grandmothers were cousins."

Baffled, I stared at the graceful handwriting. "The date is surprising."

"What do you mean?"

"Well, when I interviewed my mom for my documentary, she told me my grandmother, Stella Goss, graduated from nursing school in June of '42 and joined the Navy shortly after, but according to the date on this photo, she was off by a year."

Dan shrugged. "The mind plays tricks on time. If you read the diaries, you'll find those were tough years to remember with clarity. One year in particular made me cry."

"What year was that?"

"1943."

Looking up at Dan's face, my eyes filled with tears. "This is a priceless gift, Dan. Someday I'll share it with Celia, and she'll see history through a very personal lens."

Dan's moody-dark eyes seemed to lighten.

"Oh, I think you'll share those stories sooner rather than later. In fact, I predict you'll be halfway through your second novel by this time next year, and the heroine, no doubt, will be a nurse."

As I covered my mouth to stifle another laugh, I spied Jake and Oliver at the door.

"Hey, everyone is downstairs wondering where you are," whispered Jake.

I whispered back, "Celia just fell asleep. We're coming down to join you right now."

"When do I get to hold little Miss Summers?" asked KOMI's handsome vice president in a hushed voice.

Brushing past him, I whispered, "As soon as she wakes up...in about an hour, Mr. Hayden."

When he didn't respond, I realized he was focusing on my cousin, Dan. They were obviously renewing their friendship.

* * *

The moment I stepped onto the braided rug at the bottom of the stairs, Moose rushed up to me. Apparently, he had been looking for me and felt a need to cover me with slobber. Jake was behind me and immediately took command.

"Sit, Moose. That's enough love for now," he said as sternly as he could.

Moose obeyed. However, when he sat down and looked up with sad eyes, Jake melted and rubbed his ears.

"Good boy," he said.

I looked over my shoulder and grinned.

"He's fine, Jake. Moose's kisses are awfully wet, but they're also sincere. I don't mind them at all."

Shaking his head emphatically, Jake replied. "Yeah, but he has to behave. Ever since Celia arrived, he's been acting like someone stole his spotlight."

I raised an eyebrow. "Well, that's kind of true, don't you think?"

He patted Moose. "Mind your manners, Moose. You had your turn as king of the hill. Now it's Celia's turn to be the princess, but we still love you…too much."

Moose was happy to be noticed and caved after one pat on the head.

Dan and Oliver came downstairs and immediately suggested a few cold beers to help us relax.

"Not for me. I'm nursing. But I'm famished, and I can smell that pulled pork from here so I'm heading out to the patio."

"We'll follow," said Jake.

Once outside, I made a beeline to the buffet table and Garrett appeared at my side.

"Sunrise Farm agrees with you, Anna. You've lost your baby weight and you look fantastic."

"Really, Garrett? I've lost my baby weight?"

"What? I can't notice how good you look?"

I shot him a look that screamed *enough!* and said, "You flirt too much. Didn't you come with Maggie?"

"Yes, we're friends."

"I wish I knew what you were looking for."

"Truth be told, I don't know. I've been lost since my wife died."

I paused, then I said, "Maggie is a gem. She's true-blue. If you're ready, she can help you write your next chapter."

"I'll think about it."

"Good. Now enjoy the party."

"Okay, boss. I'll do that."

When I reached the end of the buffet table, I turned and saw my mom standing close by. She seemed to be waiting for me.

"How's our little rosebud?" she asked.

Stepping toward her, I replied, "Sleeping at last. Dan helped me put her down, and he also gave me some photos that I have to show you. He found them at his parents' house."

"You mean in New York?"

"Yes; remember I was telling you about our uncanny connection? Have you ever been to Greenport?"

My mom stared off into space as if her mind was flying away. After a long pause, she returned.

"Yes, I remember going there as a child. The ferry from Shelter Island still stops there in the summer. I remember taking that ferry with my parents when I was five or six."

"Mom, we need to talk and I need to eat, so let's find a place to sit."

When we sat down on a bench under a beautiful tulip tree, I told her about Penélope Leone's diaries, photos, and letters. My mother's eyes turned misty, but she didn't say a word.

"I haven't read any of the letters," I explained between bites, "but the photo is labeled Lenox Hill Hospital, June twentieth, 1941, and the three women in the photo are identified as Stella, Marie, and Penny. I'm guessing the inscription was written by Mary Rose because each word

291

is a work of art, and you once told me your grandmother had amazing handwriting and it was a shame that neither of us had inherited her gift."

Mom's eyes crinkled as she laughed with her whole body and soul.

"I'm sure I said that because I've seen samples of my grandmother's writing. Like Penny, Stella kept letters, and I found them in old shoe boxes years ago. But truth be told, I never really knew my grandmother, Mary Rose Goss. She died of a sudden stroke in 1947. Perhaps the war with all its heartache shortened her life. I think it's a miracle that you met Dan and he's given us this incredible link to the past."

Shaking my head, I asked, "How can this be?"

"I don't know," sighed my mother. "Even if we had researched our family's ancestry online, I doubt we would have made this connection. In New York, the name Leone is as common as Lyons, but impossible things happen. I believe you were destined to meet Dan, and you'll be working with him for many years to come. Maybe the next book you'll write will be about his great-grandmother, Angélica Solis Velázquez, and her Latin roots. For now, I can hardly wait to read Penny's diaries."

* * *

After all the guests and caterers had departed, Jake, my parents, and I retired to the living room. While Celia played in her bouncer, we sat on the couches by the fireplace and I read one of my grandmother's letters, dated March 15, 1943, aloud.

Dear Penny,

My tears have stained so many letters to mothers, fathers, wives, and sweethearts that I have lost count, but this time I am not writing on behalf of a wounded sailor or marine; I'm writing to express my own inconsolable grief. On the twenty-eighth of February, I received a telegram from Uncle Sam informing me that my beloved Ray was killed at the Battle of Kasserine Pass in the Atlas mountains of Tunisia. I have no idea where that hellish place is, but its fire has consumed my love. Every morning that I wake up, knowing he's gone, I find it harder to breathe. A few weeks before the telegram arrived, I received a letter from Ray telling me that he had named me as next of kin. I think he knew his time on earth was running out and he didn't want his parents to learn of his demise in the lines of a cold telegram. I wrote them within a day of hearing the news. Until now, my letter to the Mitchells was the saddest I had ever written. This one is even sadder because I am writing it without any pretense of hope. Do you remember that Spanish expression your dad taught us after your mom died? "No me queda más." Well, that is how my heart feels. "I have no more left."

I know that Sal is fighting with the Bloody First, and I desperately want him to come home to you alive and unharmed. Pray for me, Penny, because I cannot. I have lost that faith-filled voice, and I am afraid it may never return.

Love,
Stella

I folded the letter exactly as it had been folded many times before and slipped it into its tear-stained envelope. When I looked up, I saw my mother's face twisted in grief and regretted reading the words out loud. Today was supposed to be a celebration of faith and love. Revisiting sorrow from over seventy-seven years ago was not part of the plan, but we couldn't erase the pain.

Dad came to my rescue. He put on his professor's hat and gave us all some numbers to think about.

"Thirty thousand American troops participated in the Battle of Kasserine Pass; three hundred were killed, three thousand wounded, and three thousand were reported missing or captured. It was America's first fight with the more experienced German and Italian forces, and we took a terrible beating, but we learned from it and pushed back hard. Kasserine Pass was Rommel's last victory in North Africa…"

When my dad paused, Jake fired off a question. "Anna, did Dan know what happened to his grandfather during the war?"

"He did. We talked about his family after dinner, and he told me his grandfather made it out of Tunisia but lost his leg during the Allied invasion of Sicily."

Jake's reaction was visceral. He bowed his head and swallowed hard, but then he asked Mom a follow-up question.

"Ellie, do you remember anything more about Sal?"

"It's fuzzy," she sighed, "but I do remember him. He was tall and had an artificial leg. I saw it once. He showed it to me after telling me a scary story. He said he fell out of a boat when he was in the middle of the deep, dark sea, and a whale grabbed his leg and ripped it off before he could swim away. For a long time after that, I was terrified of whales."

Celia fussed. As I leaned over to bounce her seat, I thought about how frightening Sal's story must have been to a little girl.

"Mom, why didn't you ever mention your cousins out on Long Island? I didn't even know about the Leones until a few months ago."

"I don't know what to say. There was no Facetime or Facebook back then. If you lived far away from someone, you didn't see them much, and we never lived close to our extended family. I rarely saw the Leones. After my mom died, I didn't see them at all."

The room fell silent. My mother's eyes welled with tears, but it was Celia who cried. I picked her up and cradled her in my arms.

"It's getting late. I'll take her upstairs and get her ready for the night."

Mom stood up and gave Celia Rose a good-night kiss. "She's heaven sent. Maybe she'll sleep for a solid four hours."

Dad chimed in, "Let's pray for five," then resumed his lecture without missing a beat.

"The invasion of Sicily was launched on July 9th, 1943, and it was a bloodbath. By the time it ended on the seventeenth of August, close to three thousand American troops had been killed and over six thousand had been wounded, but the Allies had won. They smashed Mussolini's regime once and for all."

"On that note, Celia and I are going up to bed."

Jake stood.

My dad chuckled, "Okay, I get the message. Class is over."

"Yes, dear," said Mom as she extended her hand and pulled him up from the deep-cushioned couch. "It's time for this family to get some rest."

We all said good night except for little Celia Rose, who simply by breathing in and out offered us a sign of peace.

CHAPTER 30

November–December 1943

A s Stella filled two mugs with extra-strong coffee, Muriel spied an envelope sticking out of the pocket at her hip, and she decided to seize the moment.

"Is that a letter from the commander you nursed back to health?"

Stella handed her friend one of the steaming mugs and said nothing. As the two of them sat down to rest on metal chairs, Lt. Lonergan broached the delicate topic one more time.

"Come on, Stella, it wouldn't hurt to open one of his letters. After all, you did give him permission to write. How many letters have you stowed away in that box beneath your bunk? It must be over a dozen because we dropped him off at the hospital in New Caledonia almost a year ago."

"It's close to two," she said.

Muriel looked at her friend with owlish eyes.

"Oh, my God! Why don't you read them?"

Lost in thought, Stella rubbed her forehead and said, "I can't. It doesn't seem right."

"Oh, honey, reading those letters is absolutely right. Ray was killed months ago; we're in the middle of a bloody war, and the commander could die, too. Hell, you and I aren't exactly out of harm's way either."

"It's not that easy—"

"What are you waiting for? If it's Ray's blessing, he's already given it...I'm sure."

Stella pulled the letter from her pocket and studied the return address:

Commander Francis Donovan
FPO 95, San Diego, California

"I wonder where he is?" asked Stella rhetorically.

Muriel stood up to leave. "There's only one way to find out. I've got to make rounds. As soon as I go, open the damn letter and read it."

Stella didn't say a word, and Muriel took that as an *okay*.

Left alone in the wardroom, Stella opened the envelope and for the first time read the commander's heartfelt words.

Dear Stella,

I hope the twenty-second letter is the charm because the third, the ninth, and the twenty-first did not elicit a response. If this one reaches you, please reply. By now, you know I like to write. Don't let my boldness offend you. I realize your heart belongs to someone else, and I pray he survives, but thoughts of you keep me going, and right now that's all I need. I wish I could tell you more, but Uncle Sam prefers we do more and talk less.

The good news is I'm here, wherever that is, and because of you, my burns have healed and I'm okay. I did suffer a bout of dengue fever that beached me for longer than I care to admit. Maybe that's because the nurses in New Caledonia aren't half as pretty as you. I believe unattractive nurses can hinder a man's recovery, especially mine.

I wish I had a picture of you, something to pin up on my locker. Ouch! I can feel that slap. I'm kidding. Okay, I'm only half kidding. Are your eyes still changing from blue to green and back to blue? I love that about you. I mean I love your hazel eyes.

Don't worry. Whether you like it or not, I'll write again. In the meantime, keep sailing.

Yours in blue,

Donovan

* * *

Six hours later, after completing a grueling twelve-hour shift, Stella and Muriel lay in their bunks, one above the other, and started to talk as if they were on the phone.

"So, did you read the letter?"

"Yes."

"And are you going to read the other twenty-one?"

"As a matter of fact, I am," said Stella.

"Oh, dear heart, that is music to my ears. I was beginning to worry."

"Beginning?" asked Stella with a chuckle.

"Ha, you're right. I'm a worrywart, but your situation was becoming dire and needed to be addressed."

"Well, you can rest easy tonight."

"What did the handsome commander have to say?"

"Not too much. You know, everything is top secret in the Navy. He did mention that he was hospitalized again at New Caledonia with dengue fever, but he's back on duty now, which is code for he's been assigned to another ship."

"Sounds about right," said Muriel, turning off the lights. "The Pacific isn't really peaceful, is it?"

"No, it's not," said Stella.

For a minute, silence filled the cabin, then Muriel whispered, "Are you asleep yet?"

"No, but my eyes are closed."

"I was just wondering if you've heard from your friend Marie."

"Yes, I got a letter a few days ago. Reading between the lines, she's at a field hospital in North Africa, which means she is probably in Tunisia. She knew the Big Red One took a beating at Kasserine Pass, but she never saw Ray. She was heartbroken when she learned he was killed."

"I'm sure she was. Did she mention her doctor? Is he okay?"

"Oh, he's more than okay," answered Stella softly. "Pete trained as a surgeon after the attack on Pearl Harbor. Marie told me he's a major now and is with her unit. I suspect they're in love, but neither can say because that's against Army regulations."

"Imagine finding love in the middle of war. How's that for beating the odds? Thanks, Stella. You've given me something to dream about."

"You're welcome. Now go to sleep. We have to wake up in four hours."

"Roger that," she said with a yawn.

* * *

Two days later, Stella sat down at a small metal desk in her compact quarters and wrote her first letter to Commander Francis Donovan.

Dear Donovan,

I guess the twenty-second letter is the charm because it was the first letter I read, but not the last. In the past forty-eight hours, I've stolen time to read them all backwards from the twenty-second to the first, dated January 6, 1943, the Feast of the Epiphany, a.k.a. Little Christmas.

This war has taught us all how to hide the truth and how to read between the lines when someone can't be completely transparent for the sake of national security. From your letters, I gather you've recovered from the injuries you suffered that night you were forced to take a three-hour swim, and you've recovered from that nasty tropical fever. I've also gleaned that you're steaming along on a different boat. My new boss just returned from liberty on an island known for its pineapple. Before going on liberty, she was assigned to the hospital that treated you some months ago. Based on our wardroom chats, I'm close to knowing where you are and where you are going.

Tell me, Commander, do you prefer Quakers or race car drivers? Do you prefer a city with a bell or a city in the middle of farm country?

Now that we've played that guessing game, I have some tragic news to share. My sergeant was killed in action, and I've had trouble breathing ever since. I'm sorry I put off reading your letters for so long. Please forgive my failure to respond in a timely manner. I wish you safe sailing wherever you are. I've started to pray again, and I'm praying for you.

Fair winds and following seas,
Stella

P.S. If you continue writing, I will continue reading.

After adding her postscript, Stella folded her letter and slipped it in an envelope, but she paused before sealing it. She stood and reached under her bunk for her duffel bag. At the bottom of the bag, her hand rested on a book. She quickly pulled out her well-read copy of *Gone with the Wind* and opened it. Inside the cover were three wallet-size photos. One was her senior-year head shot from nursing school. She flipped the photo over and read the inscription: *Lenox Hill Hospital's School of Nursing, Class of 1941.* She slipped the photo inside the envelope addressed to Commander Francis Donovan and sealed it.

* * *

Every day after her shift, Stella checked to see if the *Solace* had received mail. If the answer was yes, she waited anxiously for the sailor charged with distributing the mail to hand her a letter. This routine went on for weeks. The flow of letters that had been arriving on a regular basis had suddenly stopped. As a Navy nurse, Stella knew there were only three possible explanations—death, injury, or disenchantment. She didn't like any of them.

After five weeks, even Muriel started to worry.

"Any mail today?" she asked as she passed Stella on the ward.

Stella just shook her head and continued wrapping bandages.

Finally, on the sixteenth of December, a letter arrived. Stella was updating a chart when Muriel appeared at her side looking like a woman with a secret.

"I hear the mail is on its way from the post office," she whispered.

"How would you know that?" asked Stella.

"Oh, I know a few sailors, and they keep me informed."

"Well, have any of them seen my name on a piece of that mail?"

Muriel bit her lip. "I can't divulge top secret information, but it's possible."

Checking her watch, Stella replied, "I'm off duty at 1900 hours. Meet me in the wardroom, and be sure to tell the postman to be there, too."

"Yes, ma'am" snapped Muriel. "I'll be there and so will the sailor with the mail."

At a little after 1900, sailor Lenny Reimann handed Lt. Goss a letter from the fleet post office. As soon as Stella saw the handwriting, she knew it was from the commander.

Dear Stella,

I just received your letter, and I'm writing to tell you your prayers were answered. We won a tough battle. You'll probably hear some radio reports, but we took back a few islands the Japs had fortified and called their own. The bad news is the victory came at a high price, but that won't happen again. Next time, we'll be faster and hit harder.

As I report I'm all well, I realize you have suffered a great loss and I'm truly sorry. I came into this war without a sweetheart back home, and I suppose that isn't all bad, but it's not optimum. Your sergeant was a lucky man because he had you waiting for him, praying for him, and loving him. You don't have to tell me the details. If your guy was a sergeant with the Big Red One, I know he was strong and resourceful. Above all else, he was brave. I know he led men into battle, and that demands uncommon valor. Your sergeant's death is a tragic loss; his life had meaning, and he will be remembered. Having said all that, I wish I could wrap my arms around you because hugs help more than words. I want to comfort you and encourage you. This war is going to end, and we'll be free to love again.

I must admit I was surprised when I received your letter at last. Uncle Sam has plans for me right now, but I yearn to see you. Thoughts of you have sustained me over these past twelve months. (By the way, I prefer Quakers to race car drivers.)

In case our FPO fails us in the future, I'm going to take this moment to suggest a Waikiki rendezvous as soon as we can finagle some liberty. To that end, I'm proposing a date, October 17, 1944. I'll fight to spend liberty in Hawaii with you. Until then, know I'm wishing on your star.

Yours,

Donovan

When Stella finished reading, she looked up and met her friend's gaze with a beguiling smile.

Muriel responded by cocking her eyebrow. "What did the commander have to say?"

"He's aboard the USS *Pennsylvania*, not the *Indianapolis*. They just took back the atolls, Tarawa and Makin, but now they're steaming across the Central Pacific preparing for an assault on the Marianas, then our bombers will be in striking range of Tokyo."

"He shared all that intel in a letter? How did that slip by Uncle Sam?"

Stella chuckled. "We're writing in code, but it makes sense. I've thought for a while that Admirals Nimitz and Spruance have targeted the Marianas. Now I know Donovan is aboard one of their battleships, and he's headed that way."

"Really? Was the commander able to convey any of his *personal* feelings in this coded language?"

"Oh, yes, he wants to take me out on a date."

Muriel threw up her hands. "You could have *led* with that fact! Does he have a plan?"

"He's going to put in for liberty, and he wants me to do the same."

"When and where? If he can pull this off, he's a magician."

"October seventeenth, 1944, at Waikiki Beach on the island of Oahu."

"Are you going to say yes?"

Clutching Donovan's letter, Stella winked.

"Of course, I'm going to say yes. As a matter of fact, I'm going to suggest we spend *all* of our liberty, seven days and seven nights, together. After all, that's what we're fighting for, liberty and love."

ACKNOWLEDGMENTS

Since moving to Maine in 2013, I've been driven to write maritime fiction to celebrate the families that built the best sailing ships in the world. Even though my characters are fictional, they are inspired by men and women who lived big, bold lives and helped forge our nation's history. In both *Daughters of Long Reach* and *The Maine Point,* the ships I describe are authentic; their names are recorded in the national archives. However, my writing experience has taught me that the history of a ship is easier to trace than the history of a family. For that reason, I am grateful to all those who have helped me tell the story of shipbuilding, seafaring families. I am especially indebted to my husband, Joseph Drago, and my brother, Michael Murtagh, two veterans I know and love, who have studied and lived military history and were always willing to share their knowledge. Even though I come from a family of nurses, I chose to be a teacher, so the chapters that chronicle the training of Nurse Stella Goss would have seemed less real without my cousin Mary Murtagh's counsel. Mary graduated from Lenox Hill Hospital's School of Nursing. I have her graduation picture to prove it; she's wearing the school's distinctive cap. As we prepare to celebrate Maine's Bicentennial, I am also thankful to the Sagadahoc History & Genealogy Room of the Patten Free Library and to the staff and volunteers at the Maine Maritime Museum.

Bringing a book to fruition would be impossible without the help of talented editors. I was blessed to find Karen Schneider and Genie Dailey. They have helped me to express my heart's wish coherently. I would also like to thank Gemma Cannon, a fellow author and beautiful spirit, for her kind words and encouragement. Just when I thought I had finished, I decided to include a few lines from Woody Guthrie's ballad, "The Sinking of the Reuben James," and contacted the publishing company. Anna Canoni, Woody's granddaughter, answered the phone, and that was the start of a great conversation. Thank you, Anna! At the beginning and in the end, I am grateful to Claudette Gamache for creating covers for my novels that invite the reader to enter the story.

CREDITS

I gratefully acknowledge the following sources for the invaluable information they offered me about lighthouses, square-riggers, schooners, U.S. Navy ships, maritime history, and Bath, Maine:

The History of The USS Northampton *(CA26) 1930–1942, Her Crew and Their Descendants,* compiled by Glen C. Randolph and Frankie L. Randolph (The Compilers, Long Beach, CA, 1993).

The Lighthouses of Maine, Kennebec River to the Midcoast by Jeremy D'Entremont (Commonwealth Editions, an imprint of Applewood Books, Carlisle, MA, 2013).

Live Yankees by W.H. Bunting (Tilbury House Publishers, Thomaston, Maine, and Maine Maritime Museum, Bath, Maine, May 2019).

Maine Odyssey: Good Times and Hard Times in Bath, 1936–1986 by Kenneth R. Martin and Ralph Linwood Snow (Patten Free Library, Bath, Maine, 1988).

A Maritime History of Bath, Maine and the Kennebec River Region (two volumes) by William Avery Baker (Maine Research Society of Bath, 1973).

"St. Mary's Church History." Unknown author: www.allsaintsmaine.com

I also acknowledge the following source for compelling lyrics:

The Sinking of the Reuben James
Words and Music by Woody Guthrie
Copyright © 1942 UNIVERSAL MUSIC CORP.
Copyright Renewed
All Rights Reserved Used by Permission
Reprinted by Permission of Hal Leonard LLC